THIEVES & MONSTERS

THREE FATES MAFIA
BOOK ONE

CLIO EVANS

To anyone who understands
STFUATTMDLAGG

Mortals Beware

Mortals Beware:

In this story, you will find the following:

Cock warming, humiliation, forced orgasms, biting, 'Daddy', rope bondage, size difference, bukkake, gang bangs, Dom/sub dynamics, guns, murder, mentions of suicide, somnophilia, dubious consent, breeding kink, primal, fully shifted monster sex, knotting, fated mates, and more.

If you have any questions, you can reach me on instagram or Facebook, or via email clioevansauthor@gmail.com

CHAPTER 1

DOG HOUSE

ASHLEY

Your debt will be paid, he'd said.

You won't have to worry about me killing you, he'd said.

What Hercules, the very rich and stuck-up bastard that I worked for, *hadn't* said was that breaking into this glass doghouse would be a pain in my ass.

I was one of the best art thieves in the world, yet here I was, wishing I had put on stronger deodorant.

I eyed the sign next to the door of the stairwell. I was on the 66th floor of the Helm, one of the most striking skyscrapers in the entire city, and now officially drenched in sweat.

The blueprint I had was outdated, which made this job ten times harder than it should have been. Sneaking my way up here had been challenging enough, not to mention I had to slip past countless guards with a bag that could safely transport a painting.

Not just any painting either. My golden ticket to freedom.

Pulling the door open just a smidge, I looked down the hall, eyeing the camera at the end. Despite the way my palms exuded moisture, and my thighs burned like I'd been trapped in pilates hell, everything was still working in my favor.

I watched in satisfaction as the green light on the camera turned red, my signal that the security system was now being shown a nice feed of a black and white cartoon I'd found online.

It was *go* time.

I ran down the hall, no longer needing to be sneaky with the cameras off. I made it to the door at the very end and knelt in front of it, listening for any movement.

Hercules had promised that the victims of my heist were out of the building, preoccupied with another one of their turf wars.

My stomach twisted. Stealing from humans with private collections was no big deal, but breaking into a place owned by monsters made me jumpy. This wasn't my normal gig, but I had no choice. I owed money to some real bastards, and this was how I would keep my pretty face away from their crosshairs.

Karma was actually a bitch, it turned out.

I'd never done anything *bad*. Well, unless you consider stealing priceless art bad. But I wasn't a killer. I wasn't a villain. Sure, I was *technically* a criminal, but I never did anything to actually harm others. I did my best to keep my hands clean of blood and pain.

The problem was not everyone within Moirai City played by the same rules.

That included assholes like the ones that owned this ridiculous penthouse. They rolled in their money, eating people who weren't smart enough to play dirty for breakfast. I imagined they liked to throw souls like me in with their Fruit Loops, drinking the blood of anyone with a moral compass like it was whole milk.

"Bastards," I muttered and then froze.

I listened for a few moments and found that I was still alone. The hall was empty, the camera still blinking red.

I glanced down at my wristwatch. I had three minutes to open this door and get inside the penthouse before the cameras came back online.

Fucking hell, Ash, I mentally reprimanded myself for speaking aloud. I could have just fucked everything up entirely.

My fingers trembled for a moment, and I sucked in a silent breath to steady myself. I was dressed in a black catsuit, my blonde waves drawn into a tight high-top bun so they wouldn't get in the way as I worked.

I reached into my boots, pulling out the small board and wires, along with the connector I needed to break this keypad. Within a few seconds, I had everything hooked up and was listening for a faint beep.

Three, two, one...

It went off, and I smirked under my mask as the door unlocked itself. I left the electric board and wires there, as I'd need it to lock everything back up.

Hell, if I did this right, these pricks would never know I was here. The fake painting I had was a really nice one, and most rich men didn't have an artist's eye. They wouldn't know the difference between the *Mona Lisa* at the Louvre and the one at the home goods store.

I slipped inside the foyer of the penthouse, pausing to listen. As Hercules had promised, it seemed as though I was the only soul in this place.

I'd already done a couple jobs for him, but none of them had ever been this high profile. I'd get a text on my burner phone with all the info, and then instead of paying me—the money would go towards working off my debt.

This job would be the last one though. The last time I would have to put up with Hercules, and the last time I would have to deal with the Three Fates Mafia.

I was done.

It wasn't like I had the best moral compass, but after this? I was going squeaky clean. Nun clean. I'd move to an island where I'd become an old lady that cooked pies and owned a library with every spicy book known to woman. I wanted to lay out on the beach with a margarita in one hand and a vibrator in the other, not a damn care in the world.

No more mafia. No more stealing. No more crime.

I could feel my mood improving already.

I reached into my back pocket, pulling out the spray that Hercules had given me. He'd provided very strict instructions that I was to spray myself with this, and I knew why.

I stared at the can for a moment, wondering if I was about to gas myself. I closed my eyes, spritzed it over my body, and then tucked it back in place.

It was there to block my scent, to keep me out of the noses of monsters.

Yes, *monsters* were real. Not like, *haha*—politicians are monsters. More like real life, toothy, thirsty, ugly monsters who ruled this city with an iron fist. I'd never known they were real until moving to this place and getting sucked into the under-ground but—now it was where I existed.

Just a common criminal.

At least I was dealing with the human half of the mafia and not the other side. Well, I assumed that Hercules was human.

Ever since I'd learned creatures were real, I'd wondered if my ex from eleventh grade had secretly been a dragon. The knowledge had me staring at shadows a little too long, and jumping every time someone tapped me on the shoulder. Greek myths should have stayed myths, but that wasn't the reality of my world.

I'd been here for two months now, and was still figuring out how everything worked.

Nerves fluttered through me again.

Usually, I got a thrill from stealing, especially from private collections–they gave me an even bigger hard on. The adrenaline high was a beautiful, beautiful thing when stealing from the obscenely rich.

Everything had been great, until I'd fucked up a heist and ended up in Moirai City. Hercules was the first bastard that I'd run into. He ran his own faction of the Three Fates Mafia, and since he'd found me, he'd used my debt to his advantage.

Three million dollars was a heavy bill to pay when you already had student loans, health insurance, and preferred to shop the health food aisle.

Ironically, I'd gone to art school, and up until recently—that degree had actually paid off.

The Three Fates Mafia had a reach unlike anything I'd ever seen. There were ten branches that all stemmed from Moirai, tendrils that choked the life out of cities and towns across the country. I had yet to encounter any of the other leaders within the mafia, but if they were anything like Hercules, then I wanted to stay far away from them.

He liked to use people's desires against them. He was demanding, cruel, and didn't take no for an answer. If you had a weakness, anything at all, he would find out and use it.

Which was what had happened to me.

I'd been hired by a woman, who went by the name C, to steal a golden filigree egg from the Russian *Bratva*. But, due to a stroke of bad luck, I was caught. I managed to escape and found myself in Moirai, with a whole brigade of Bratva goons breathing down my neck. Hercules interfered, paid my ransom and debt, which in turn put me in debt to him. I had yet to hear from the infamous C and assumed she was dead at this point.

Initially, I'd been thankful for Hercules' interference. Unironically, the kindest mafia boss I had ever met was a liar and adept at tricking others into trusting him. Hell, he'd convinced me to trust him.

I gritted my teeth, moving swiftly through the foyer and living room. Turning a corner, I went down a hallway with four doors, creeping as quietly and quickly as possible.

This place was like a maze. I scowled as I came to the end and went through a doorway that led to yet another hall. This one looked more like what Hercules had spoken of. There were black marble pillars every few feet, with different objects encased in glass domes sitting atop each.

My eyes widened and my fingers itched as I went past them all.

No. No shiny objects. Do not touch.

In and out, like always. That was the plan.

I'd dump this painting in Hercules' lap, take whatever sassy, degrading things he had to say, then fly my ass out of this country.

Three million. Three million dollars.

I was done being a chew toy for men like him.

Not a man, I reminded myself, *a monster.*

Bingo.

I finally came to the door I'd been looking for—one that had an ornamental golden three-headed dog door knocker.

Weird-ass rich people, I swear. I bit my tongue and knelt in front of the door, inspecting the lock. A streak of excitement coursed through me because this was an easy one. I moved fast, pulling the lock pin out of my other boot and working as quickly as possible.

My fingers were nimble, even in the darkness. Finally, I heard the little click, and the door creaked open.

Fuck. I froze for a moment, listening for any movements, sounds, breaths, or growls.

Yes, growls.

Monster men growled a lot.

All I could do was hope that Hercules hadn't been lying to me.

The penthouse was silent, so I pushed the door open a little more and slipped inside. This room had no windows, unlike the rest of the house. There was one light, a golden spotlight, that was a beacon straight on my prize. *Yahtzee.*

I crept closer, assessing the artwork to make sure it was the original.

In front of me was a gold-framed oil painting, one that reminded me of a 17th-century piece, but with brighter, more vibrant colors. My breath hitched as I stared at the subject, my cheeks flushing under my mask.

It was a painting of three werewolf creatures ravaging a woman, and she was having the time of her life. There was no mistaking that look on her face, and for a moment, I felt jealous.

It had been an eternity since I'd done the deed with someone, but my trust issues meant I did a level four background check on anyone who looked at me for too long, and that didn't help my lady bits' cause.

I shook my head, kneeling and letting my black bag shift forward. I unzipped it quickly and pulled out my tools, along with a canister I'd roll the canvas into. I had wax paper that would go on top of the painting to prevent damage, and once I replaced the original with the forgery, I'd be on my merry way.

I couldn't wait to wipe Hercules' smug grin away.

I let out a calming breath and stood, carefully taking the

painting off the wall. I worked in the amber light of the small space, only taking a moment to glance up.

This must have been an office at some point, though now it was mostly empty.

Strange.

I worked fast, popping the canvas out of the floater frame. The oil painting was on an inch-thick canvas and stapled to the wooden brace on the back. I laid the painting face down on my wax paper and then grabbed my tools, popping the staples free as quickly and carefully as possible.

God, I was dripping with sweat. Did they have to keep this place hotter than hell? Had they heard of air conditioning?

I drew in a shaky breath, trying not to think about everything that could go wrong. I loosened the last staple and moved both frames, swiftly rolling up the original painting. I popped it into the canister and shoved it into my bag.

Now to put the forgery on the frame.

I fell into the rhythm of it, my brain finally turning off and allowing me to go on autopilot. This was my jam, stealing art. I'd broken into museums, mansions, banks. You name it, I'd probably broken into it, and if I hadn't—then I could.

Fucking Bratva. My ego was still slightly bruised from being caught.

I'd been taught from an early age how to pick locks. I had survived like this for years. It was time to retire, though. The monster-free beach life was calling to me.

I finished securing the fake painting and placed it back into the gold frame. I hung it up and stood proud for a moment, admiring my work.

Damn, I really was the best.

"How long are you going to let her go on, Damon?"

The hair suddenly stood up on the back of my neck, I was frozen to the spot, all of that sweat turning to ice.

No. No, no, no.

I turned, my heart dropping.

A man stood in the doorway, only I knew he wasn't a man.

No.

Humans didn't have eyes of fire or pointed teeth.

They also certainly weren't that damn good looking.

The monster cocked his head, swirling a glass of whiskey in his hand as he leaned against the doorframe.

"I was waiting to see if she'd notice me first, but she's just a dumb little thief." The voice dripped with sweet disdain.

My head swung to the left.

How had I missed him?!

Standing in the corner of the small room was another who was just as fine as the other, except he had a silver scar that tore through his black brow and high cheekbones. His black hair was cut short, his face shaved and smooth.

He had the same eyes as the other. Ones that burned like embers in a tartarus pit.

A shiver ran up my spine.

I'd just fucked up.

In all the years I'd been doing this, I had never been caught. Never. Well, besides that *Bratva* job...

I took a step back, my heart pounding. "I..."

"Now, I can smell her," the one from the doorway growled, giving me a fiendish grin over the rim of his whiskey glass. "And I think she smells like our next meal, Damon."

"Minos," the other purred, stepping towards me. "We can't eat mortals, remember?"

I continued to back up as they spoke and realized I was pressed against the opposite wall. My eyes darted around the room.

There was no escaping this. No escaping them. The one that blocked the door was already twice my size in whatever human form he was in. Even beneath the expensive suit, I could see the bulge of muscles.

I could also see the gun on his hip.

"Listen," I said quickly. "I have money."

"Look at the way her vein trembles in her neck when she *lies*," Minos chuckled, taking a step toward me as he sipped the alcohol.

His gaze swept over me. Undressing me. Reading *everything* about me. I felt a lick of heat between my thighs, which confused me more than anything else.

Both of these monsters were dangerously hot, conjuring thoughts of how sirens would draw men in. I couldn't let their looks deceive me.

I'm going to murder Hercules.

"You know, the last thief that was sent at least had the decency to hang the painting straight. Then again, the last thief hadn't been careless enough to leave their electric equipment hanging from our keypad."

"I want a lawyer," I blurted out.

This time, Damon was the one to sound cruel as his head tipped back with a rough laugh. "We don't abide by your trivial laws. We are the law in Moirai, or have you never heard of the Three Fates Mafia?"

I didn't have time to explain that yes– *yes* I had heard of the Three Fates motherfucking Mafia.

I looked from one to the other and decided the only way out was to fight.

Fuck the painting. I had to get out alive. Hercules could take his three million dollars and shove it up his pompous ass.

Minos recognized my decision right as I moved, a growl ripping from his chest as I shoved him. Damon lunged for me, but I managed to squeeze between them both, darting out the door.

A crazed laugh left me, as that had been lucky, and I ran as fast as I could. I had to make it out.

I still had to make it past all the guards.

My heart burst in my chest, the adrenaline kicking in. The penthouse was pitch-black aside from the glow of the city lights outside the windows.

"Come back, you thieving bitch!"

I ran, heading straight for the front door.

I reached for the handle just as a dark figure slammed into me, pinning me against the wall. A clawed hand wrapped around my throat, cutting off all my air.

Glowing eyes met mine, teeth shining like daggers. "Look at what we found," he snarled, "Our next chew toy."

My vision began to dot, and then with one more slam against the wall, I was out like a light.

CHAPTER 2

POMEGRANATE SEEDS

DAMON

The very last thing I had wanted to deal with today was a human breaking into our penthouse to steal from us.

The fucking gall. I was pissed. I seethed over the thought of anyone, especially a *mortal*, breaking into *our* home.

This week had already been a shit show, and this was very much the thing that could tip me over the edge.

I watched as Aaecus finished tying up the little thief. For such a big guy, his fingers had always been nimble with rope. He had a patience for it that I had never been able to find.

He dropped her onto the rug and ran his hand over his bald head, scowling at her. Her breathing was steady, although she was clearly still knocked out. He'd been the one to catch her. She'd slipped right between Minos and I, which had put me in an even worse mood.

There were three things in this world that made me happy. Fucking, killing, and collecting art. The last part was something

I kept private, as being one of the heads of a mafia meant that you couldn't look weak.

A pathetic thief managing to sneak past all of our men in this building, disabling our security system with piece of shit equipment, and then almost getting out the door made us look fucking weak.

It made *me* look weak.

There were three things in this world that made me angry, and looking weak was one of them.

"You could have been a little more gentle," Minos grunted to Aaecus, regarding the woman with an almost soft look.

"What the fuck do you care?" I spat.

I narrowed my eyes, pulling my gun out and cocking it. I aimed it at her, but Minos stepped forward with a growl.

"*Wait*, hold on," Minos said. He raked his fingers through his dark hair, drawing it back into a loose bun. He had that look on his face, the one that I didn't want to see right now. "Put the gun down, Damon. I'm not done with her. I want her *alive*."

"I'm two fucking seconds away from putting a bullet in her head, and three from tearing her limb from limb."

"I want to fuck her," Minos said darkly, meeting my cold gaze. "Her scent appeals to me, and I want to take her."

His words settled over the three of us. Aaecus shook his head, already frustrated. Minos had always been somewhat of a man whore–my whore–but this was taking it too far.

"And I don't care what happens after that. But I want to fuck her. Her scent is appealing, even with that stupid spray toning it down."

Was he being fucking serious? Minos, the monster I'd seen gut mortals, murder monsters, and fight the gods themselves— was asking me to spare a useless woman because he wanted to *fuck* her?

I pressed my lips into a thin line, the vein in my temple

pulsing. It was almost midnight, and I couldn't remember the last time I'd actually slept or even eaten a proper meal. One night a month, the three of us liked to have beers and watch a show together. It kept us at least on friendly terms even when we wanted to rip each other apart.

Tonight was that night, and some thieving bitch wasn't going to steal that from me.

I took a deep breath, attempting to calm myself. I looked back down at her. She had yet to wake up.

I'd spent almost a million dollars on anger management at this point, specifically for times like this where I could feel my pulse in my temple. Still, I couldn't keep the anger from my voice. "Normally, I *might* comply," I said. "But not today. We kill her, chop her up, and then ship her back to whatever cunt sent her to mess with our dinner plans."

"It was Hercules," Aaecus said, his tone deadpan. He was still looking down at the woman, his gaze never leaving her. "I'm certain of it. He's been on our ass ever since we gutted three of his men for setting Echo on fire."

"Well, you did send him their cocks in a box, Aaecus."

"It was Valentine's Day," Aaecus said, shrugging.

He said it so matter of factly, that it was hard to tell if he'd done it out of humor or just because the whim had struck him.

That was the thing about Aaecus. He was steady and patient until that switch flipped in him–then he became a crazed beast that would do things no one could predict.

Running our faction of the Three Fates Mafia had its challenges, starting with how the demigods were always crossing lines. Undoubtedly, this woman had been sent by one of them, and I would ensure that they'd think twice about it before trying again.

I was almost certain it was Hercules though, as Aaecus had said.

"I'm hungry and ready for a beer," Aaecus grunted, giving Minos a sour look. "If you're gonna fuck her, then do it while I get the TV set up and Damon orders food."

Minos let out a frustrated sigh. He shrugged off his suit jacket and then tie, tossing both items over one of the couches. He wore a black shirt that hugged his muscles, a line of sweat tracing his spine. The three of us had been *educating* some of Jason's mortal dumbasses on why they weren't allowed to simply walk into one of our clubs, and he'd worked up a sweat.

The *education* had been bloody, but satisfying. Causing suffering like that worked up an appetite while satiating a different kind of hunger.

She let out a soft whimper, drawing my attention again. I felt a pang of sympathy, and then buried that feeling. She was a thief. A dead thief.

"I have a different idea," Minos said. "There's something about her scent. Let's keep her alive... maybe get some information before killing her."

"The only info you want is between her legs," I snarled. "So, no. We will not keep her alive. She's just another criminal, nothing more than a mosquito sent to annoy the fuck out of us."

Minos shrugged, giving me the most charming grin he could muster. It was an easy going one that he had perfected over hundreds of years. He went from being an annoying fuck to Mr. McDreamy, and I hated when he did this because out of the three of us, he'd always managed to roll the most charisma.

It was hard to tell the asshole no.

This was a fucking mess. My answer was still no, even with his smile. I aimed the gun, pointing it straight at her head, despite the growls it brought from Minos.

"No," I snarled. "We're doing this my way. I'll call one of the women who like taking your monster form, and we can call it good. I'll even pay the bill."

"Don't you fucking dare," Minos growled. "You put a bullet in her head, and I'll tear down every single one of your plans for the next century."

I kept the gun pointed at her, my finger on the trigger. The temptation was strong. She was a problem. This whole thing was starting to unravel right before me, and I fucking hated loose ends.

The tension grew in the room, the sound of the city below drowned out by the pounding in my skull. I focused on her, ignoring the tiny voice that made me want to listen to Minos.

"*Damon,*" Minos growled again.

He was very serious about keeping the human alive, and that was...concerning. He never argued with me over a mortal's life—so why now? Because she had nice tits? A nice ass? A nice...fuck, she was hot.

I gritted my teeth, feeling the monstrous part of me rise up. Still, if Minos was so certain she should stay alive...

"I don't understand you." I let out a disgruntled sigh, lowering the gun and moving to the leather chair. Taking a seat, I propped my elbows on my knees and glared at the human.

I couldn't take my eyes off her.

I didn't like that. It made me feel uneasy.

"I'm not asking for permission to have her," Minos snapped.

"If we keep her alive so you can fuck her, then she's your problem. And yes, you are asking my permission. I am the leader, I am the boss. What I say, goes. End of story."

He growled again, a deep one from his chest, stepping towards me. His human form glimmered, his hellish one almost breaking free. "As if I would listen. Your curse fucked all three of us over, and sure—you're the middle head in our form—but that doesn't mean you get to say who I fuck. I'm taking this little thief to my bed, and you can drool over her cum on my sheets after she's left."

I fought the urge to flinch when he said '*your curse*'. It *was* my curse, though, that had changed everything for the three of us.

All because I'd let a woman get to me. She hadn't even been worth it. Because of her, Hades cursed me to be bound with Aaecus and Minos. We had become Cerberus, and while we were still individuals, we were bound together for eternity. Most of the time, the curse wasn't as bad as Hades had intended. Other times, the three of us wanted to murder each other.

"After she's left?!" I yelled, waving the gun. "Left to where? We're just going to let one of Hercules' toys wander off without punishment? That's not how our world works, Minos, and you fucking know that."

Aaecus moved closer to the human, nudging her leg with his boot. He didn't typically involve himself in our arguments, which was why I was surprised when he interrupted me and Minos. "Her scent is intoxicating. I'd like to have her too. Make that her punishment, Damon. Being our slave for a week. We can fuck her however we want and then move on."

The three of us were silent, the weight of his words settling.

For fuck's sake. Did he really want her too? Was she truly a human or a little witch that had cast a spell on the two of them?

"Both of you are thinking with your cocks," I said. "This is ridiculous."

"I fucking want her," Aaecus said again, his voice holding a warning. "You're not the only one who gets what he wants, Damon."

The three of us had gone too long without a good fuck apparently. Perhaps we'd been going too hard, which was easy to do in our line of work. We owned all of the clubs in Moirai, including the strip clubs, ran several online enterprises, and moved the kind of money that would make a mortal's head spin.

I groaned, closing my eyes for a moment.

The three of us were once Hades' hounds–keepers of the gates to hell, monsters that lived off of screaming souls. We'd lived in the Underworld, had seen the mortals come and go for ages. There would always be a part of me that longed for the darkness and the screams. I had fucked up, gotten the three of us cursed, and we had become one monster known as Cerberus.

We had stayed in the Underworld for hundreds of years after that, but it had never been the same. And now?

Now, monsters had moved into a new era.

Allowed to mingle with humans. To take a mortal form.

We obeyed the rules and made our own, to an extent. If only the demigods weren't such a massive pain in the ass, then I'd even say our lives were more enjoyable than ever before.

We hated each other. For centuries, demigods and monsters fought repeatedly—a cycle that could not be broken. I was certain it was to the amusement of the gods, as they had only ever pitted us against each other.

The good news was there hadn't been a new demigod for at least a few hundred years. And none of them, aside from the five in the Three Fates Mafia, had been allowed to live for long.

I wasn't sure which was worse. Being a monstrous pawn of the gods, or one of their half blood children.

The Three Fates kept everyone in line, even though the ten branches fought for power. I'd never met the three old hags and didn't care to, as that would mean I was about to truly die.

Out of all the demigods—there was one we sparred with

the most. Hercules, the curly haired cunt that mortals praised. They'd made movies about him, songs about him, books about him.

They had no idea how much of a piece of shit he was.

The fucker was annoying. He should have been buried in Tartarus, but *noooo*, the old demigods were never allowed to die.

I scoffed as the human's scent hit me, the spray finally wearing off.

Minos and Aaecus were right, which only irritated me further. My mouth watered as I opened my eyes, studying her.

She looked so damn innocent, tied up the way she was. She wore all black, her curves hugged by the soft fabrics. She had long blonde hair that had unraveled from the tight bun she had earlier and a dusting of freckles over her face. Long legs and love handles that were perfect to grip during a hard fuck. I found myself staring at her ass, wishing I could lick her—

Fuck.

Fuck NO.

Not with a human. Not just a human either, a fucking thief. And one of Hercules' pawns.

Aaecus had said I wasn't the only one that got what I wanted, but this situation was different.

"No," I said again.

"We take a vote then," Minos growled. "And go from there."

"Not a chance in hell!" I exclaimed, rising. "Both of you know this is insane. She's a human. Her body can't fit your cock, Minos, and I highly doubt she'd want to."

"I'm sure she'd come around," he purred, squatting down next to her. The way he looped his finger through one of her wavy strands made my blood boil, and I found myself tempted to kill her again.

I also felt a twinge of jealousy. Our relationship was always complicated, and seeing him so intrigued by her...

Minos never took his eyes off her, his smile becoming devilish. "We'll make a contract. For one week, she'll be our slave. We'll feed her seven pomegranate seeds to ensure she can't break the contract. In return, she gets to keep her stupid human life. And then one day we'll meet in the Underworld, and I'll devour her precious little soul."

I wasn't sure if the longing in his voice was for the Underworld or for her soul.

"Oh, so now you don't even want to kill her?" I sneered.

"I'm sure Hercules will take care of that," Minos said.

Aaecus snorted and shrugged. "Damon, I think you will lose this argument. I have needs and I quite like the idea of making her our dumb little whore. So, can you put the gun down and finally order some fucking food? She can sit on my cock while we watch a superhero movie or something."

I fought the urge to shoot him, my jaw ticking, and instead lowered the gun enough that both of them relaxed.

"Great," Aaecus said. "I'm getting hangry."

"So am I," Minos sighed. "I want steak and wine. Order food while we wait for her to wake up."

"I should have them overcook your steak," I muttered, pulling out the phone in my pocket.

"No, I hate it when it's not red," he pouted.

I rolled my eyes, fighting off a smirk as I pulled up the restaurant menu. They'd get the food to us fast, which would be nice.

There were some aspects of humanity I did enjoy, such as all the technology. In the old days, you'd have to write a letter and pray to Hermes for it to be delivered swiftly. Now, you just pulled a magical device out of your pocket and it sent messages instantly.

Of course, I was certain Hermes owned all of the phone companies.

Then there was the fact I could order whatever I wanted to eat and have it delivered quickly.

"What do you want, Aaecus?" I sighed.

"I want a brisket sandwich, chips, and a soda," Aaecus said as he grabbed the remote.

"You know they don't have that on the menu at this place."

"And? Have them add it," he grumbled.

"I swear to Hades," I muttered.

Within a few minutes, I had called in our order, reminded the restaurant who owned them, and made myself another whiskey to bide the time.

The human began to stir right as I went back to the living room—gun still in one hand, alcohol in the other. I moved closer, leaning over her.

Her eyes fluttered open, and all three of us watched as she realized her predicament.

I leaned in close enough to press the gun's barrel against her temple, earning me another growl from Minos, but I didn't care.

I wanted her to wake up knowing I could kill her. I wanted to scent her fear and hear her heart pound in her chest.

"*Fuck*," she whispered hoarsely, blinking rapidly as she came to.

She was so fucking fragile looking. All humans were, but seeing her on the floor surrounded by the three of us—I was reminded just how breakable a mortal was. "Fuck, indeed," I snarled. "What's your name? Or should I just call you thieving little bitch?"

"*Damon*," Minos snapped.

I ignored him, making a mental note for later. I would

punish him for this, especially for disrespecting me in front of a mortal.

"The only way you're getting out of this is if you talk," I said, pulling the gun away. She sucked in an audible breath as I moved back towards the chair. I waved the gun as I plopped down, never taking my eyes off her. "Stand her up and strip her. Search her for any hidden weapons. I want her facing me as we speak."

Minos rolled his eyes, but knew better than to argue. We might have words when no one else was around, but when someone was—the three of us were back in villain mode.

I watched as he pulled her to her feet. She was still becoming aware of everything, but her eyes widened and she yelped as Minos ripped open the front of her shirt, letting the fabric fall to the floor.

Aaecus let out a dark chuckle as he watched, his gaze fixated on her. I found myself smirking too.

"Fuck you," she growled, attempting to pull away. "Don't touch me!!!"

Minos snarled, grabbing her face and forcing her to look at him. "Don't you dare try to fucking fight me, thief," he spat. "I just saved your life."

She glared as he continued, removing her clothes where there wasn't rope binding her. Within a few moments, we had a very angry and nearly naked human standing in front of us.

"You left her bra and panties," I said. "Off with them, Minos."

"Listen, I have money—"

All three of us snorted. She didn't have more money than we did, and we didn't need a dime from her. I raised a brow as her gaze fell on me, all of her anger focusing in as two bright blue daggers.

"Save your lies," I said. "You work for Hercules, no? Or another one of the demigods?"

"Hercules," she seethed, her cheeks scarlet now. "Although saying that I work for him is a stretch. He's an asshole."

"Then why are you working for him, huh?" Aaecus asked.

She glowered at him, holding her chin high as Minos unclasped her black bra. "Money. Why else? And seriously. Demigods? What do you mean *demigods*?""

"A lost little thief, pawn of Hercules," I said, disregarding her ignorant questions.

If she had worked for Hercules without knowing what he was, then that was her problem.

Her breasts were freed as her bra fell to the floor. Minos knelt down in front of her, letting out a barely suppressed groan as he slid her underwear down.

"Search her," I said. "Every crevice."

"I have no weapons!" she cried. "Don't you fucking touch me."

Minos glanced back at me, giving me the *look*.

I cocked my head, letting out an unamused *hum*. "Fine," I said. "I'll be kind. But if you act up, thief, I'll let him do whatever he pleases. And I'm sure there are *many...many* things he would like to do to you."

She paled, her eyes darting between the three of us. Her chest heaved with panicked breaths, and I caught the delicious scent of fear.

I relaxed in my seat and became aware of everything about her. Her body couldn't be hidden now that we had every light in the goddamned house on, and she was naked. Her skin was smooth, her muscles taut. There were some scars here and there, and that made her even more attractive.

"Turn her around," I said, gesturing with the gun.

Minos turned her with an amused chuckle. She attempted

to twist back, but he smacked one of her ass cheeks hard enough to make her cry out.

I watched it jiggle, which damn near short circuited every thought I had.

Minos looked back at me again, this time with the hint of a sly smile. He knew that I was going to give in to his request.

"What do you want, you fucking creeps?" she asked. Her voice was strong, and she did well at hiding the tremble there.

It made me wonder how many times she'd been caught like this.

"We have a proposition," Minos said, giving her ass a squeeze where he'd just spanked her.

She gasped and tried to move away, but had nowhere to go. Aaecus snorted, as amused as I was.

Aaecus' voice came out gruff and menacing. "You'll listen to us, thief. Because either way, we're going to devour you. This is the only option that will give you a chance to live... unless Hercules finds you, of course."

Convincing.

I watched her digest his words, then her gaze slid back to me. Filled with so much hate and defiance.

Fuck. I wanted her to look at me that way while I rubbed the tip of my cock against her lips.

I wanted her to hate me while I fucked her.

I dug my fingertips into the whiskey glass, aware that it might crack in my grip.

"Tell us, little thief. Who are you? And why did he send you? What terrible things did you do to put yourself in this position?"

She looked from me to Minos, to Aaecus, and then to the floor.

"Chin up," Minos tutted, giving her hair a rough tug.

She shivered again, and this time I caught...

A scent.

A *different* one. One that made my blood heat.

"Human," I said, my voice dangerously low. "Start talking. Or else I'm going to let them tear into you."

"She'd like it if we did," Minos grunted. "Wouldn't you, little thief? Taking all our cocks at the same time."

She glared at him, but I noted the way she swallowed hard first before talking. "I'm an art thief. He hired me to steal that weird painting for him."

"It's *art*," I scoffed, offended that she'd called it weird.

Minos and Aaecus both rolled their eyes. They didn't have the same appreciation for art like I did, just like I didn't give two shits about Aaecus' affinity for working out or Minos' gaming habits.

"Sure, the artist is talented. But, that's it. I'm known for stealing art and not getting caught. I've been doing this for years now. Even if it's from *monsters*."

The three of us stiffened, and I leaned forward, glaring at her. "Got something against monsters, sweetheart?"

"Many things," she said, not breaking our locked gazes. "And the list is growing the longer I'm stuck here with you."

Minos chuckled, obviously enjoying this way more than us.

"I see. And how many monsters do you think would give you an option to live after breaking into their home to steal from them?" I asked.

"Not many. But what's the catch? The three of you don't strike me as the type to do something for free. All you rich mafia monsters are the same."

"The same, huh?" Aaecus chuckled.

"Hmm...first, tell me more about you. How did Hercules find someone like you, *sweetheart*?" I asked, smiling at her.

Oh, how she hated that. I grinned even more, wishing I could bend her over my knee and make her scream. Spank her into submission and then fuck her until all she could say was my name.

As if she could ever take us in our fully shifted form.

The thought made me feel uncomfortable, and I fought the urge to touch my cock.

Fuck, she was making me hornier than a goddamned nymph.

"You ever been fucked?" Minos asked, leaning in to breathe in her scent.

If the ropes had not bound her, she would have slapped him. I watched as pure hatred rolled through her, her expression becoming feral.

"Tell us your name," I commanded.

She was silent for a moment, but Minos wasn't having that.

"Tell us your name. Now," he growled.

She looked at him like he was an annoying fly she wanted to swat. "Ashley. What about you, captain my-dick-is-bigger-than-yours?"

Aaecus barked out a laugh.

Minos gripped her hair, forcing her head back. For a moment, I thought he would kill her.

I wouldn't stop him if he did.

"*Ashley,*" Minos said in an almost sickly sweet tone, his lips inches from touching hers. I envied that he could taste her breath and touch her. "Are you ready to hear the proposition that could save your life?"

"And what is it?" she gasped.

He let go of her slowly, offering her a demonic smile. "One week. You do everything we tell you. You let us have you however we please. And then you leave here, free of Hercules and monsters. No more debt. No more mafia."

"You can't just cancel my debt with him," she whispered. "Hercules took care of a debt of mine and then bought me like some whore. That's how I ended up here in the first place, and after this, I'm done. Just give me the painting, and I'll go."

"Nice try. I'm not giving you my painting," I said.

"And we aren't like that fucking twat. He's one head of the Three Fates Mafia, as are we. A demigod asshole. We have just as many men, just as many guns, and probably even more money. He's just fucking with us by sending thieves like you. But this time, we'd like to keep one around," Minos said.

"We won't torture you," Aaecus chuckled. "Unless you beg us to."

She looked around, wide-eyed. "You want me to *fuck* you in exchange for you letting me live and waiving a *three million dollar* debt?"

I damn near spit out my sip of whiskey. Minos and Aaecus muttered curses.

"How the fuck did you end up with a debt like that?" Minos asked.

She sighed and then went silent for a moment, thinking through what she wanted to reveal. "Answer my question first," Ashley demanded. "Is that the deal? I sleep with you monsters, and I get to walk free after a week? My debt paid, no strings attached?"

All eyes turned to me. I pressed my lips together, mulling it over.

I couldn't touch her, even if I wanted to.

"I won't fuck you," I said. "I'd rather not touch someone as worthless as you. But Minos and Aaecus can. Then, I will pay your debt and you will leave the city. No tricks. No strings attached."

She was silent for a moment, then she blew out a sigh. "I want it in a contract. I want it signed. I do what you want for one week, and then I'm free of all this monster mafia bullshit."

"Contract, and you will consume seven pomegranate seeds

from the Underworld," I said. "They will enforce the contract, just as they did with Persephone to Hades."

"Whatever. As long as they're not acid or something," she said. "Deal."

I scowled. "Deal," I said, standing. I hit the safety trigger on my gun and holstered it, aware of how her eyes tracked me.

Minos and Aaecus both glanced at me. They both had good poker faces, but I knew that they were surprised.

They obviously wanted this, and....what could it actually hurt? Maybe I'd get a break from their constant bitching. Besides, I had other things to worry about. Men to run into the ground, deals to seal, and a city to own.

One little wench would mean nothing. And it would be nice to have someone at our every beck and call.

"Aaecus and I will go draw up the contract. Minos will show you to your room."

"Room?" she echoed.

"Once you sign it, your contract will begin. But he can give you a taste first, right?" I said, stepping right up to her. She stared up at me, her defiance a lightning bolt straight to my cock.

I wouldn't touch her.

I wouldn't fuck her.

If I did, I knew I would lose control.

And after M, after my curse, after everything... I couldn't risk that again.

"We'll be back," I growled, her presence irritating me.

Maybe by the time I returned, she would choose death.

CHAPTER 3

UNDERWORLD CONTRACT

Ashley

I had a three million dollar pussy, and that was officially the highlight of my shitty day. The deal I'd just struck was a crazy one, but at this point I'd sell part of my soul to get away from this world.

At least I'd break my dry streak.

A monster stood right behind me, one of three that looked human—but definitely were not. There was an air of power surrounding all of them, a dark and forbidding one that made me want to run.

I'd stood in the same room as mafia men and bosses before. From the Russian *Bratva* to the Italian *Cosa Nostra*, I'd had my fair share of run-ins with scary men.

But this was different, even from Hercules.

All three of them made me feel like I was out of my depth. I felt like a drop of blood in an ocean full of sharks.

My head pounded as I drew in a breath, the scent of

alcohol and sweat filling the room. My eyes kept wandering around, my mind developing a map of their penthouse.

A shiver worked up my spine, my nipples hardening as Minos ran his hands down my body to my hips. I clenched my thighs together, tensing as he touched me. I could feel the rough calluses of his palms against my skin, the tension between us making me bite my lower lip.

"You were the one that wanted this," I whispered.

"Yes," he said, his voice sultry and soft. "Your scent makes me want to bend you over and rut you, little thief. Normally, I'd just slit your throat, but I can't bring myself to do it."

My pussy had no right to throb from a threat like that. I glowered, pressing my thighs together.

Fucking mafia men. Fucking monsters.

"So for three million dollars, I'll have to do whatever the three of you want?"

He chuckled as he yanked me back, his hard cock fitting against my ass. *Gods, he's huge.* I could feel him through the fabric of his pants, a soft restless groan against my ear.

The fucked up part about all of this was the heat that spread between my thighs. I'd never been ashamed of sex, never shied away from it. There were things I enjoyed that made it hard to find a compatible partner, but something told me Minos might just work...

He bought you, dumbass. Not partner material.

His breath was hot against my neck, his voice husky. "My brothers would love to merge with me and fuck you. I bet you could take our cock with some magic. I bet you'd beg for it, beg to service us."

"Fuck off," I breathed. "I won't beg you for anything."

"Sweetheart, you're going to beg me for *everything*." He grinded his cock against me. "You wanted to know about demigods, hmm? Did I hear you right?"

I glared, but my curiosity was too much to ignore. "Yes." When I thought of demigods, I thought of the cartoons I'd seen growing up. Ones that had heroes battling monsters, saving mortals, fighting the gods.

But they were just myths and legends, right?

"They're real," Minos said. "Only five left in the world. The Hercules you've been working for, he's one of them. The same Hercules you mortals sing ballads about."

"We don't sing about him," I muttered.

He let out a soft groan, his cock rubbing against me.

The ropes around my hands kept me from hitting him, and the rope around my ankles kept me from kicking. This wasn't my first time being tied up, but the way that bald asshole had done it, I wasn't able to loosen the binds.

He cupped my breast and squeezed, pinching my nipple and making me growl in response. "I think we'll have fun, don't you? You ever fucked a monster? A hell hound? I've served Hades for thousands of years, and I remember hearing screams from his palace before Persephone. All the little mortals he'd fuck over and over again. And I remember the way their slick dripped down their skin, their bodies betraying them...."

Oh, god. His low tone had me gritting my teeth as he squeezed my other breast, continuing to grind his cock against me.

It was distracting me from the revelation that there were more than just monsters out there in the world. I was very familiar with Greek history, as it overlapped with the art world, and now my mind was falling down a rabbit hole.

How much of it was real, and how much of it was just a story?

"It's funny because I knew. I watched you enter our penthouse. I watched you think you got the best of us, all the while I hunted you like prey. You were so blessedly oblivious and I knew the moment I saw you, your body would betray you. That you would belong to me."

Minos' fingers slipped between my thighs, running over my clit.

"Hey," I gasped. "I haven't signed the contract yet."

He began to rub me, circling my clit and drawing a helpless cry of pleasure from me. The tension between us created a rift between the part of me that already hated him and the part of me that wanted to cum for him, and I found myself arching against his chest like I was in heat.

He growled in my ear, pulling me tight against him. "You really think you can survive seven days of sin, little thief?"

"I'm going to," I gasped. "I'm going to survive it and then get the fuck away from all of you!"

He turned me around, tipping my face up to make me look at him. He was too fucking pretty for a monster. His dark brows were drawn together, his irises pitch black with flickers of orange and yellow like burning embers. His soft dark brown waves were still pulled back in a bun, but some strands had loosened and framed his chiseled face.

Minos leaned in, his words a seductive promise. "I'm going to fuck you until you're dumb, little thief," he whispered.

"You can fucking try." I glared at him, wanting to kick this pretty boy so bad.

"Tell me to stop," he whispered, lowering himself down in front of me.

My heart pounded in my chest, my pussy pulsing as he knelt. Even on his knees, his head was at my chest. I'd never considered myself short, but he was a giant. I sucked in a breath as he pressed his face against my pussy, immediately tightening my thighs together.

"No," I rasped. "Not until I'm under contract. Keep that fucking mouth to yourself."

He laughed and leaned back, looking up at me like I was a silly toy he wanted to play with. "If I take your ropes off, are you going to run? Or are you going to be a good little mortal?"

Running sounded nice, but I'd already seen how crazy all three of these fuckers were. Monsters, demigods, gods, mortals. All of it sounded insane.

The theme for the next seven days was *survive*, which meant not running from them—even if that's what I wanted to do.

Right?

Three million dollars and sex for seven days.

Sex with monsters.

"I won't run," I said, even though I wasn't certain that was true.

"Excellent. Is there anything I should know about that would actually cause you harm?" Minos asked, reaching around me to start undoing the knots.

The vibrations of the ropes sliding over each other made goosebumps rise over my skin, my nipples hardening. I blushed, which pissed me off, so I decided to choose a place in the room to fixate on until he was finished.

"What do you mean?" I asked. "I thought you were going to do whatever you wanted."

Minos paused for a moment. "I'll fuck you how I please, but I still would like to know. I'm a monster, but I have morals."

I snorted, and the moment my hands were free, I crossed my arms over my breasts. *Morals.* The mafia monster supposedly had morals.

I'd chosen to focus on the massive TV across from us, and wished there was something on so I didn't have to see our reflections on the empty screen.

I was selling myself to monsters. I felt a sense of frustration, but at least this was cut and dry. I knew exactly what they wanted and didn't have to guess like I did with Hercules.

Damn it. Hercules would be pissed, especially if he'd texted me without an answer.

"Where did my phone go?" I asked, trying to keep any hint of panic from my voice.

"I'm sure Aaecus confiscated it," Minos said as he untied the ropes around my ankles. "Why?"

"I'm certain that Hercules has messaged by now."

"And?" Minos asked, standing up. He tipped my chin up, pulling my gaze from the TV to him. "You belong to us now. Not him. *Our* pet, not his."

"I was never his pet," I growled. "I hate him and he used me. This is the third job I've done for him, and I should have trusted my gut about it."

I thought about the bottle of Tums I'd downed. My gut had told me one thing, and I'd ignored it.

He raised a brow, but didn't say anything. Instead, he continued to hold my gaze until I felt like running again.

"If I really need a break or for you to stop, then I'll say 'lock'," I whispered. "That's my safeword. And I do have limits..."

"Make sure to put that in the contract," he murmured. "Or else we might break you. Write your limits too."

My glare faltered for a moment. One minute he was cackling like a goddamn evil clown, and the next he was practically dry humping me. Now, he was handling me like a lamb.

"Any other advice for a contract with monsters?" I asked bitterly.

Minos shrugged. "Maybe add a clause about getting eaten. Sometimes Aaecus loses control, you know."

I paled, swallowing hard.

Minos snickered, that evil grin coming back. "Just kidding. I don't think he's ever eaten a human unintentionally."

"Fuck you," I muttered, turning away from him. "I hate men like you. Monsters too."

I looked around the penthouse, taking everything in. This living room dripped with money. The soft charcoal rug beneath my feet probably cost more than my yearly rent. There were two black leather sofas and the chair that Damon had perched on, watching me like he wanted to put a bullet through my head.

Aaecus and Minos had some type of weird attraction to me, but *that* monster? He wanted to kill me.

"What kind of monsters are you?" I asked, turning back around. Minos' eyes fell straight to my breasts and I narrowed my eyes. Fucking perv. "And can I have something to cover up with?"

He grabbed a blanket from the couch and threw it at me, his eyes never straying from my breasts until I'd wrapped myself up.

"Eyes up here," I snapped.

He chuckled. "We are the three hellhounds that form Cerberus."

Cerberus.

Fuck. Not only had I messed up this job, I'd ended up in the claws of three monsters from the Underworld.

When I had first come to Moirai and discovered monsters were real, I spent days pouring over everything I could find about them on the internet.

Well, the internet had one thing wrong about Cerberus. Not one fucking article had mentioned that Cerberus wasn't just a massive monstrous beast, but also three men that looked like Greek models.

"Cerberus?" I whispered, my head swimming.

"Yes. You know the myths and legends?"

"Yes. The three-headed dog," I said. "The right-hand creature of Hades himself. Guardian of the Underworld, devourer of souls."

"Mhmm." Minos leaned in, his breath tickling my ear. "I'm going to enjoy fucking you a little too much, I think."

I shivered and was about to take a step back when I heard Damon and Aaecus come back into the room, this time not alone.

I turned to see a very hardened man, with tattoos covering his entire body and a cigar in his mouth. He was holding three bags of food and a receipt.

"Food is here," Aaecus grunted, running his hand over his bald head. He had rolled up his sleeves, tattoos now showing. I lost count of how many covered him.

He was even taller than Damon and Minos. The bastard that had caught me.

"Just in time too," he said, narrowing his gaze on me. "I was getting hungry for a mortal snack."

I pulled the blanket tighter around my body, but didn't ease up on my glare. At the end of the day, I was still a thief. I wasn't a wallflower, or someone that would freeze. I was smart. A fighter. I'd been in and out of criminal worlds for years, and threats didn't quite do it for me like I'm sure these assholes expected.

I would make it out of this situation, just as I had every other situation I'd ended up in.

Damon stood in the center, the aura of power around him palpable. The scent of the cigar smoke curled around the living room, followed by the scent of food.

My stomach grumbled, and I bit back a curse.

Damon's lips tugged into a cruel smile.

Out of all of them, he was the one that made me the most nervous.

I could handle the lust that Minos and Aaecus had for me. But I wasn't sure I could handle the disgust Damon obviously held for me. He didn't even know me, yet he acted like I wasn't good enough to be a foot stool.

"This is Hector. He's one of our bodyguards. He will be taking your measurements after you sign the contract," Damon said. "Put the food down."

The bodyguard glared at me, which meant word had already spread that all the monster's men had been bested by me. That gave me a hint of satisfaction, and I found myself smirking.

"Yes, boss," Hector grunted, putting all the bags on the floor.

"Not on the fucking floor," Minos snapped. "Take them to the kitchen and then come back. For fuck's sake, we're not dogs."

I snorted, which drew four not so happy gazes to me.

Damon glared as Hector disappeared and then came back with a measuring tape, the cigar still burning in his mouth.

I took a step back from him, raising a brow. "Measurements? For what, a body bag?"

"No. For what you'll wear in our presence. Although, sure, a body bag too," Aaecus said.

What the fuck had I gotten myself into?

"Come on, little thief, let's sign the papers so I can fuck you," Minos growled.

Three million dollar pussy, I reminded myself as he shoved me forward.

My heart pounded a little harder, nerves working through me as I followed Damon to their massive kitchen. It looked unlived in, and I noted the trashcan was open and full of takeout bags.

"Does anyone know how to cook?" I muttered.

"Sorry, Hades doesn't typically give cooking lessons in the Underworld," Minos snarked, while chuckling to himself.

I found myself smiling even though nothing about this situation made me happy.

The four of us crowded around the black marbled island at the center. Damon set down a stack of papers, along with a clear glass vial that held what I assumed were pomegranate seeds. The juice had pooled at the bottom, vibrant red.

Hell, that could be poison.

"I'd like for you to add that I can use a safe word," I said firmly. "If it's used, all activities stop immediately."

Damon scowled for a moment and then shrugged, "I already added that. Now, read over it, sign it, eat the seeds, and then Minos will take you away so I can eat my food in peace. Everything is getting cold."

Wow. The big bad boss had added in a safeword for me. I was surprised and did everything I could to hide it. I leaned over, scrutinizing the pages. One was just a copy of the other, and the contract was short and simple.

The following will outline our agreement and summarize the terms of the arrangement that we have discussed.

You have been detained by Damon, Minos, and Aaecus Cerberus as a servant for the dates of February 17-25 (2/17-2/25).

You will be responsible for successfully completing tasks the three aforementioned ask of you, to whatever specifications are within the policy guidelines discussed.

In exchange, you will receive life protection from Cerberus

Inc. and, by extension, the Three Fates Mafia. Any debts previous to the Three Fates Mafia will be null and void upon completion of the above arrangement.

The use of a safe word will be permitted, but must be used earnestly.

Sign and return one copy of this letter for our records. You may retain the other copy for your files.

Agreed:

Ashley the Thief

There was a place for all our signatures and at the bottom of the page, there was an eye with a circle for a pupil.

The Three Fates Mafia symbol.

A shiver worked up my spine. I'd seen that eye everywhere, always watching over everyone in the city of Moirai.

"Hector is our witness," Aaecus said, a little too cheerfully for my taste.

I really had no choice, did I?

"Fine. Give me a pen."

Damon gave me an annoyed look as he reached into his jacket and pulled one out, because of course he was the type of guy to have one on him. I snatched it and scrawled my signature on both pages, ignoring the way he stared at me.

I had just sealed my fate for the next week. I would do whatever they asked, whenever they asked. I'd sold my body and soul to three monsters, all so I could live to see another day.

Minos pressed himself against my back as he leaned over, signing his name. His cock was still hard against me, and he didn't do anything to hide it.

Aaecus signed next, then handed the pen to Damon. His

gaze darkened as he held the ink to the page, scrawling his signature.

It was done.

I swallowed all my fear and reached for the glass vial. I popped open the top, holding the rim to my lips.

I'd never liked pomegranates, but now I really hated them.

I threw it back like a shot. The seeds filled my mouth and I chewed them as quickly as possible. As I swallowed them all, my throat became an inferno.

My heart began to beat faster and I gasped, leaning over the counter. My head burned, my tongue feeling as though someone had pressed a brand to it.

What the fuck was that?

All the sounds in the room deafened aside from a soft voice I'd never heard before bleeding through my mind, a symphony of dark whispers.

The Thief, The Thief.

I realized that Minos was shaking me and looked up, all other sounds returning.

"What the fuck was that?" he growled. "Are you allergic to pomegranates?"

"No," I gasped. "I don't know."

A heavy silence hung over our group, then Damon growled, interrupting my thoughts. "Take her measurements, Hector. And then go to the places M used to shop," Damon said.

Minos scoffed. "I don't want her even wearing the same brands as that bitch."

"M is not a bitch," Damon growled.

"She absofuckinglutely is," Aaecus said. "She fucked you over, Damon, don't act like she didn't. Hector, don't go to those stores. I don't want our slave wearing anything from them either. Besides," Aaecus said, stepping closer to me. "She should be in more leather than lace. The shiny kind that I can rip with my teeth."

I felt like I was burning from the inside out, my mind spinning as I listened to their banter.

What the hell was happening to me? I could feel the seeds inside of me, the heat becoming almost unbearable. I felt like I was running a fever, my blood boiling.

Was this what it felt like to eat food from the Underworld?

"Well, let me measure her so I can get back to training the newbies," Hector grumbled.

"Good. Tell them her measurements too, so they know that this little thing managed to take them down. Now, show her to her room, the spare one between Minos and Aaecus."

"I'm a bodyguard, not a goddamn butler," Hector muttered. "Surely you don't expect me to serve this *criminal?*"

"Hey," I scoffed, even though I was barely keeping up now. "You got a lot of nerve, pal, considering who's in this room."

Maybe the seeds had been poisoned.

I was still for a few moments, trying to digest everything that had happened. I looked up and let out a soft squeal when I saw the way Damon was looking at me.

"Go, little thief," he whispered, his gaze darkening.

He didn't have to tell me twice. I left with Hector, following him down the hall I'd snuck through earlier.

This day had really gone south.

Hector led me to a room and kicked open the door. "In you go," he said gruffly. "Go on and measure yourself." He tossed the tape at me, along with a pen and paper. "Write them on this piece of paper and slip it under the door. I'd rather not even touch you after seeing how they look at you. I like livin' too much."

"Great," I whispered. I gave him a thumbs up, which made him snort.

"I'll give you a minute," he said, stepping out of the room.

I found myself frozen again, my mind spinning.

Had I really just sold myself to three monsters? To Cerberus? Out of all the creatures I could have ended up doing it with, it was *that* thing? Would they be as hideous as some of the art depicted Cerberus to be?

My stomach roiled and I felt like vomiting. I had been on a rollercoaster since breaking in. From the absolute fear of being caught to being tied up, to having a gun shoved against my temple...

To feeling Minos against me...

I let out a breath, my hands trembling.

He'd devour me.

A sharp knock at the door had my head snapping up. I stared at it in a daze that had come over me ever since consuming the seeds.

"Hurry up, girl, I've got shit to do."

I drew in a shaky breath and took my measurements. I then scrawled them on the piece of paper and crept to the door, sliding it under.

"Good. Give me the pen too."

I ground my teeth but obeyed, rolling it under the crack.

"Good luck, girl. If you're smart, you might survive."

With that, I heard the door click, a key in the lock. I gasped, reaching for it. I tried to yank it open, but was now locked in.

The lock was an easy one to pick, but I still found myself sliding to the floor.

"Take a shower. There's a nice one in there. I think there's some extra clothes too. Oh, and try not to die," the bodyguard called, followed by a cruel laugh.

This was a nightmare.

I'd sold myself to three demons. I was nothing but a chew toy to them, one they wanted to tear limb from limb.

Even Damon. *Especially Damon.*

He would be the cruelest of them all.

I swallowed hard, holding back the tears. I thought about the contract that I had just signed, thinking back to every word... and then realized that the contract had said nothing about keeping me here. I turned slowly, looking at the lock again. It was the easiest kind to break.

The fact was—they couldn't tell me what to do if I wasn't here.

CHAPTER 4

PUNISHMENT

MINOS

The romance action movie Aaecus put on had finished. I sighed as the credits rolled, sinking back into the couch. It was absurd to me that he liked movies like that, but maybe he secretly hoped we'd end up like the heroes in the movie–with defeated bad guys and the girl. Maybe I hoped we would too.

The three of us had managed to have dinner together, even though it was obvious all of us were distracted. Damon still looked angry, even after food and the film.

The mortal that had broken into our penthouse was on my mind. I drummed my fingers on my thigh as I thought about her, glancing back down the hall from the living room.

Her scent lingered throughout our home. I could hear any movement in the bedroom, even over the music from the tv, and found myself listening intently.

Was she crying yet? Was she cursing our names? Praying to the gods to set her free?

Damon lifted the remote, turning the screen off. There was a heavy pause and then he cleared his throat.

"Are you certain she's a human?" he asked, looking directly at me.

His gaze bore into me, crawling over my skin. Even after knowing him for centuries, he still made me nervous when he was like this. On edge and *hungry*. The scar over the left side of his face gleamed, his dark brows drawn together.

"Why are you asking *me*?" I challenged.

"Because you wanted to keep her."

"So did Aaecus," I said, narrowing my eyes.

Aaecus held up his hands, standing up. He pushed up his sleeves and then rolled his shoulders. "I'm not getting involved in your bickering," he grunted, giving me a grim smile. "I'm heading over to Larry's to check on some of his work. We should have a two million dollar deal going through with some electronic currency exchanges and I don't want him to fuck up. There's also the issue at one of the Nymph clubs."

Damon regarded him warmly, relaxing as he spoke. "While you're out, swing by and check on some of the men we have in our cells right now too."

"Fine," Aaecus said.

"And let me know if I need to come talk to them."

"Will do," he chuckled, giving me one last look that said *good luck.*

I watched as he sailed out of the living room, jealous that he was always able to do whatever he wanted without pissing Damon off.

The front door opened and closed, leaving me alone with my mate.

How long had the two of us been together? I didn't even know at this point. Our bond was ancient and beautiful, but also made us fight like an old married couple.

Damon moved two fingers, gesturing for me. "Come," Damon said. "And kneel."

I gritted my teeth, but didn't dare disobey. Not after the day we'd already had. I went to him and sank to my knees at his feet, looking up at his menacing face.

"You made me look like a fool in front of her," Damon growled, his voice low. He was careful, making sure that whatever he said wouldn't carry down the hall to *her* ears. "In front of a *mortal*. Why the fuck do you want her to be alive?"

"Her scent," I answered. "There's something about her, Damon."

I didn't know how to explain it exactly.

He leaned forward and I felt the shift in his mood, like how the pressure in the air changed as a storm rolled in. His hand shot out like lightning, grabbing my jaw and gripping.

"What is it about her?" he snarled. "She's just a woman. I can call twenty strippers over that would literally throw themselves at your feet and worship you like a god. If you want pussy—"

"I'm well aware that I can have any woman in this city I want," I said, cutting him off. "Hell, I've probably had every woman in this city." I started to pull back, but he held me firmly.

How did I explain that for whatever reason, I wanted *her*? I'd watched her break in and there had been something in the way she moved, so sure of herself. She believed she had cut off the cameras, but I had several installed that weren't connected to the main system of the Helm, and could watch on my phone. Still, the fact that she'd been able to hack our cameras with her equipment impressed me.

And when we caught her, she hadn't cried, hadn't begged. She'd tried to strike a stupid deal and get her way out of the problem.

She was a survivor, like us.

Not to mention her scent made me want to hunt her. I wanted to chase her, fuck her, breed her. Her voice made my cock hard, and her bright blue eyes felt like daggers straight into my soul.

I wanted her.

None of that would appease Damon. Ever since M, he'd been more callous with me. There were times he felt like a stranger, times that made me wonder what the hell the two of us were anymore. Sure, there were moments he was tender with me, but our relationship hadn't been what it used to be for a long time.

I loved him, but I hated him too. I still wanted him, even when I wished I could shove him out the window.

"We can use her," I said simply.

Damon's hand began to change and I felt his fingers turn into claws, piercing my mortal skin. A low, beastly growl rumbled in his chest,

"We can," I insisted. "She was sent by Hercules, so we can use her to get more information about him and his faction. We haven't yet been able to infiltrate anything to do with him."

Hercules was one of the demigod crime bosses we had to put up with. One of five, and the only one that actively let his men kill ours or attempted to sabotage our plans. We had more businesses under our control than him, more wealth, more power—and the idea that a monster might be better than *him*, the hero of Olympus, had never sat well.

He hadn't been a hero for quite some time, though.

"He'll know she's been compromised," Damon said. "Her phone has been lighting up, but obviously, she hasn't responded. This was a job, and Hercules isn't dumb. He knows we have her."

"And he expects that she will die at our hands," I said. "But maybe she's a good thief and able to escape us. We could make him believe she got out, and use her then. She was able to bypass all of our security."

"No," Damon said. "And that reminds me, we need to follow up with security and figure out how the fuck this even happened." He sighed, his shoulders finally relaxing. "I thought you wanted to fuck her."

"I do. That doesn't mean she can't benefit you too."

I was still kneeling in front of him, our gazes locked. Blood rolled down my jaw, my neck, dripping onto the polished tips of his shoes. Bargaining with Damon was never easy, but if there was reasoning to your words, he at least listened. That's part of what made him a good leader.

His grip loosened and he let out a breath, his eyes softening. "Sorry," he muttered. "I'm frustrated with you. You've never fought me for a mortal. And you know better than to challenge me like that."

The cuts were already healing. I stretched my jaw and leaned forward, resting my head in his lap. He combed his fingers through my hair, loosening my bun until my hair unraveled. I relaxed against him and had to fight to focus.

The human was driving me mad. I took in a deep breath, practically tasting her through the walls of the penthouse. Her room was next to mine, and it would be impossible for me not to go to her tonight.

I wanted to hear the little thief scream and beg.

"I always challenge you," I said. "Aaecus does too. We have to. It doesn't mean I don't respect you, Damon. Or love you." I looked up at him, holding his gaze. "You know if anyone else disrespected you though, Aaecus and I would be the first to cut them down."

Damon raised a brow, his expression unreadable.

I leaned up, our lips almost touching. "Do I need to show

you how much I *respect* you?" I whispered, sliding my hand up his thigh.

"Maybe," he whispered, the corner of his mouth tugging. "It's been awhile, hasn't it?"

I chuckled and slid my arms around Damon for a moment. His mortal form had become one of my favorites, though I still preferred his monstrous one. I ran my fingertips over his hard muscles, *feeling* him.

The two of us had been dancing this dance for centuries now. "I don't like it when you're mad."

"Then maybe you shouldn't be such a dick," he muttered, his breath hitching as I pressed my mouth against his neck.

"I'm going to cover myself in her cum and then let you fuck me this week. Wouldn't you like that? I know you found her scent appealing too."

I was testing him, and the way he stiffened told me I had struck a nerve.

So, Damon *did* want her.

"Minos," he warned. "*Behave.*"

"No," I whispered, kissing his skin. His scent was like a drug, and I breathed him in, desire rising like a tidal wave. "I can't."

I loved turning him on like this. I loved to push him as far as possible until he became hard and needy, desperate to fuck me.

"What if I got her pregnant?" I whispered, listening for a growl.

"Do *not*," he snarled, gripping my hair and yanking me back.

That had been the wrong button to press. I grunted as I was shoved back onto the rug, Damon pinning me down. His knee parted my legs, his forearm pressing against my throat.

The air was forced out of me in a *whoosh*, a moan following. My cock immediately hardened, straining against the zipper of my pants.

I loved it when he was like this, even though he was absolutely more feral.

"Listen, you little fuck. You will *not* get her pregnant. You will use safety, and you will not create more problems for all of us!"

"I want to," I choked as he applied more pressure, cutting off my air. "I want to fill her with my monster cum and breed her. I want to shove my cock into her little human cunt and give her every drop of my seed."

"*You will not!*"

"I may not want to give her up," I confessed, gasping for air. "I may just want to leave you and only be with her."

Now, I'd done it. The crazy part of me loved it, too.

I lived to see Damon lose his temper.

His human form broke, his body shifting and tearing his Brioni suit. I laughed maniacally as he began to grow, letting out a ferocious noise. His jaws unhinged and I was faced with his massive teeth, his body becoming a hellish wolven monster the size of a car.

My cock continued to pulse, aching to be stroked now.

His massive clawed hand slammed against my chest, knocking the breath out of me. I wheezed, and even through the pain, I let out a laugh, now trapped beneath a wolfish monster.

"*You're a bitch,*" he snarled.

"Yes, but I'm *your* bitch," I huffed, looking down between us.

All our clothing was off, his cock free. He was pulsing, his cock a crimson red with golden veins. Cum dripped from the tip, splattering onto me. His shaft had ridges every inch or so and a knot the size of a baseball towards his balls.

"See," I gasped. "I knew you wanted this. I'm not the only one with a breeding kink."

Damon snarled and stood, dragging me up and onto my knees by my hair. His claws raked against my scalp and I felt the skin tear, blood dripping down from the wounds. His cock slapped my cheek, precum smearing over me.

I opened my mouth just as he shoved the tip of his cock into it, filling me. I choked as he hit the back of my throat, my eyes watering. This mortal form wasn't meant to be taken by a monster, but I enjoyed the pain. I loved it when he broke me.

"*Cunt*," he growled, his hips pulling back before thrusting into me again.

I gagged, tears streaming down my cheeks as he fucked my mouth. He was brutal, taking his anger out on me. I took it, reveled in it, desired it.

Finally, I felt his body shudder, and I looked up through my tears, watching his expression as he came. I swallowed quickly as the heat shot down my throat, drinking his cum.

I would only ever kneel for him. I liked it when he took me, when he lost that clean edge of control.

It was my way of breaking him, even if I had to give up my own control.

He slowly pulled back, his breaths harsh. I fell forward, catching myself on my hands before I hit the floor. I stared down at his clawed feet, at the soft midnight black fur covering him.

"Get up," he growled.

I moaned, focusing on the pain in my throat. I could taste a bit of blood in my mouth, and I smiled, looking back up at him. "I think you needed that."

He began to take on his mortal form again, shifting until he was no longer a monster. He knelt down, digging his fingers in my hair and yanking my head back. "Are you going to behave now?"

"No," I snorted. "Never. And you like that about me."

He didn't disagree. We both knew he had a soft spot for me, and that I liked to use it to my advantage. At least I was honest about it.

Damon shook his head, still annoyed. "How did I end up with the world's biggest slut as one of my mates?"

"I don't know," I said. "How did I end up with someone that has a stick up his ass?"

He rolled his eyes. "Get dressed. That human is your problem. I'm going to go out and help Aaecus take care of some things."

"What about resting?" I asked. "You haven't slept in three days."

"Are you tracking my sleep now?"

Yes, I was. Because when Damon hit day four of no sleep, he was a raging bastard.

"Go do what you want, but come home and sleep," I said. "I'll be here with the mortal."

"Fine," he reluctantly agreed. He looked down at the floor, seeing the shredded remains of his clothes. "Fuck. That was an expensive suit."

"I know," I said, not even hiding my smirk. "I'll buy you a new one, *daddy*."

He muttered under his breath, leaving the living room and heading down the hall to his room. His human form made my cock hard all over again, his lithe muscles perfect and toned.

I much preferred his monster form, but couldn't complain about the mortal one he'd chosen.

He halted halfway, turning to look at the mortal's door.

Alarm bells went through my head as a low growl left him.

I rolled to my feet, walking down the hall to meet him.

"She's gone," Damon said as I stopped next to him.

The door was cracked open, and I found myself rushing into an empty room. I went to the dresser with an open drawer, seeing the spare clothes were gone. The throw blanket was all that was left of her, everything else untouched.

"Motherfucker," I whispered. "She snuck out on us."

Damon let out a low laugh. "Your problem, Minos. Go get your three million dollar pussy, bring her back here, and show her what will happen if *I* ever have to retrieve her."

I ground my teeth, anger working through me. "I'll take care of it."

Damon snorted, his mood almost cheery at seeing my rage. "Have fun. Let me know if you need some help finding her."

"Fuck off," I snarled. "I don't need help finding a mortal thief."

Damon chuckled, leaving me standing alone in the room. I rushed back out to the living room, grabbing my phone off the floor and sending a text to Aaecus.

The thief escaped. BOLO

With any luck, I'd have the mortal in my bed screaming as she took my cock within the hour.

CHAPTER 5

OUT OF LUCK

ASHLEY

The image of Damon shoving his monster cock down Minos' throat was seared into my brain, but that didn't slow me as I burst out the alley door of the Helm. The skyscraper towered above me, the sounds of Moirai at night surrounding me.

That was the thing about this city, it was never truly asleep. Especially in this neighborhood. The sounds of traffic echoed, horns blaring as pedestrians crossed streets on their way to clubs.

I took off down the alley, ignoring the sting of the asphalt on my bare feet. Hector had been right about the spare clothes in the room, but I hadn't found any shoes. I'd managed to knock out one of the guards, but his boots had been way too big for me and would have slowed me down.

I hit the sidewalk and smacked straight into a couple of people, knocking them back. I almost lost my balance, but managed to catch it before taking off again.

"Watch where you're fucking going!"

"Hey!"

I ignored their shouts as I ran.

Everything had gone wrong today. My luck had run dry it seemed. The *Bratva* job had fucked me up, and now this.

No more stealing. No more mafia.

I ducked down a different alley, tracing my way back to the car I'd stashed this morning. The one that was supposed to have carted me and that painting away.

I ignored the shards of glass that stabbed into my bare feet, cursing as I ran down another street, took a left, and then found my chariot.

A silver 2001 Impala sat unbothered on the street. I glanced around as I yanked the driver-side door open, slamming it shut behind me.

My heart pounded in my chest, my blood rushing in my ears. They had to have realized I'd escaped by now.

Would they come after me? Would they hunt me down in those hideous monster forms like the one I'd seen Damon in?

I sucked in a breath and leaned over, reaching beneath the seat and gripping the screwdriver stashed beneath it.

The keys were still with the things the monsters had taken, along with my phone.

"Son of a bitch," I mumbled.

Well, this would be the Impala's last ride, but at least I could make it to my hideout.

I slammed the screwdriver into the ignition as hard as possible and cranked it, the car sputtering. It took a moment, but it came to life.

"Thank the gods," I muttered, putting it in drive. "I just need a little more luck to get home."

The wheels screeched as I lurched forward, my hands shaking as I drove. Pain flared in my feet and I winced.

Maybe running barefoot wasn't a good idea. At least, I'd be able to treat myself at home. Being in this type of world had taught me some good medic skills.

I looked behind me, making sure that no one had followed. All I saw were strangers on the street and sidewalks.

I blew out a breath, sinking back as I sped out of the most congested part of the city. Every red light turned green right as I came up to it, the traffic seeming to clear a path just for me.

I felt a wave of heat again, my head throbbing as I crossed one of the bridges to the east side of Moirai. I gripped the steering wheel until my knuckles were white, forcing myself to breathe.

Within a few minutes, I was parking my car again. I turned it off and stared at the windshield for a moment, letting the events of the night take root.

It was all a blur.

Maybe leaving had been a mistake, but I was an opportunist. I'd had the chance and I had taken it—but now, undoubtedly, I would need to hide from not one mafia man, but four. Hercules *and* the Cerberus monsters would be after me now.

Fuck. My life really kept tumbling down hill, despite how hard I worked to get to the top.

I willed myself to get out of the car. My apartment was on a quiet street, one that was uneventful. I pushed open the squeaky gate, went up the steps, and through the front door of my building, hissing as I took the stairs to the third floor.

Once I made it to my door, I arched up on my tiptoes, grabbing my spare key from its spot on the frame. Bloodied footprints trailed behind me.

The moment I stepped inside, I slammed the door behind me, locked all of the locks—good, state of the art locks—and sank against the door.

"Fuck monsters," I whispered, squeezing my eyes shut for a moment.

I didn't have time to just stand here, though. I needed to take a quick shower, sanitize and bandage my wounds, get dressed, grab my backup wallet, and grab a taxi out of Moirai.

I went through my apartment and flipped on every light, ignoring the fear that iced my veins. Everything seemed to be in place—the patched sofa was still ugly as hell, and the kitchen was still a mess from cooking dinner last night. I had all my electronic equipment spread over the floor, along with a couple of blueprints of the Helm.

I stripped off my clothes as I limped to the bathroom. The pain in my feet was getting better, which meant my adrenaline had kicked in. I plopped on the edge of the tub, pulling my foot onto my knee.

"What the fuck?" I mumbled, watching as shards of glass fell to the floor.

All of the cuts closed before my eyes. My blood wasn't dark red like normal, instead it was a weird shade of orange.

Fuck, maybe those seeds had been laced with something.

All the pain went away and I let my foot go, checking the other. It looked the same, all of the cuts and wounds gone.

I was losing my mind. I mean, it was bound to happen eventually, right?

I turned and cranked on the shower. I didn't have time to process everything that had happened tonight.

I wasn't even sure that running had been the right decision. They would come for me. I knew they would.

The way that Minos had touched me had been almost possessive, which told me that he wouldn't let me go.

My stomach growled as I stepped in, but the heat of the water washed away all thoughts.

What the hell is happening to me? I closed my eyes as the

water ran over me, rinsing all the tension down the drain. I showered and it wasn't until I turned off the water that I heard the movement in the bathroom.

"*Hello, little thief.*"

A scream left me right as the shower curtain was yanked open, and I grabbed my shampoo bottle like it was a weapon. The massive tattooed mafia boss stood on the other side, looking especially pissed.

"You'll never be able to run from us."

I screamed again, only for him to slam his hand over my mouth and shove me against the shower wall.

His chest was heaving, his eyes burning. Every tattoo on his skin almost looked like it was moving, his form wavering like it was about to break.

Fuck, fuck, fuck. They'd found me so fast.

He stepped into the shower, barely fitting. His shoulders were massive, his body pressing against mine. I hadn't realized just how big this man, this *monster,* was.

He leaned in, his voice menacing against my ear. "If you run from us again this week, I will *personally* rip your soul into strips and feed it to demons in the Underworld. Nod if you understand."

I nodded, tears filling my eyes.

He grabbed my hair and yanked, forcing me to look up at him. "I had three fucking jobs to check on tonight, and instead I had to track you down. After you signed a fucking contract that you'd be with us for the week. Let me tell you something," he snarled, forcing a cry out of me as he pulled my hair again. Pain burst through my skull, his hand over my mouth muffling any noises I made. "Minos wants you alive. Damon doesn't give two shits. But me? I want you dead. I want to fuck you and kill you, because there is something *wrong* with you."

I had no idea what he meant, but it didn't matter. He

dragged me out of the shower and I stumbled, my knees cracking against the tiled floor. I grunted in pain, my eyes wandering around the bathroom for some other kind of weapon.

Aaecus turned to say something, but froze as the sound of wood crunching and the front door breaking open echoed through the apartment.

His head snapped up, his grip loosening. "For fuck's sake," he muttered. Letting go of my hair, he motioned for me to be silent.

That meant only one thing.

Someone else had found me too.

These bastards really didn't fuck around.

I stayed on the bathroom floor, watching with wide eyes as he pulled a gun from his belt and cocked it. "Up," he whispered, motioning for me to stand.

I obeyed him, not knowing what else to do. I reached for my robe and pulled it on, earning an eye roll from him. Voices carried through the apartment, followed by sounds of things being broken.

"Stay," he said.

"I'm not a dog," I scoffed.

Aaecus ignored me and slipped out of the bathroom. For such a large man, he was silent as he moved.

I pulled my robe tight and followed after, sneaking behind him through my bedroom.

The sound of footsteps and voices grew louder, and the door flew open. Two men burst through but froze at the sight of Aaecus.

Aaecus growled. "Get the fuck out of here. She belongs to me."

"By order of the Three Fates Mafia—"

Aaecus fired his gun and I screamed as a bullet went

straight through the man's head. Blood and brains sprayed on the wall and door, his body collapsing.

The other man took a step back, holding up his hands. "We're with Hercules! He will destroy you for killing one of his men!"

"Destroy *me*? Do you know who I am?" Aaecus laughed, his body flickering again. For a moment, I caught a glimpse of his other form.

The same one that Damon had taken.

The monster beneath the mortal shell.

Hercules' man startled, taking a step back, but that only seemed to amuse Aaecus. He let out a low laugh, stepping forward. "He doesn't give two fucks about his goons," Aaecus said. "Get the fuck out of here before I shift and eat you alive."

The man's hand fell to his waist, reaching for a gun. Aaecus moved in a blur, grabbing and slamming him onto the floor. I stared in shock as bones crunched, my stomach rolling with nausea.

The man cried out as Aaecus snarled, pinning him down easily. "Take a message back to Hercules," he said. "Tell him that if he comes after this bitch again, I will personally fucking gut him. We *bought* her. We *own* her. She is contracted to us."

He let the man up and shoved him down the hall.

We watched as he ran, disappearing into the night.

Rage rolled off Aaecus in lethal waves. He turned slowly, his gaze falling on me. Blood speckled him, blending in with the tattoos that crept up his neck. He licked his lips, his fangs gleaming in my bedroom light.

I was shaking. I couldn't stop it. I'd been in the underworld of society for a long time, but I'd never killed someone.

He chucked, a dark amusement. "A little bunny caught in the wolves' jaws," Aaecus said, stepping closer to me. "Stand up."

My legs were like rubber bands, but I still found the strength to stand. He stopped in front of me, tipping my chin up with the cold nose of his gun.

"Look me in the eyes."

I did. I looked straight at him, and for the first time in my entire life–I wished that I could kill someone.

"Who owns you?"

Tears blurred my vision again, but he only growled out a warning.

"Answer me, Ashley."

"You do," I whispered hoarsely.

"*We* do," Aaecus said. "We own every single part of you. This stupid little brain, this body, and this pussy."

His hand slid down, pushing open my robe. My entire body flushed with heat as his calloused fingers pressed between my thighs, drawing a squeal from me.

"Fuck you," I whispered.

"If a single tear falls right now, I'm going to bend you over my knees and spank you until you can't sit this week. I don't have time for tears."

His threat was enough for me to hold them back, even as he explored me. He paused, raising a brow as he ran his fingertips over me.

"You're wet," he whispered, drawing his hand back.

"I was just in the shower."

He gave me a *knowing* look, his lips pulling into a twisted grin. "Our pet likes a little violence then, huh? Or maybe it was me surprising you in the shower..."

Fuck. I glared at him, refusing to admit anything.

He chuckled, holding his fingers to my lips. They glistened with my wetness, which only humiliated me further.

"Suck them off."

I hesitated, and he forced them into my mouth.

I hated him, but I wasn't going to crumble. I sucked his fingers, only to realize that I could taste blood on them too.

"Good. Maybe we can break you into a submissive little pet. Wouldn't you like that? Keep sucking and don't fucking cry."

I continued to suck them, squeezing my eyes shut.

"Clean them good and then spread your legs."

I ran my tongue over them, opening my eyes to glare at him. I hated him so fucking much. But what I hated more was the way my pussy started to throb.

He leaned in closer, whispering in my ear. "You can't hide your arousal from any of us, little thief. We're monsters. We can smell you. And you're like a bitch in heat around violence it seems."

I jerked back, releasing his fingers with a gasp, glaring. "Fuck you."

"Spread your legs."

I swallowed hard and widened my stance, my breath hitching as he moved his hand down again. This time, he pushed a finger inside of me, and I bit down on my bottom lip to keep from groaning.

"Don't fight it," he said. "You're gonna cum on my hand, and then I'll deliver you back to Minos. And you can tell him every single thing that happened here tonight."

"No," I gasped, reaching up. I clutched his shirt for balance as he slid another finger inside of me, working them in tandem.

Pleasure began to build even with me wishing I could kill him. I arched back, gasping as he stroked me deeper. I couldn't escape him.

This is what I had sold myself to do this week. My escape plan had failed, and now I would be forced to do whatever they wanted for the next seven days.

"You're so fucking tight. Our cocks are going to split you in two, little thief."

I panted, letting out a curse as I rode his hand. I gripped him harder, gritting my teeth as an orgasm crashed into me.

I cried out, my head falling back as I came. The rush of pleasure was overwhelming, followed by the realization that my captor had just made me cum with his fingers.

I shoved him back, his hand pulling free. I was still panting as I looked at him, words failing me.

"I can't wait to fuck you," he said. "I'm going to make you scream."

"You're disgusting," I whispered, feeling another wave of nausea.

"And you're nothing but a thieving whore. Now, let's go. I need to deliver you back to Minos before he tears the city down. He's going to be pissed I found you first."

A shiver worked up my spine. I felt a mixture of terror and satisfaction, which led to self-loathing.

"I'll put on some clothes—"

"Did I say you could?"

He couldn't be serious.

"I'm not leaving here naked," I whispered.

"Yes, you are," he said. "We'll give you clothes when you earn them. You're going to come as I want—naked and owned by the Three Fates Mafia."

CHAPTER 6

BROKEN BONES

AAECUS

I pulled up to the Helm. It was 3am, but the city was still very alive.

This was going to be fun.

I stepped out of the car and walked around to the passenger door, opening it for the human. She was in my front seat, naked and angry. Just like she had been when I'd found her.

"Out."

Her bright blue eyes had gone dark and stormy, her blond hair still damp. She looked at me with loathing, her gaze darting to the front doors of the Helm. "I'll get in trouble for public indecency."

That was amusing. She had no idea that every cop in this fucking city was on our payroll.

"Get out of the fucking car," I said. "If I have to tell you again, then you will be crawling all the way to the penthouse."

That seemed to change her mind about arguing with me.

Her cheeks flushed as she got out of the car, her nipples perking up from the chill in the air.

She had a perfect body for breeding. Curvy hips, soft thighs, long legs, and breasts that were large enough to bite. There were scars here and there as well, which I enjoyed even more.

I wanted to leave marks on her too.

I slammed the car door shut and shoved her forward. There were murmurs and catcalls from the people around us. Her steps became quicker as we made our way towards the Helm's front doors.

The lobby was all beige marble and gold, decorated with fake plants. There were marble pillars with engravings, and a statue of Zeus with a bolt of lightning at the entrance.

I hated that guy.

The women at the front desk gasped, but no one said anything. They just watched as we walked through the lobby, Ashley's tits and ass bouncing with each step.

I pulled out my phone and opened the camera, snapping a photo. I smirked and sent it to my group chat with Damon and Minos.

BRINGING THE PET HOME.

I tucked my phone away as they both began to text back.

Ashley went to the elevators and pressed the button for the penthouse, her shoulders tense. I reached for her, gripping her shoulder and turning her to face me.

"The elevator will take a couple minutes," I said.

Her eyes widened as I ran my hand down her body, searching out the heat between her thighs again.

"Please don't," she whimpered. "Not here. Not in public."

I heard a couple of laughs from some of the men standing guard, and didn't care.

"Why? You belong to me," I said. "My toy to break. I can touch this cunt whenever I want."

Her eyes watered again and she pressed her lips together. I began circling my fingers around her clit right as the elevator dinged.

She was still so fucking wet.

The doors slid open, and I looked up to see Minos on the other side.

Our gazes met and he growled.

Oh, this would be good.

"Here's your pet, Minos," I said, shoving her back.

She stumbled, and he caught her against his chest. Her eyes were wide, her naked body leaning into him.

"Thanks," he said, his voice stoic.

I was a real bastard, but Minos was even more of one when he lost his temper. Based on the tick in his jaw, I knew he was close to giving into his rage. He didn't like being taken advantage of, especially after promising Damon she wouldn't be a problem.

"Hercules sent some men after her," I said. "I killed one and sent the other back to him, with the message that we own her now ."

There was a 50/50 chance that would actually keep him from coming after her again.

"Have fun getting bred," I said, smirking as the elevator doors closed.

Fuck, the look on her face might just stay with me forever.

I stood there for a moment, my fingertips itching for a cigarette. I needed something to inhale that would distract me from her. Her scent clung to me now, invading everything.

There was something about her. Something that made me

want to lose control. I wanted to forget about all of my responsibilities and take her over and over again until the sun rose over this cursed city.

I let out a breath, forcing myself to let her go.

I had to get back to work. My night had been interrupted by her twice now, and it was fucking with my schedule.

Not to mention, my cock was throbbing.

I stared at my reflection in the polished elevator doors for a few moments, doing everything I could to rid my mind of her. All I could think about was the way she had cum on my hand at her apartment.

She'd squeezed me so tight. I wanted to feel her squeeze my cock like that.

"Fuck," I sighed, annoyed.

I turned and strolled through the lobby, straight back to my car. I wasn't going to fuck her yet, but I needed to work off this tension.

Luckily, there were three men we had imprisoned at the moment that I could use as punching bags.

Echo was one of the night clubs we owned, and it thrived on nights like this. Downtown Moirai was flourishing and as I went inside the club, I was met with the scent of sex, drugs, alcohol, sweat...

And blood.

Music pounded, men and women moving against each other. Neon lights flashed around the room, interrupting the darkness. The walls were painted black, and there were tables with patrons on an upper balcony that overlooked the entire club.

It wasn't uncommon to find Damon there, watching over our world while someone serviced his cock.

I had different preferences. Despite humiliating Ashley in front of everyone at the Helm, I preferred to fuck in private. Damon liked to make a show of things though, as did Minos.

Unless it was the two of them.

Their relationship was complicated, messy, and annoying. For those reasons, I'd never initiated anything with either of them. I didn't want to be emotionally involved in a way that could end up hurting me. After centuries together, I knew them better than any other souls and in some ways, they were like brothers to me. Other times, they were more like friends. And while we occasionally fought like enemies, the three of us worked well together, even with a curse breathing down our necks.

I blinked, focusing on the movement around me. There was a long stage at the center of the club with stripper poles and four dancers, two men and two women. I gave them an appreciative glance before making my way to one of the employee doors, which led to a dark hallway.

I passed by several couples making out and grinding on each other, arriving at yet another door and made my way down a set of stairs. The sounds of the nightclub disappeared, my hearing focusing on the groans below.

The musty smell of being underground filled my nostrils, blood and fear following. I could feel it on my tongue, the metallic taste. I hit the bottom of the steps, meeting one of our men.

"Boss," he said, giving me a subtle nod.

"Have they talked?" I asked.

"No, sir. We've tried several methods, but they haven't squealed."

"Excellent," I said, cracking my knuckles. "I think I'll spend some time with them. If I haven't come up in an hour, knock three times on the door."

That would pull me out of this headspace. The thought of Ashley seeing me down here made my heart beat a little faster, and I shoved that image away.

I couldn't think about her right now.

"Yes, Boss," he said.

I nodded and opened the door, stepping inside a cool room with one overhead light. The walls and floor were concrete, blood staining the gray with rust colored splatters.

Three men were tied to chairs in a row. Bags over their heads and their bodies completely bound. I could see the outline of the headphones that covered their ears, and knew that static white noise was playing.

They'd been like this for at least a few hours.

Bastards.

They were part of the Hydra faction initially, but were discovered to be working for Theseus, one of the demigod cunts we had to deal with. The Hydras and us went way back, and they had sent these three over to us for a bit of torture.

The way our mafia was split up was simple. Each of us controlled different businesses, and on the monstrous side, we tended to work well enough together.

There were the Hydras, the Chimera, the Colchian, and the Gorgons. The Hydras, like us, were a monster made up of three ruthless men. The Colchian, however, was just one monster—a dragon that had survived like us. The Chimera had two leaders, a set of twins. Then there were the Gorgons—run by Medusa. Of course, she didn't go by that name anymore, unless in ancient company. To the rest of Morai, she was known as Madeline Winters, a famed sculptress.

Most of the city believed her faction was run by someone else, but *we* knew the truth.

I'd never liked her very much, but her art amused me. I wasn't a collector like Damon, but I still found her continuous supply of sculptures of men with their cocks broken off to be funny.

Then there were the demigods. The five of them opposite us, the pricks the Fates had allowed to live past their time. They'd been a thorn in our side for centuries. When monsters had been allowed to reside in the mortal world, they'd been sent to 'keep us in line'.

I hated demigods. Whenever I had a chance to kill one, I did.

Jason, Theseus, Hercules, Perseus, and Orion.

All cunts.

I undressed, folding my clothes in a neat pile before allowing myself to completely shift. My bones and muscles cracked, fur sprouting over my entire body as I grew into a massive wolven beast.

I looked down and cursed, realizing my cock was hard.

Fuck. I could still smell Ashley's scent clinging to me.

This torture was going to be awkward, but maybe they'd talk in the face of a massive hellish cock.

I ripped the bag off one of their heads, watching as the man blinked repeatedly. I yanked off the headphones, his voice muffled behind the fabric stuff in his mouth. I pulled that out too, enjoying the terror on his face.

He let out a string of curses as I leaned in, saliva dripping from my jaws. *"Why did Theseus hire you?"*

The man shook his head, sweat dripping down his face. He had the same crazed look that prey did when it was in a trap, his dark hair sticking to his skin.

He clamped his mouth shut.

I sighed and moved to the guy in the middle, removing the

bag, headphones, and gag. He looked around wildly, seeing who he was next to.

Then his eyes went to me, then down to my cock.

"Oh fuck," he groaned. "Fuck, man. We didn't get paid enough for this."

The first guy's eyes widened at his buddy.

"I just wanted you to see what happens when you refuse to speak," I said.

I grabbed the first man's jaw and ripped. The sound of flesh tearing and his screaming made me grin. I watched blood drip down his body, his tongue lagging.

The middle man cursed. "Fuck! Fuck! I'll fucking talk!"

I held his friend's jaw and turned, ignoring the noises the other was making. "*Talk.*"

"There are rumors, man. Rumors that more demigods have been born and are in the city. Theseus hired us to infiltrate Hydra and find out if they have one in holding. They have a woman they call their niece, but she's not really their niece. She was sent to live with them when she turned eighteen, and it was thought she could be one of them. A demigod. We were never able to see her though."

My blood ran cold.

There was no way that was true.

"Liar," I growled.

"I'm not lying! It's the truth. We're supposed to be keeping an eye out for them."

Them? What he was suggesting was impossible. The Fates had stopped allowing demigods to be born centuries ago. Still, I knew he wasn't lying. I could hear it in his voice, in the way it trembled.

"Is that all?" I asked.

"Yes."

"What was the woman's name?"

"Lyla."

"And you think she is a demigod?"

"Those were the rumors, but we never got close to her. The Hydras have her hidden. They protect her."

Argos, Bash, and Pierce were the leaders of the Hydras. They were fierce like us and, for lack of a better term, snakes. If they had something in their control, such as a fresh demigod, I wouldn't put it past them to not tell anyone.

But why keep it alive?

I stared at the human as his friend bled out, thinking everything over. I needed to tell Damon and Minos.

I threw down the chunk of jaw and shifted back into my human form. I pulled my clothes back on, grabbed my gun, and turned—putting a bullet in all three of them. Their bodies sank into the chairs, their deaths quick.

Well, two of them had been quick.

I opened the door and stepped out. "Clean up in here," I said.

"Yes, Boss."

I left the guard standing there and went back up to the club. I paused, looking over the crowd—searching to see if Damon was near.

"What did you find out?"

I paused and slowly turned. Fucking hell.

Pierce was standing against the wall, clearly waiting. He reminded me of a Ken doll with snake eyes, and was my least favorite of the Hydras. Maybe because he was more fucked up than me.

"Come," I said, nodding towards a staircase that led to the VIP balcony.

He followed me and I led him to a table in a dark corner, deciding how I would play this.

I reached into my pocket and pulled out my phone as we sat down, sending a single text to Damon, just the number '1.'

It meant get his fucking ass to Echo now.

I slid onto one of the leather seats and Pierce took the opposite. His bright green eyes met mine, his scars glinting like scales on the right side of his face.

"Who's Lyla?" I asked, holding his gaze.

He stiffened. It didn't matter how good his poker face was or how great of a liar he was, I could see the shift immediately.

"Who?" he asked.

"Pierce," I growled. "The mortal just told me that Theseus sent him and the others to spy on her. To find out if there are new demigods. Surely, if that were the case, Argos would alert all of us." Argos was their leader, Bash was the brains, and Pierce was the killer. Their group was much more divided than Minos, Damon, and me.

Pierce leaned back in his seat, arching a pale brow. "He would. As I would expect Cerberus to."

"I don't know what you mean by that."

"Surely, you do," Pierce chuckled. "Or is a dog's nose not as good as snake's?"

I started to lunge forward, but a smooth voice interrupted us.

"Aaecus, Pierce. Was I not invited to the party?" Damon interjected, coming to our table.

When the man wanted to act, he sure could fucking act. Pierce looked up at him, giving him a subtle nod. "Damon."

"What brings you to my club?" Damon asked.

"I was checking on what information those mortals had, and it seems I got it," Pierce said, standing from his seat. His gaze slid over to me, his lips tugging playfully. "See you around, Aaecus."

Damon and I watched as he left.

"What was that about?" Damon asked.

"Nothing good," I said, mulling everything over.

If I understood what he was insinuating, he meant that Ashley was a demigod. But that was impossible.

"According to the man I just killed, there are new demigods and the Hydras have one. And according to Pierce, so do we."

Chapter 7

Beasts and Goddesses

Ashley

"You never put in the contract that I couldn't leave, so that's why I did."

My explanation was pointless. My words didn't do anything to soothe the monster in front of me, made apparent by the way his muscles tensed and jaw ticked. He looked like he was two seconds away from turning me into his next meal.

After Aaecus had humiliated me and shoved me from the elevator, I'd been taken to the room they'd kept me in before. Minos had locked the door and now stood in front of me, glaring.

My heart raced as I sat on the edge of the bed, looking up at him.

"We'll be sure to add it," he said. "I can't believe you snuck out."

"I can't believe you can take a cock that big down your throat."

We stared at each other until Minos let out a humorless laugh, his eyes darkening. I sensed the aura surrounding him change, and had a feeling that I might have just fucked up. Again. For the billionth time today.

Nevermind that I was still reeling from witnessing a man's brains get blown out of his skull, or from the humiliation of being forced to walk naked in a lobby full of people.

"Undress me, little thief," he demanded. "We're going to find out how much you can take. If you can suck me off better than I can suck off Damon, maybe I'll let you brush your teeth after you swallow my cum."

"I don't swallow," I snapped.

"*Woman*," he snarled, lunging forward.

I gasped as he grabbed my hair, my head burning with pain as he yanked me up like a rag doll.

"You fucking do now. Undress. Me. *Now*."

"Okay!" I yelled, wincing.

He let go of me and I reached up, starting with his shirt. I undid the buttons, holding back tears.

Fucking rich motherfucking monsters. I hope they rot in hell...

"You can cry," he whispered softly, almost sweetly. "After the day I've had, I wouldn't mind seeing you cry."

Unlike Aaecus, who would gut me for shedding a tear.

"Oh, you're scared to, after Aaecus," he chuckled as I pushed his open shirt off his shoulders . It fell to the floor, and I lifted the hem of his soft undershirt. "No, little thief. I like tears. It would be even better if you had mascara on, so it could run down your face while I fuck your mouth."

"I hate you," I breathed, leaning up on my tiptoes so I could pull the shirt over his head. He helped me, his chest now exposed.

He was hot, and that made me hate him even more.

"That's okay, baby," he said. "You can hate me and still take my cock like a good girl."

I started to tell him to fuck off, but before I could get the words out he cupped my face and surprised me with a kiss. Without realizing it, I was leaning into him with a groan.

What was I supposed to do? He was too fucking pretty. If we'd run into each other in a bar, I would have been begging him to let me taste his cock.

My head was spinning, my blood searing my veins. His hands roamed down my body, cupping my breasts as his tongue tangled with mine. He tasted sweet, his mouth hot and body even hotter.

He broke the kiss, the two of us breathless.

Of course he was a good kisser.

"On your knees, princess," he whispered hoarsely. His voice almost sounded desperate, his words softer than before.

I went to my knees and reached for his belt buckle. He stared down at me, his cock throbbing in his pants as I released the clasp of his belt, followed by his pants button. I pulled them down, and discovered he had gone commando. His hard cock sprang free, the veins bulging along the shaft.

Holy fucking gods. This man was packing.

I stared at his cock for a moment, blinking as I processed that I was going to have to fit that thing inside me.

"That's just the human version," he chuckled.

"You're gonna break my fucking jaw."

"Not if you fucking relax."

He gripped my hair, pressing the head of his cock against my lips.

"Come on, little thief," he whispered. "Do you even know how to suck a cock? Open up like a good girl, and I'll reward you with some dignity."

I pressed my lips together for a moment, and then mentally

said fuck it. I was exhausted and wanting to sleep, and if sucking this monster's dick helped me get into a bed in this prison, then so be it.

The head of his cock slipped between my lips, and I groaned as I began to suck him. His breath hitched, his fingers gripping my messy waves as I took him all the way to the back of my throat.

Fuck. Tears filled my eyes, followed by a wave of need. I pushed my hand down between my legs, feeling how wet I was.

Gods damn it all.

I loved sucking cock, and hated that I hated him because this was the best one I'd ever had in my mouth.

"You feel so good," he grunted, thrusting forward. "You're not even gagging."

I took his cock, closing my eyes as I tumbled further and further down the path of need and desire. My head bobbed back and forth, his cock sliding in and out. He began to pump a little harder, his breaths becoming desperate pants.

I ran two fingers over my clit and groaned around his cock.

He suddenly pulled back with a growl. My eyes flew open right as he leaned down and pulled my hand away from my pussy.

"*This* is mine," he snarled. "Only I may touch you, little thief."

I bit my bottom lip, my entire body feeling like a firecracker that had been lit but wasn't able to pop.

"Minos," I gasped, staring up at him.

His body began to shift and I stared in horror as the beautiful man in front of me became a monster. The same type of monster I'd seen in the living room earlier. The sound of bones snapping and crunching made me feel nauseous, but then I felt shock seep through me as he became a creature that reminded me of a werewolf.

He cocked his head, staring down at me.

Fuck. He was a monster but all I could think about now was taking his monstrous cock. There was a knot at the base, it was thicker and longer than before, and was dark red with throbbing veins. Cum dripped from the head.

"You're even more turned on," he growled, his voice deeper. "I can smell you. Do you like fucking monsters, little thief?"

I didn't know what to say, but the way my pussy pulsed was answer enough. I leaned forward and he stiffened as I flicked my tongue where his cum dripped, his curse sending a stab of need through me.

"Just admit it," he huffed, his claws slipping gently into my hair.

"No," I scoffed, but I licked the head of his cock again. I couldn't stop myself.

"You want to know what it would feel like."

"No," I said again. "I hate everything about this. You're making me do this."

"Does that help you believe that you don't want to be fucked by a monster? I'm not forcing you to lick my cock like it's a fucking ice cream cone."

My eyes fluttered as I took the head between my lips again, swirling my tongue as I tasted him.

"I'm asking you," he rasped as he gripped my hair. His claws scraped against my scalp, sending a shiver down my spine and drawing a moan from me. "I'm asking you to. Will you, Ashley? Will you let me bury my cock inside of you?"

I looked up at him, and he slid a claw over my bottom lip, the tip scraping gently. I parted my lips, surprising us both as I allowed him to slip it inside of my mouth.

"I need you," he rasped. "Contract or not, I won't force you."

Fuck. Contract or not, I did want this. Maybe it was because I'd had a shit fucking day, or maybe it was because part of me wondered if he would do the type of things I liked. Either way, when in Rome...

I swirled my tongue over the tip of his claw, sucking carefully. Knowing that one wrong movement from him could cut me turned me on even more. His breaths became uneven as he fought for control, his monstrous form looming over me.

We stared at each other now, a monster and a human. The air shimmered with lust, our needs growing.

"You look so good on your knees for me," he said. "Sucking on a claw that could tear you to shreds."

I licked and sucked harder, the noises filling the room. The razor sharp edge glided over my tongue and I gasped at the feel of a small cut, drawing back as blood filled my mouth.

He growled. "Show me your tongue."

I opened my mouth, sticking my tongue out so he could see the cut he'd just made.

He leaned down, his wolfish jaws parting to reveal rows of teeth. I kept my mouth open as he leaned down. His tongue darted out, meeting mine before pushing further into my mouth.

His jaws were large enough to fit around my head.

He drew back with a low growl and then a groan. "Your blood..." he whispered. "Fuck. There's something about you."

He leaned in again, and this time it was more like a kiss— only he was doing his best to clean up any blood welling up from the cut. I reached up and began to stroke his cock as his tongue invaded my mouth, my body humming with more and more pleasure.

He pulled back again, staring at me with the same confusion I felt.

I wanted him. This mafia monster that had bought me.

I needed him.

"You're stunning," he whispered.

I felt stunning, I realized. No one had ever called me that. No one had ever looked at me the way he looked at me.

Like he needed me.

Like he wanted me.

"Everything about you reminds me that a beast can worship a goddess," he murmured.

His words sank into me, but he didn't give me a moment to respond. I yelped as I was scooped up and lifted against his furry chest. "We're going to shower," he said. "Get the scent of death off you." He carried me across the room, into the sprawling bathroom I had yet to explore.

My emotions were on a fucking roller coaster. Being reminded that a man died tonight because of me didn't exactly make me feel warm and fuzzy inside.

"Aaeceus shot someone," I whispered.

"Yes, I'm sure he did," Minos said, shrugging. "I shoot people too."

They shot people. Killed them. Kidnapped them.

"Do you torture them?"

"Sometimes," he said. "Sometimes we have to."

"You never have to hurt someone like that."

"You're wrong," he said. "You don't understand. The worst monsters are not monsters. They're humans. I've seen terrible things done by the hands of mortals. Things that no one should ever do."

I knew that better than I would admit.

My thoughts turned deeper and darker the longer he held me. I'd never seen someone shot before, but I wasn't unfamiliar with death. There was a reason I had ended up in the world of criminals.

The bathroom was all black and gray, with gold-veined marble counters and a walk-in shower fit for a monster. It reeked of wealth—the kind of money I would never have.

The kind of money that hired me to steal.

I'd done so many jobs in the last few years. I'd learned from the best until he hadn't been the best anymore.

Tears filled my eyes.

I'd promised myself I wouldn't think about the past any longer, but I was breaking apart. The monster who held me in his arms had done so many terrible things, but who was I to judge when I'd done them too?

He carried me into the shower with ease and flipped a switch. I looked over his shoulder and stared, shaking my head.

"You have a fucking fireplace in your shower."

It was true. The walk-in was huge, with the type of shower head above us that would feel like rain. The warmth from the fireplace chased away the cold, the black tiles polished and reflecting the flames that roared to life at the flick of a mere switch.

"Yes? And? Enjoy it," he chuckled. "Maybe instead of running away and fighting us, you enjoy the luxury of this penthouse and have good sex."

"If only it were so easy to behave exactly as you please."

He chuckled as he leaned back and turned on the shower.

"Are you going to smell like a wet dog after this?"

That made him laugh, his head falling back for a moment. His whole chest rolled with the sound, and I found myself smiling.

"No," he finally answered. "Gods, woman, I don't know what to do with you."

He stepped us under the water and let out a soft groan as

the water hit him. He shifted me in his arms, and I wrapped my legs around his hips, yelping as he turned and pressed me against the tiled wall.

It was cold against my skin, my nipples hardening.

"Fuck," I groaned, grinding my hips against him. "I don't know what I'm doing with you. One moment, I want you. The next, I hate you."

"I want to kiss you," I moaned.

Minos leaned in, his tongue parting my lips. This was unlike any kiss I'd ever had before, far more primal. Aggressive. He held me as his tongue began to thrust down my throat. His teeth scraped my lips, nicking my skin.

He drew back for a moment and made me gasp as he lifted me even higher, placing my legs on his bulky shoulders.

"What the fuck are you—"

My words were cut off. I gripped the fur on top of his head, letting out a scream as that insane tongue dipped inside of me.

"Oh gods!" I cried, heat filling me.

Contract or not, this was the best fucking sex I'd had in my life.

His tongue moved in and out of me, lapping me like no man had before. I groaned as pleasure filled me, the pressure building.

I was going to come. I was going to come on his tongue, straight into the mouth of a beast. A monster.

Fuck, his tongue felt good.

Another cry left me and my head tipped back as my orgasm unraveled, pleasure shooting through my entire body. I felt my muscles squeeze his tongue, every part of me hanging onto the wave of relief.

He withdrew with a soft grunt. "You taste like nectar," he said, licking his mouth. "I'm going to devour you again and again," he growled. "First, let's get clean. Then, bed." He let me down carefully.

My head was spinning as I looked around for the soap. I grabbed a bottle off the wall, poured a copious amount into my hands, and then began to wash him like my life depended on it. I gave him very firm rubs across his body—lathering up the soap in his fur.

"You're incredible," he moaned.

He hadn't asked me to do this. He hadn't asked me at all. I found myself wanting his tongue again, and wondering what his hot cock would feel like pulsing inside of me.

I washed everything, even kneeling in front of him and cupping his balls. I blew a warm breath against his cock, watching as it throbbed.

"Your pussy will never be the same after you take my cock," he growled, pulling me back to standing. "I'm going to mark you as *mine*."

The water rinsed over the two of us as his mouth found mine again, the soap chasing away the horrors of today.

"I'm going to dry myself off," he whispered. "I want you in bed, waiting for me, face down and ass up. Do you understand?"

"Yes," I whispered.

"Go," he said. "Be ready for me, little thief."

I left the shower, grabbed a towel, and went straight for the bed. I dried off quickly, the anticipation of taking him driving me wild.

I listened to his movements in the bathroom as I crawled onto the mattress. I grabbed a pillow and put it under my stomach, positioning myself with my ass up.

I needed his tongue back inside of me. Coming once for him hadn't been enough.

I wanted him to do things to me that no one else would do.

I felt the darkness within me for a moment, the dark things that I desired turning from a craving to a desperate need. I wanted him to choke me, to fuck me, to make me scream.

I wanted him to give me every inch of his massive cock even if I begged him to stop.

But I couldn't tell him those things, could I? I had to keep those dark desires secret.

I wouldn't tell him that if he put me on my knees and slapped me, it might just make me come.

Minos came out of the bathroom and I turned, my gaze following him over my shoulder.

"Good girl," he praised. "Look at your wet little cunt. Dripping just for me. And to think you didn't want me to fuck you."

I let out a helpless moan, squeezing my eyes shut.

I felt him get onto the bed, but then the sound of a door slamming echoed through the entire apartment.

"Minos!"

It was Damon, undoubtedly.

Minos let out a low snarl. "What the fuck does he want?"

"MINOS!"

That was Aaecus.

Minos let out a string of curses and left the bed. "Stay here," he said. "Exactly as you are now."

I heard footsteps coming for the door.

"They're going to come in," I argued, turning over.

Minos shot me a dark look. He slowly began to shift back into his mortal form, although his eyes still burned like before.

"Minos! Get the fuck out here. NOW!"

He snatched up the towel I'd brought into the bedroom and wrapped it around his waist. My heart raced as he went to the door.

"I'll be back," he said, and then he went out to the hallway.

I listened intently. Their voices escalated, but I couldn't make out what they were saying.

What the hell had angered them so much?

Had Damon decided he wanted to kill me instead? What if they went back on the contract and sent me to Hercules?

Hercules would murder me.

Especially since one of his men had died today.

I reached for the edge of the blanket and slipped beneath the covers, sinking into the bed. The voices grew quieter, and I wondered if Minos would come back.

Did I even want him to?

I had been about to let him take me. I had given myself over to him so easily, and all because he'd been a little bit nice.

I lifted my head as the sound of footsteps came down the hall again, stopping at the door. I expected Minos to walk in, but instead heard the sound of the lock turning.

Whatever had just happened, I was right back to square one.

—

CHAPTER 8

DEMIGODS

DAMON

The sun began to rise outside, filling the kitchen and living room with warm light. My gaze was fixed on Minos, a mixture of anger and worry driving every word of mine.

"Did you fuck her?" I asked.

"No," Minos growled. "I was about to when the two of you interrupted. What the fuck is going on?"

Aaecus was gripping the bar so hard that his knuckles were white. He glowered at Minos too, his muscles tense. "I tortured the three Hydra men today. I found out they were sent to discover if the Hydra leaders were holding a demigod. I now have reason to believe they were."

"Which demigod?" Minos asked. "I can't imagine one of the demis going missing without—"

"A fresh one."

Minos stared unblinking, his breath hitching.

"A new demigod that the gods are unaware of," Aaecus

said. "I saw Pierce. He didn't deny what I said, but insinuated that the thief we have is one as well."

"That's impossible," Minos whispered.

"Is it?" I asked. "Is it impossible?"

"Zeus and the Fates have prevented it," Minos said, clearing his throat. "There is a written command. The gods are not allowed to procreate with mortals."

"The Fates do as they please," I sighed. "They always have. If they decided to bring new demigods into the world, then a contract wouldn't matter."

"Why would they?" Minos asked. "What good are demigods now? The world isn't the same as it was. There's no need for heroes to stop monsters from devouring humans. Most monsters are dead."

"To overthrow what's left of us," Aaecus suggested. "Who knows? New demigods could ruin us and the world we've built."

"What if she knows? The thief. What if she is playing with us?" I asked.

"No," Minos said. "She's not..."

"Your cock is blocking your mind," I hissed. "She could be."

Minos paled, his gaze falling to the counter. "I fucked up, then. I tasted her blood."

"You *what?*" Aaecus and I snarled in unison.

"If she is a demigod, then I don't believe she knows," Minos said. "I swear, I didn't know either. And Pierce could have just been fucking with you. Who would even be her parent? The god of bad luck?"

"The god of thieves," Aaecus speculated . "Hermes."

His words were like a guillotine. I shook my head, feeling a numbness wash over me.

Could Hermes be her father? I hadn't seen Hermes in ages.

The god of thieves, luck, gambling, and messaging was an evasive one. He was a trickster. I had never liked him.

If anyone had fucked a mortal and managed to dodge a contract made by Zeus and the Fates, it would be him.

"She has bad luck," Minos said.

"Bad luck or is this exactly what the Fates intended?" I asked.

That was always the grand question.

I liked to be in control. I did everything as I pleased. Mortals and monsters obeyed me, the world around me molded to my will. Everything was exactly as I wanted it—unless I thought about the Fates.

Then I began to wonder if what I wanted was really just part of their bigger scheme. Was I in control of my own destiny or was Lachesis spinning me along?

Was she at work right now? Bringing a daughter of Hermes into the house of monsters?

"If she is a demigod, then she won't die," I said decidedly.

"Let her sleep tonight," Minos whispered.

My head snapped up and I stared at him like he'd lost his mind. "Are you serious, Minos? You're already under her control, aren't you?"

"No," he snapped. "I'm not. But we've already had so much happen since last night. Let her rest, and we can test her tonight."

"*I* will test her tonight," I growled. "Not you. Not even Aaecus." I turned, glaring at him. "Don't think I can't smell her cum on you."

He stiffened, as did Minos.

"Did *you* fuck her already?" Minos asked.

"I fucked her with my fingers," Aaecus bristled, glaring at him. "Why does it matter? I signed the contract too. I can fuck her whenever and however I please."

I already knew the answer, and it only made me angrier. "Minos wants to be her first, apparently. Take her monster virginity. Isn't that it?"

"Fuck you, Damon," he said.

I shook my head, my rage intensifying. "It's disgusting. She's nothing but a criminal whore, yet you stand before me, asking me to spare her. I fucking own her like a cheap piece of trash. Her life is in *my* hands."

"There's something about her—"

"If you bring up her scent one more time, I'm kicking you out," I said. "Maybe its because she's a fucking demigod! How the fuck else would someone manage to sneak out on us like that?"

I hadn't even heard her, which infuriated me. I'd been focused on fucking Minos of course, but I still should have heard something.

"We were preoccupied," Minos seethed. "Or have you forgotten about fucking me already?"

We stared at each other, and then I gave him a cruel smile. "You're forgettable almost all of the time, so perhaps."

"Listen," Aaecus growled. "We all need to rest. Especially you, Damon. Minos, do not fuck her. Let's lock up, sleep, and decide what to do in the morning, once we've had some space from each other. She won't get out, I'll make sure of it."

"Put a shock collar on her," I said.

"*Damon,*" Minos growled.

"I'm fucking serious. Collar her and give me the remote when you're done. And Minos, do not—or so help the gods I will fucking murder you—do not taste her blood again. Never again."

Minos shook his head, his anger clear. "What difference does it make now?"

"Minos," I warned, my spine straightening. "I will kick you out of our mafia if you disobey me."

"How?" he asked. "You're cursed with me."

I moved in a blur, grabbing his jaw with a snarl. "I'm cursed with you, but that doesn't stop me from keeping you locked up for an eternity."

"I hate you," he hissed.

"I don't fucking care. Tell me you won't take more of her blood."

"What are you afraid of? A mating bond? With a potential demigod?"

That was exactly what I didn't want to happen.

"You belong to me," I reminded him. "Mine. Even if you hate me."

Aaecus sighed. "For fuck's sake, get a room, you two. I can't take this."

"Jealous?" Minos asked, giving Aaecus a sly smile as he stepped back from me.

"Far from it," Aaecus grunted.

"I'm going to my room," I said. "Get the collar for me."

"Fine," Aaecus acquiesced. "Get some sleep, Damon. You look like shit."

I ignored him and left the two of them standing there, wishing they'd stop looking at me like that. I went down the hall, pausing at her door.

I listened. I could hear her heart beating, slow and steady.

She had fallen asleep.

I resisted the temptation to pound on the door and continued down the hall. Her scent haunted me as I locked myself in my room.

I undressed as I mulled everything over. My clothes ended up in a pile on the floor and I went to the shower, rinsing off before plopping onto my bed.

What if she had Minos under her spell? What if she was a demigod sent to ruin us from the inside out?

I would punish her for that.

She wouldn't make it out alive if she was a demigod, contract or not. Demigods were evil beings with too much power.

Killing her would be hard too, if she was one of them. Even if a god like Hermes was the parent. He wasn't quite as powerful as one such as Zeus or Hades.

I should have known by her scent. That's why it was so enticing to the three of us—yes, enticing to me too. Demigods always drew us in that way, their blood calling to us.

It had caused so many problems in the past. They would invade a monster's space and it was difficult to fight the blood frenzy they could cause simply by existing.

Countless monsters had died at the hands of demigods.

Countless demigods had died at the claws of monsters.

If Ashley was truly one of them, I would hurt her.

I would use her.

I would make her do things that would break her.

Seven days of sin. Seven days to find out if I had a demigod in my possession.

Seven days to find out just how well a demigod could beg for their life.

I stared at the ceiling, letting my anger take over.

I was losing my grip on Minos. And Aaecus wasn't far behind. There had been moments where he had doubted me.

All of this was her fault. It had only been a few hours, but she'd managed to hook them in.

I closed my eyes and thought about her, bringing the images of her face to my mind. Her dirty blonde hair, smooth skin, and bright blue eyes. She was nothing but a fuck doll.

What was her past? What was her history? If she was a mortal, then she had a life I could find out about.

I rolled out of bed, ignoring the exhaustion clawing at me. It didn't matter now—I had to know. I went into the office that was connected to my bedroom, taking a seat at my desk. The walls were windows in here, and with the sun now risen, there was a bright glare on my computer.

I pressed a button to close the curtains, the machinery humming as they automatically shut, submerging me in cool darkness. My computer screen glowed as I logged on, casting a bright blue light over my body.

Who was Ashley, the thief?

I pulled up our camera system and grabbed a snapshot of her face in the lobby earlier. I paused, seeing her entire naked body on display for everyone and the smug look on Aaecus' face.

I hated that. I didn't want the mortals to see her.

Why does it matter?

Disgust and frustration had me grinding my teeth as I pulled up another website, one the city's police used. I uploaded her image and waited, wondering how long it would take to find out exactly who she was.

The loading process didn't take long. I raised a brow, leaning forward as a match appeared.

Found you.

I read over all the info about her, making notes as I sifted through.

Ashley Galani. Twenty-six years old.

Father unknown.

Mother died when she was ten.

Grew up in a small midwestern town with her aunt and uncle.

Aunt died when she was sixteen.

Went to college for a degree in the arts before disappearing seven years ago after the death of her uncle. Cause of death unknown.

She was wanted for questioning about his death.

"For fuck's sake," I muttered, leaning back in my chair.

Demigods and their missing parents.

And their bad luck.

Her life looked like a string of misfortunes, which was common for those with blood of the gods. This world rejected them, hurt them, fought against them until they claimed their power within.

If she wasn't a demigod, then someone had fucked her over before she was brought into the world.

I felt a pang of sympathy, then buried it back into the hellhole that was my heart. I could not have sympathy for her.

I had to find out if she knew of demigods. Hercules could have sent her to infiltrate and manipulate us. She could be part of his plan to bring us down.

A frustrated sigh left me and I leaned forward, bringing up social media to try and find her. She barely shared anything, but I did manage to find three pictures of her that she'd posted.

Ashley stared back at me, a soft smile on her face. She looked so carefree in all of them, a girl enjoying the heat of the summer. There was an older man in one of the photos, I assumed he was her uncle. They had the same crinkle around their eyes when smiling. I could see how much they loved each other, how much they cared for one another.

Would he have known if she was a demigod?

Did he know he'd die and leave her to such a cruel world?

I leaned back in my chair, staring blearily at her photos. I either had a mastermind demigod thief in the bedroom down the hall or a woman with extraordinarily bad luck.

Either way, she would die at my hands.

My eyes began to drift closed as I continued to stare at the screen, her pictures plastered over it.

She was pretty.

It was a shame.

The Fates were cruel.

CHAPTER 9

COLLARS AND SILK

ASHLEY

My stomach burned as I sat up in bed, the blankets falling around my waist. I was naked, of course, and alone. I closed my eyes for a moment, listening intently for any sounds outside my door.

Darkness engulfed my room aside from the sparkling lights of the city below. It was night again, which meant I'd slept the entire day away.

The monsters had let me sleep too.

The door to the bedroom opened, and to my surprise, Damon came in. I tensed as he shut the door behind him, his muscles strained.

"Morning," I said hoarsely.

"Evening," he answered drily. "You and I need to talk, and if you're honest with me, you'll get clothing." He held up two bags. "Which would be useful considering you'll be going to one of our clubs tomorrow night."

"You wouldn't make me go naked," I said.

Surely he wouldn't.

"I would," he said. "Do you think I care what the world thinks of you? Did Aaecus not already prove that *none* of us care about you?"

His words cut like glass, and I did my best not to wince. No, of course he didn't care. He was right, too, Aaecus had already paraded me around through the lobby.

My cheeks flushed, but I did my best to keep my voice steady.

"What do you want to know?" I asked bitterly.

Damon set the bags down and walked to the foot of the bed. His gaze seared me the same way it had when he'd caught me stealing from him.

"Are you a demigod?"

What? Was he serious? I stared at him like he'd lost his mind. "What?"

"Are you a demigod?" he asked again. "Be honest with me."

"No," I answered, shaking my head. "No. I'm not. What the hell would make you think that? I'm not one of *them*."

The fact that Damon was entertaining such a ridiculous idea, and believed it enough to question me, infuriated me. Hercules had ruined my entire fucking life, had used my debt and past against me. I had reason to hate him, almost more than the three monsters that had captured me.

"Did you know your parents?"

I felt my throat close up. I stared at him, my thoughts spinning. "My mother died when I was ten," I whispered. "But you already know that. Did you look me up, Damon? Did you see how many people have died in my life? Did you see how the only people that want me are the police?"

"I did," Damon answered stoically, his eyes narrowing slightly. "So. Did you kill them all?"

Horror washed over me, followed by rage. How fucking dare he. Accusing me of killing everyone I've loved.

I launched myself toward the foot of the bed. I reached for him, but in one swift motion, he slammed me back down onto the mattress, pinning me with his weight.

"How dare you!" I rasped.

He grabbed my neck, squeezing hard enough to make me gasp for air.

My pussy throbbed in response.

Now is NOT THE FUCKING TIME, I mentally berated myself.

"Answer me," he snarled.

"No," I spat. "I didn't fucking kill them, you stupid son of a bitch."

He squeezed harder, cutting off my air supply completely. I became painfully aware of how it felt to be pinned beneath him like this, unable to get free. I shoved against him, but it was no use.

My ears started ringing, my head spinning. I raked my nails down his chest, but he only chuckled.

"Another question," he said casually, as if he wasn't choking me. "Were you sent here by Hercules to get pregnant by one of us?"

He eased the pressure on my neck, allowing me to drag in air. I gasped for it, my heart beating rapidly. I felt the rush of adrenaline and chided myself for how being choked by him made me feel.

I was in a perilous situation and I couldn't stop thinking about him fucking me while he choked me.

"Answer me," he demanded.

"No," I wheezed. "No! He sent me here to steal the painting, that's it. That's all I am. I'm just a thief for hire." Tears filled my eyes as I stared up at him. "I didn't kill them. I didn't.

I swear I didn't. Someone killed them. Anyone I love dies. I'm fucking cursed."

He stared at me, his dark brows drawing together. He eased the pressure more and all of that sexual frustration turned on me, melting into something much sadder.

I'd been so good at running away from everything, shoving down all the pain and sadness. But it all came rushing back, filling my entire body with the type of pain that was almost ethereal. It wasn't my muscles and bones that were broken, it was my heart. My soul.

"I didn't kill them," I breathed again.

It would have been easier if I had. If I was a secret serial killer, some evil mastermind without a heart. I wasn't like that though. I had never enjoyed hurting others and that trickled into my life as a thief.

Hell, that's probably what had fucked me when it came to the *Bratva*. I left too many witnesses alive.

If I was more like the mafia I was now tied to, maybe I wouldn't be here and in this position.

"I believe you," he said, finally letting go of my neck. He sat up and was now straddling me. "You are a demigod," he stated. "I know you are. You never knew your father, death has haunted you, and you're a thief. A good thief, *supposedly*. You've stolen items that no one should be able to steal, from places not even I could break into so easily. Your luck is volatile, and it's because the world of mortals is meant to break you. To test you. You're like them, like Hercules."

"I'm not a demigod," I croaked. "That's wrong. I'm not one of them. I'm nothing like Hercules."

"You are," he said. "And now my mate has tasted your blood. If you didn't do this on purpose, then you truly have been singled out by the Fates to live a miserable existence. And I don't envy you."

"Do you mean Minos? Why does it matter that he tasted my blood?"

"Because, if you are a demigod, then tasting your blood creates a bond. Even if it's not a mating bond, it is still a bond."

"I didn't taste his," I retorted. "So—"

"That's even worse," Damon seethed. "You've stolen more than one thing from me now. First, you stole my art."

"I didn't actually steal it. I attempted to."

"Now, you've stolen my mate."

"Is he your mate?" I snapped. "I saw how you fucked him in the living room. You didn't care if you broke him."

"You bitch," Damon hissed.

"Am I wrong?" I asked. "When was the last time *you* sucked his cock like that?"

He scoffed. "We have a dynamic I don't expect you to understand," Damon said tightly.

"Why? Because I'm nothing but a whore to you?"

I was testing someone I knew had a bad temper, but I didn't care. "Eye for an eye. You just asked me if I murdered the only people I've ever loved. So I'm asking if you love the person you call your mate. Are you even capable of love?"

"No," he replied, moving off me. "No, I'm not. I'm a heartless mafia leader. A monster." He let out a chuckle, but there was no humor in it.

"I'm not a demigod," I stated again, but he clearly did not believe me.

Damon grabbed one of the bags and reached in, pulling out a black box. "Come kneel in front of me, Ashley."

Hearing him say my name sent a shiver through me. I slid off the bed and went to him, kneeling on the cold hard floor.

He loomed over me, his expression menacing. He removed the lid and withdrew what looked like a dog collar.

"Pull your hair up," he requested as he took it into his hands.

"I will not wear a collar like a dog," I hissed.

"Lift your hair. Now."

Fuck. He was really going to collar me like I was some mutt.

"I hate you," I spat as I swept my hair up, holding it in place as he leaned down. His face was inches from mine, our lips almost touching as he looped the collar around my neck. I felt the clasp against my skin, and the bite of the collar too. There were metal bits every inch or so, and they were cold against my neck.

"This is a shock collar," he informed me. "If you attempt to take it off, you will be shocked. If you attempt to leave this penthouse, you will be shocked. If you refuse to do anything I ask of you, you will be shocked. In the event that you try to use our contract against us, you will be shocked. You are my slave. I am your master. You belong to me for the next week," he said. "I am the leader here, the boss. Everything that happens is because I have commanded it."

"Seems like you're overcompensating," I mumbled.

"Would you like to find out? I can give you my cock right now. Collaring a pretty woman has always made me hard. Even if she's nothing but a lowly criminal."

He grabbed my hand, placing it over the hard outline of his cock in his pants. I sucked in a breath as I felt the heat from it, felt him throbbing.

"You're horrible."

"I am," he agreed, tipping my chin up and forcing me to look at him. "Are you going to behave, Ashley?"

"I can certainly try," I responded bitterly.

"Good," he purred softly, sending another shiver down my spine.

He was dangerous and cruel.

"If you step out of line, I will fuck you and then I'll kill you," he threatened.

"You mean you'll rape me," I fumed.

"No," he said. "I don't rape women. You'll be begging me for it. You'll beg for my cock to be inside your demigod cunt, and then you'll beg for me to take your pathetic life."

"I will never ask or beg you for either of those things. I'm a lot stronger than you think."

"I'm sure you are," he quipped, smirking.

He ran his thumb over my lips, all while holding my hand to his cock.

"Open your mouth."

Fuck. Was he going to make good on his threat now? I felt a flash of fear as I slowly parted my lips. He slid his thumb inside my mouth, tugging on the side like it was a hook and I was a fish.

"Bite down for Daddy," he instructed.

I recoiled, but he held me in place. His eyes danced with amusement and I felt heat flare through me the same way it had when I'd been pinned beneath him.

I remembered his threats about shocking me. Would this motherfucker actually use a shock collar on me though?

"Three, two, one—"

I bit down on his thumb. Hard. As hard as I fucking could, and kept biting down as I glared up at him. I put every ounce of anger into it, wishing I could crush his bones with my mouth.

"Good girl," he said. "See? Is that so hard, Ashley? To be obedient? You like it too, don't you?"

I bit down harder, but he only chuckled.

"Your teeth are so soft compared to mine," he whispered. "Now. Release."

I held on a second longer, then let go of his thumb. I swallowed the saliva in my mouth, sitting back on my heels.

"Good," he praised. "So obedient."

"*Daddy?* Really?" I sneered.

"You'll be calling me Daddy before the week is up. Then maybe you'll understand Minos a little more. I could break his jaw with my cock, and he'd thank me like a good boy."

I glared at him, but he only smiled and walked toward the door. He paused with his back to me.

"I do love him, for the record."

"And I'm not a demigod, for the record." I retorted.

"We'll find out," Damon said cryptically. "Tomorrow, you're running a heist for me. Tonight, I'm leaving you to Aaecus and Minos. They can fuck you, breed you, use you. I don't care. But tomorrow, you belong to me, demigod."

He grabbed the door and I yelped as he yanked it off the hinges. Part of the door frame cracked, and he turned to face me.

"No secrets in this house," he scolded, leaving and taking the door with him.

He was a fucking asshole.

I sat there for a few moments stunned, staring off as I ruminated on everything we'd just discussed.

He believed I was one of them. It was absurd, insane, and honestly disrespectful. How could he think that?

What if it were true?

"Are you hungry?"

I blinked, clearing away my thoughts. Minos was standing in the destroyed doorway, a soft smile on his lips. A feeling spread through me, an unwelcome one. I shouldn't be glad to see him, but I was.

"I ordered some food," he offered. "Figured you could use something to eat."

My stomach grumbled in response and I nodded silently. I reached for the bags that Damon had left, seeing that there were some clothes in there.

"Wear the beige silk dress," Minos requested. "I want to see it on you."

"Okay," I murmured.

Minos nodded and left, heading back down the hall.

I dug through the clothes until I found what he meant. I pulled it out, running my fingers over the fabric. How much did this cost? How was it possible that someone had so much money they bought something like this for someone they were holding hostage?

I slipped it over my head and stood, adjusting the fabric as it slid down my body. It was soft, thin, and just a couple shades darker than my skin. It had an open back, the fabric draping across my lower back and ass. There was a slit up my right thigh, the kind that barely kept everything hidden.

I walked into the bathroom, the lights coming on as I entered. I was startled by that, and even more startled to see myself in the mirror.

The collar around my neck was black and looked more like a necklace. The dress they'd chosen for me fit perfectly. I ran my hands through my hair, then opened the drawers of the vanity, looking for a hair tie.

I found one and pulled my hair back, pressing my lips together.

I was so lost. So tired and lost.

Drawing in a deep breath, I exhaled and headed out to their den. I was greeted by the scent of food and my stomach rumbled in response as I made my way to the kitchen.

Minos was pulling to-go containers out of a plastic bag, a plastic knife hanging from his mouth.

"Is it just us?" I asked.

"*Soon*," Minos said through clenched teeth. He grabbed the plastic ware from his mouth, smiling at me. "How'd you sleep?"

"Well enough," I replied. "I can't believe I slept the entire day."

"I did too," Minos said. "Should be good to go for a couple weeks now."

"A couple of weeks?" I puzzled.

"Yep. Sit down. I'll get you some water and a plate."

I stood still for a moment, then pulled out one of the barstools. I slid onto it, eyeing Minos carefully as he got me a glass of water and piled food onto a plate.

"Fried chicken?"

"Plus mashed potatoes and okra," Minos added. "There's a place down the street that makes the best southern style food in Moirai. It's called Mama's Chicken. I'd never had this kind of delicacy before we came to this city."

I doubted it was the best, but I didn't say no to a plate full of hot food. I'd eat anything at this point.

"I see Damon put the collar on you," Minos noted. He slid onto the stool next to me and began to dive into his food.

"He did," I said. "Made it very clear if I'm not the picture-perfect obedient bitch you all want, I will be shocked. Oh, and he accused me of murdering my family when I was a child. *Also,* he mentioned that he thinks I'm a demigod sent to fuck you."

Minos nodded, his eyes wide as he chewed. "Well. At least he's honest about what he thinks and wants."

"*Really?*" I asked, shaking my head. "Not to mention he ripped the door off its hinges. That was truly the cherry on top."

"He has his reasons," Minos sighed.

I stared at him as I began to eat. He wasn't wrong, the fried chicken was really fucking good. The mashed potatoes were yummy, and the fried okra was crispy. I wasn't sure if this was *the best*, but I grew up in the Midwest, not the Underworld. Not that those two were much different from each other.

Silence settled over us as we ate. Sitting next to him, all I could think about was how if I did anything wrong, I might end up getting electrocuted.

It was absurd that this had even happened, and I was furious that Damon had put a collar on me. Did he really believe I was a demigod?

There was no chance in hell that was true. Then again, there were things he was right about. I didn't know who my father was. My mother had taken her own life when I was ten years old. I had gone to live with my aunt and uncle, then my aunt had died when I was sixteen. My uncle had been a thief, a really good one. He was who I had learned from.

When my aunt died, he ended up walking away from his office job and becoming a thief for a gang that promised him loads of cash. He was a damn good thief and a fool. Her death had truly sent him down a darker path. He did jobs that got him in trouble, and that was how I had ended up getting pulled into doing such things. He had taught me how to get out of almost every single situation, and soon I was running the jobs myself.

He tried to do the best he could, even though after the death of my aunt, he had been haunted by sadness.

Then he was murdered by the hands of the people that made those pretty promises. It wasn't much longer after his death that I was sucked into a world I couldn't escape. My reputation as a thief who could steal almost anything spread, and soon I was being contacted by people willing to pay me enough money that it would put me through college. Enough money to get me into a new life. Eventually, a job came along that I should have refused. When it went wrong I ended up in the clutches of Hercules

This city was demented. It drew you in and held you here. A place for monsters and demigods to roam freely, believing they were the rulers of the entire world. It made me wonder if they ever left their little bubble.

When I had first met Hercules, I thought he was charming. He'd been easy to talk to, and was kinder than I expected for someone so rich. Knowing now that he was a demigod, everything made more sense, but I wanted to know more about them.

"Is your silence because you hate the food or because you're thinking about the big what if?" Minos asked.

"What if *what*?"

"What if you *are* a demigod?"

I shook my head in disbelief. I'd already told Damon several times, but I'd say it over and over again if I had to. I was *not* one of them. Even if I'd had bad luck my entire life. Even if I didn't know my father, and everyone that I ever loved had died.

"I can't be," I answered so quietly, I was surprised Minos heard me.

"But what if?"

"You tell me," I implored. "What if I am? You tasted my blood last night."

"I did," he agreed.

We stared at each other. He slowly raised an eyebrow, his eyes dancing with amusement. Was this funny to him? The idea that he had tasted the blood of a demigod?

I didn't even know what that would mean, but Damon hadn't made it sound good.

"What is a demigod?" I asked. "I went to school and I'm familiar with mythology. But up until I landed in this hellhole of a city, it was just that. Myth. So can you please explain everything to me?" I added the please, hoping that would work its magic.

"A demigod is exactly what you think they are. One parent is a mortal and the other parent is one of the gods," Minos explained. "Zeus, Hera, Athena, Ares, Hermes, Dionysus, Apollo, Aphrodite, Poseidon, Hades, and more. For centuries, they were allowed to have relationships with mortals, which sometimes resulted in children. Many of those children never lived to be adults. This world was cruel to them. We were cruel to them. Their blood taunted us, made us hunger for them. Made us hate them. Monsters and demigods, villains and heroes. Many of the tales are true and many are not. For one, they were certainly not as nice as the stories made them sound."

I took a deep breath, digesting all of the information. "And monsters? Why are monsters and demigods running a mafia?"

"Because the Three Fates gave us a second chance," he continued. "We were finally allowed to live amongst mortals without being hunted or hated. We were allowed to break the chains the gods had bound us with for so long. That's why we are here. And why we are ruthless."

I swallowed hard, pressing my lips together. Minos shifted in his seat, his shoulders relaxing. He watched me, his eyes drawing me in.

"If you are a demigod, and I tasted your blood, that means you will have some control over me. Not a lot of control, but enough to make me do things I maybe don't want to do. The only way to even this out would be for you to taste my blood as well. But who knows what other side effects that may cause," Minos finished, shrugging.

He leaned across the counter, grabbing a styrofoam cup with a straw. He let out a happy sigh as he sipped whatever he was drinking, shrugging his massive shoulders.

"Maybe I don't care," he added. "Maybe I want you to ruin me."

"You don't actually mean that," I said, but I found myself smiling.

Once again, I wished that our fates weren't so twisted. What if I had met him at a bar instead? What if we had to run into each other on the street and offered apologies that led to a conversation? Would we have had the chance to explore the chemistry between us as just two people, instead of a potential demigod and monster?

I wanted him. That was undeniable.

In just a few days though, I would never see him again.

Minos winked at me. "Finish your food. I'd like to finish what we started last night."

I felt my pussy pulse, my cheeks flushing.

"If you'd like to," he added .

I nodded. "Yes."

"Good," he said, his voice becoming hoarse. "I'm desperate to taste you again."

CHAPTER 10

KNOTTY

MINOS

The two of us finished eating and cleaned up together. For a few minutes, I was able to forget she was our prisoner. I was able to forget what Damon had told me last night and the threats he had made.

I was not allowed to give her my blood under any circumstances. Damon made it clear that he would force me to leave, if that happened.

Honestly, I wasn't sure he'd go through with it. He had only slept for a couple of hours, which led me to believe he was up to more than he wanted Aaecus or me to know.

But, even with his threats, I found myself not caring. I wanted her. I wanted to fill her with my cock, to feel her pulsing around me. I had lain awake last night for hours thinking about fucking her over and over again, and when I'd fallen asleep—she'd been in my dreams too.

All I could remember of my dreams was how hot her cunt had felt around my knot.

I wanted to take her repeatedly and explore that sweet little body.

I was desperate to touch her. To taste her.

I hungered for her like I had never hungered for anyone else before.

Demigod or mortal, I didn't care. I needed her now.

Ashley turned and looked at me. My gaze roamed over her body, over the dress I had chosen for her. It hugged her curves, and I could see her nipples pushing against the fabric. The collar Damon was forcing her to wear clung to her slender neck and I was frustrated that I wouldn't be able to choke her now.

At least not with my hands.

Her eyes darkened the longer I stared at her, her hands curling into fists.

"I don't like it when you look at me like that," she whispered.

"Like what?"

"Like you want to eat me."

"I *do* want to eat you," I said, stepping close to her. I cupped her jaw, forcing her face up so that she was looking at me. "I want to fill you. I want to breed your little cunt with my monster cock. I want to hear you scream while I knot you."

Her breath hitched. I slid my hand down her neck, careful not to push against the collar. I could feel her pulse under my fingertips and could hear it too.

"I want to be so deep inside you that I can feel your heart beating around my cock and both knots," I purred. "That's how I'm looking at you."

"Minos..."

"What?" I asked.

She pressed her soft lips together and then closed her eyes, taking a moment. I didn't know what she was thinking, but I wished that I did. I wished I knew what was happening in her mind.

"Fuck me," she groaned, her eyes flying open. "I want you. I'm not sure why, but I don't hate you as much as the others. So fuck me."

"As you wish," I whispered.

I scooped her up, throwing her over my shoulder as my body began to change. She squealed as I grew taller, my nails becoming claws, my shoulders becoming even broader.

I'd never felt like this about anyone before. I'd been with countless men and women over the years, but when I was with Ashley, I felt light again. I wanted to savor every moment with her.

I carried her down the hall to my room, kicking the door shut behind us. I slid her down my body until her legs wrapped around my hips and her fingers tangled in my fur.

Fuck, I needed to feel her. She reached up and grabbed my face, her lips parting so our tongues could meet in a kiss. She let out a soft moan, one that made my cock immediately harden.

She was *ruining* me.

I carried her to my bed, desperate for her scent to mix with mine. She laughed as I plopped her down in the center.

Her eyes went to my cock, her swollen lips pulling into a smile.

She was beautiful when she smiled like that.

"I need you inside of me," she rasped. "Please."

I stopped for a moment, her plea tapping into the most primal part of me. A low growl rumbled in my chest and I leaned down, grabbing the silk fabric of her dress and ripping. She gasped as it tore, her breasts spilling free. I immediately leaned in, flicking the tip of my tongue over her nipple.

She cried out, her scent becoming increasingly aroused. It

was like a drug, and maybe Damon was right—maybe I was under her control now.

Maybe I liked it that way.

I cupped her breasts, my claws leaving angry red marks that had her making all sorts of delicious noises. I played with them, worshiped them, my tongue playing with her nipples as her scent surrounded me.

I licked down her body until I came to what I wanted. She was so fucking wet for me already, and I breathed her in.

She was a drug, I was an addict, and I couldn't get enough of her.

I pushed apart her thighs, dipping my tongue between them before shoving it inside of her. She arched against the blankets, her throaty moan making my cock and knots throb.

"*Minos.*"

I loved hearing her say my name. I groaned as I plunged my tongue inside her again, the taste of her pussy driving me wild. She tasted like Elysium, like heaven.

I worked her cunt, driving my tongue in and out. She squeezed around me as I lapped her up, drinking in her essence. I rolled her over onto her stomach, dragging my claws down her back.

Her gasp was sweet, a moan following. The way my claws marked her made me feral.

"Do you like a little pain?" I huffed.

"Yes," she breathed.

Thank the fucking gods. I raked my claws down her spine again, watching as the red marks from the sharp tips deepened. She hissed as I slowed the movement, really digging them into her.

I reached down and knotted my fingers in her hair, splaying out the blonde strands. They reminded me of silk, and I brushed them out with my claws.

"Fuck," she whispered.

"You're my little fuck doll," I said softly. My control was hanging on by a thread, forcing myself to slow down with her was the equivalent of keeping myself from coming.

Not yet. Not yet.

"Your gorgeous ass and beautiful blonde hair. You're perfect," I said. She sucked in a breath, letting out a whimper. "You're going to feel so good taking my cock, baby."

I pulled her ass up, her breasts pressing against the blankets as I moved behind her.

"Please," she begged. "Please. Please fuck me now."

I tipped my head back, drawing in a sharp breath. Her scent was drawing out the most primal part of me, the part that had wanted to breed her the moment I saw her.

I had taunted Damon with this moment, with me filling her little mortal cunt with my cock and giving her every drop of my cum.

"Please," she begged again.

I gripped her hips, my claws digging into her skin. She didn't cry out because of the pain, but because the sting of it brought her pleasure.

The Fates had brought someone to me that was absolutely perfect.

I spread her ass cheeks, wanting to see all of her as I pressed the head of my cock against her pussy. She cursed, gripping the blankets as I gave her the first couple of thick inches.

"Oh gods," she groaned. "You're so big. I've never taken something so big before."

"You're taking me so well too," I praised. My claws dug into her more, desperately holding onto my restraint. "I can feel you squeezing me, little thief."

She simply moaned again, her pussy pulsing around me. I gave her another couple inches, easing inside of her. I needed to stretch her around my cock before fucking her the way I wanted to.

After a couple sessions, her pussy would be trained to take me all the way.

"Oh gods," she rasped. "Is that all?"

I looked down and chuckled.

I was only halfway inside of her.

"No, sweetheart," I said, giving her more. She cried out, her pussy gripping me like a vice. "You're only halfway there."

"You won't fit all the way," she protested.

"I know," I said. "But I'm going to keep going until your body physically can't take me. And then we'll train this pretty asshole too so you can take it all."

I pulled back, my cock sliding out of her before I thrust forward again. The two of us groaned together, and I repeated the motions. With my next thrust I gave her as much of my cock as possible.

Her back muscles rippled, her gasps edging me.

"Ashley," I grunted. "Fuck."

I couldn't keep going gently now. I needed to fill her, to breed her.

I gripped her hips and began to pump in and out of her, the head of my cock bumping against her cervix. She cried out, every thrust giving her as much of my cock as her body could take until she was taking it all.

A brutal rhythm overcame me, lust driving me wild as I fucked her. The sound of our bodies slapping against each other, along with our cries and moans, filled my room.

"I'm going to come," she panted. "Oh gods. Minos!"

If she wanted me to stop, it was too late. I growled as I kept filling her until she screamed, her entire body tensing as an orgasm crashed into her. I watched in awe as her body clenched around me. The sounds she made were ones I never wanted to forget.

I was going to come. I was so close and couldn't stop myself. I fucked her harder, letting out a low growl and giving her one last thrust before my cock burst inside of her.

She gasped as my knots popped into her, sealing every drop of cum shooting from me. I leaned over her, dragging in harsh breaths as I filled her.

"You came inside me," she whispered, eyes widening.

"I did."

"What if..."

"I want you pregnant," I admitted.

She immediately tensed around me, which only made me moan more. Her little pussy squeezed my cock, now hot with all of my cum.

"What the fuck are you talking about?" she yelled, trying to pull away from me.

My knots ensured she wasn't going anywhere.

"Woman," I growled. "I'm still coming."

"I can feel that!" she yelled, trying to crawl away from me.

I snorted and gripped her hips, holding her in place.

"I don't want to be pregnant!"

"I know," I grunted.

She squirmed beneath me, but I only pushed her down into the bed, forcing her to stay still under the weight of my body. She turned her head to the side, that defiant look already on her face.

"Why?" she whispered.

"Because," I said. "If you're a demigod, then we'll make beautiful children. And if you're not, well..."

"What the fuck is wrong with you? You fucking bastard. This wasn't in the contract!!"

"You're right," I said, grinning. "You never said anything about birth control."

"I have an IUD," she blurted .

She was lying.

I leaned down, my breath hot against her neck. I felt her pussy pulse again as a low growl left me, a soft warning one. "Okay, I'll schedule an appointment to have it removed so I can breed you properly."

"Fuck you," she hissed.

"I'll find the best doctor. I'll take you to all the appointments and after I'll take you for ice cream . Then we can have breeding session after breeding session and..."

"I hate you," she cut me off.

"Don't lie to me," I warned. "You can't tell me you don't like how it feels to be filled with all my cum. I can smell how turned on you are."

I closed my eyes, listening to her breaths. I could feel her heartbeat with how deep my cock was inside of her, and it was glorious.

"Damon will kill me," she whimpered.

"Not if you're pregnant," I said, smirking.

She shook her head, shivering beneath me. I held her there, more cum filling her.

I could feel her hatred, and I didn't care. She could lie to me, hit me, try to kill me—but she was *mine*.

No matter what Damon had said, I'd made my decision.

Ashley was going to be mine.

"I can protect you," I promised.

"No you can't," she said. "You can't. You won't. You're a monster who doesn't give a shit about me."

"A monster that wants you."

"I'm not a fucking trophy," she hissed. "You can have me,

fuck me, breed me like a god damned cow—but you will never actually have me. Not the real me."

That's where she was wrong.

I would win her over. I would steal her heart, make her love me. She would not be able to escape me. Not after this.

I couldn't let her go.

She had no idea just how much I needed her, wanted her.

"I hate you," she spat again.

I chuckled and in one swift motion, rolled over onto my back and seated her on top of me. She gasped, leaning forward and planting her hands on my thighs. I began to shift my body back into my mortal form, but kept my cock the same.

She rocked against me, letting out a frustrated sigh. "You can shift select parts of your body?"

"Yep," I said. "Might be fun."

She scoffed, which made me smile because my distraction had worked.

I let my cock slowly begin to shift, my knot going down. My hot cum began to drip out of her, and she groaned as I was finally fully back in my human form.

My cock was still hard.

I sat up and turned her so her legs would wrap around my waist. She tried to pull away, but I hugged my arms around her, holding her in my lap.

She growled, pulling an arm free and slapping me.

"Slap me again," I provoked, looking up at her. "Slap me all you want."

She did. She slapped me harder this time, but I lifted her up, pressing the head of my cock back against her pussy.

Ashley sneered, trying to shove against me, but I brought her back down on my cock again. She gasped, a guttural groan leaving her as she grabbed my shoulders for support.

"Gods damn it all," she huffed in exasperation.

I grinned, thrusting up. "Slap me again, princess."

She bit her lower lip as she began to ride me, still glaring at me. "No. You like it."

It was true, I did.

"I bet you'd like it too," I challenged, filling her pussy all over again.

Her nails dug into my skin as we fucked, her breasts in my face. I leaned forward, sucking on her nipples with a growl. I was tempted to shift inside her, to let my form take over again, but I was enjoying having her so close like this.

Her arms wrapped around my neck and I looked up at her, her body fitting against mine perfectly. She panted as she took me until finally, she cried out again. I groaned as I felt her come around me, and I did the exact thing I wasn't supposed to do.

I leaned up, kissing her neck as she kept coming.

And then I sank my teeth into the soft skin of her shoulder, her blood filling my mouth.

She didn't even scream, still so caught up in the pleasure that was rushing through her.

I moaned, drinking her blood, swallowing it. She growled at me, rocking on my still hard cock.

"Two can play at that," she snapped.

Before I realized what she meant, she sank her little human teeth into my neck like a god damned vampire.

I yanked back from her, but she held on, digging her teeth in further. "Fuck," I yelled, pain flaring as she broke my skin. "No! FUCK!"

It was too late.

I'd said I wanted her, but I didn't want *this*.

The moment my blood hit her tongue, I felt the mating bond snap into place.

Three things happened next.

One, I realized that I'd just found the mate I'd been searching for since I knew soul mates existed.

Two, I now knew she was undoubtedly a demigod.

And three, I felt a rush of power. Not from me, but from her. It was like a sonic *thump*, one that mortals might not be able to hear—but every being, god, demigod, or monster would.

She drew back, falling onto the bed with wide eyes. My blood wet her lips and her blood dripped from her neck.

I watched as the red began to turn gold.

"Oh Ashley," I whispered. "We really fucked up."

THREE FATES MAFIA

MINOS

Chapter 11

Knives

Ashley

"Damon is actually going to murder you, Minos."

Aaecus stood across from the two of us, glowering like he always did. Minos was pacing back and forth, running his fingers through his dark hair.

I was torn between feeling smug and being terrified. On one hand, seeing Minos freak out gave me an intense amount of satisfaction. On the other, he'd just filled me with his cum and then we'd apparently created a mating bond—which had triggered something inside of me.

That something being my blood now resembled liquid gold, I felt like I could arm wrestle Aaecus and actually win, and my senses were heightened as if I was high on some of the best drugs.

"Remove her collar," Minos commanded. "We need to get her out of here before Damon gets home, then I'll talk to him."

Aaecus snorted. "I'm not getting involved in this."

"You already are involved in this!" Minos shouted.

The two of them started to argue, so instead of standing there and listening, I walked to the kitchen. I picked out one of the massive knives that was shoved into the butcher block and pulled it free. I started to work the edge of the blade against the collar until a massive hand came around and plucked it from me.

"Stop," Aaecus snarled. "For fuck's sake. Are you trying to get electrocuted or stab yourself? What if your hand slipped?"

"Aw, it sounds like you actually give a fuck. So cute. I'm trying to get free," I snapped, twirling to look up at him.

He rolled his eyes and turned. Minos was standing in the doorway, still obviously stressed. Rightfully so. This was the fuck up of the century apparently, but I felt a little smug knowing I wouldn't be the only target of Damon's temper now.

Mates, bonds, and Minos' breeding kink. Three of my favorite things if it meant Damon murdered him instead of me. I gave him another glare, hoping he realized this was his fault.

"Go talk to him," Aaecus said. "And I will stay with your whore."

"She's not my whore," Minos growled.

"Nope, just your demigod *mate*," Aaecus scoffed. "The one that has your cum dripping from her cunt, and gold blood dripping from your mating bite."

Minos hissed between clenched teeth. "I didn't know she was going to bite me *back*."

This time I laughed. "You're fucking kidding me, right? You do realize it's not normal to just *bite* someone during sex, don't you?"

"Maybe you're just having vanilla sex," Minos quipped.

"Shut the fuck up," I snapped.

Aaecus snorted. "Actually, based on how your cunt felt on my hand, I'd say you haven't been having any sex—"

I lunged for the knife in his hand, but he outmaneuvered me, slamming me against the kitchen island. He held me there, his body pressed against mine. His tattooed muscles rippled around me, a low growl leaving him.

He grabbed my hair and slammed my head down on the bar, holding it there as he leaned in. "Do you want to fight, baby girl? Is that what you want? Now that you think you're a big bad demigod, you're going to take on the terrible monsters?"

"I would kill you if I could," I seethed. "All of you."

Scratch all the sentiments I'd had about not being a murderer. All three of these men made me feel like I wanted to stab them.

"What about the thing that might be growing inside you, huh?"

Fuck. I was silent, but tried to shove back against him. He pushed harder, holding me in place.

I could feel his cock hardening against my ass.

I looked up at Minos and wondered if he knew his friend's cock was pressing against me.

"Go beg Damon for forgiveness while I watch her," Aaecus snarled.

Minos was silent for a moment, watching the two of us. His dark brows drew together, his jaw stiffening. "Don't kill her. Please."

"No promises," he teased.

I felt his cock throb, his grip on me tightening.

"Behave, Ashley," Minos growled before turning around. "Aaecus isn't as nice as me."

I stayed still under Aaecus as I listened to him walk towards the door. It opened and shut, leaving me alone with the bastard that had humiliated me last night.

"Did he know your cock was hard?" I asked, shoving my ass against him. I grinned as I felt his muscles stiffen. Whatever I could do to throw him off, I would do.

"You little bitch," Aaecus cursed.

"Did he?" I asked, my voice ragged. "Maybe you're jealous that he fucked me first."

"Maybe I am," Aaecus said, reaching down to hike up my dress.

"Hey," I shrieked, trying to push against him again. "Stop!"

He lifted me onto the counter, surprising me as I ended up on all fours, my pussy and ass right in his face.

"Do you really want me to? Say your safeword if you want me to stop."

"Aaecus—"

He drove his tongue inside of me and I gasped. Pleasure made my toes curl, every thought disappearing.

Fucking hell, I really *really* hated him. And on top of that, I hated how much I loved the way it felt to be manhandled by him.

I could feel him laugh against me, his tongue stroking me deeper. He pulled back for a moment, humming to himself. "What were you saying, princess?"

I had no clue. Every goddamn thought and worry had flown out the window. "I don't know."

"What was that?"

"*I don't know*," I growled.

"Right, because you're our dumb little whore, aren't you?"

Every part of me screamed *fuck off*, but the words never found their way to my mouth. Instead, I moaned as he began to lick me again, a shiver of pleasure working up my spine. It wasn't fair that his tongue felt this good after everything that had already happened.

His hand slid up, his fingers finding my clit as he kept going. I cried out, arching my back.

He was going to make me come.

"Aaecus," I pleaded. "Stop!"

His fingers circled my clit faster, drawing out another cry from me. His tongue hit *that* spot perfectly, and I groaned as an orgasm crashed into me.

My entire body trembled as the pleasure became more and more intense. Aaecus pulled back as I relaxed, breathing hard.

"Minos came in there," I rasped.

"I know," Aecus replied.

I looked back over my shoulder as he licked his lips.

For a moment, it felt like he didn't absolutely hate me, which left me feeling confused.

"Help me get this collar off," I pleaded.

"Absolutely not," he chuckled, his gaze holding a hint of wildness. "Damon may come home and kill you, who knows."

I scoffed, turning over and sitting on the counter.

"You could thank me for the orgasm," Aaecus snarked.

"Minos gave me more," I quipped.

His eyes darkened and he stepped closer, my legs on either side of his waist. I held my breath as he lifted the knife from earlier, using the tip to push my chin up.

"Thank you," I said quickly.

"Mmm," Aaecus hummed. "I don't think you meant that."

"I did," I lied. "Of course I meant it."

He smirked now, leaning in closer until his lips were almost touching mine. There was tension between us that was wicked and enticing, the kind of burn that teetered on the edge of madness.

I wanted to hate him, to murder him.

I also *wanted* him.

"You made me walk in a lobby naked," I hissed.

"I would do it again, too," he said. "You have a perfect ass. Perfect breasts. I liked the hungry looks you got from all our men. I bet they went home thinking about fucking you, wondering what terrible things you did to end up as a prisoner to us monsters."

"Fuck off."

"You ran away from us after signing a contract. I had to punish you somehow."

"You said you don't care if I die."

"And?"

"You also just gave me an orgasm." He was a confusing motherfucker.

"You were passed out when I said it, but I told Damon I wanted you when you were caught. Minos isn't wrong about you—your scent is delicious, and I want my cock in your cunt."

"But that's all I am to you," I seethed.

His eyes narrowed, the tip of the knife digging into my skin. "Of course," he said softly. "Do you really want a murderer to think something more of you?"

"Of course not," I snapped back.

He gave me a ruthless smile, studying me. "If I knew any better—"

"Shut up," I sighed.

He chuckled, licking his lips again. "Lift your hair up."

I raised a brow, but listened to him, sweeping my hair away from my neck. He stepped closer, his fingertips searing my skin as he reached around. I sucked in a breath as I felt a small shock, but it was almost nothing compared to the relief I felt the moment the collar came free.

"That's all it took?" I inquired.

"Well, you wouldn't know how to remove it," Aaecus said. "We're going to go save your boyfriend before his boyfriend murders him for disobeying, but if you disappear from my side at any point, this collar goes back on—and I'll make sure to be the owner of the remote. Understood?"

"Yes, *Sir*," I replied, smiling.

He paused, letting out a low growl. "Don't call me that unless you want my cock in your mouth, princess."

"Am I *princess* now or still *little thief?*"

"You're a little *whore*. Now, come on. Go put something on that will convince Damon not to murder you, then let's go."

I grinned and slid off the counter. Maybe he wasn't *that* bad.

I went to my room and dug through the bags of clothes they'd bought me, again ignoring the fact that the fabrics in this bag were stupid expensive.

I sighed, pulling out a deep crimson dress that was covered in sequins. I stared at it for a few moments, wondering which of the three of them had picked this out. Or had their body guard been the one to?

Either way, it would look good on me.

I changed into it, not quite as shocked this time to discover it fit perfectly. I slid into some black heels and wobbled for a moment.

It had been a long time since I had worn heels and a dress like this. Being a thief meant you didn't exactly go out much.

The heels clacked as I walked into the bathroom. I ran my fingers through my wavy hair, studying myself in the mirror.

I wasn't sure if this would convince Damon not to murder me, but it was worth a shot.

Sucking in a deep breath then exhaling, I turned and made my way back to the living room. Aaecus was standing there waiting, wearing a black suit jacket and pants.

How many weapons did he have hidden?

I studied him for a moment before approaching , noting the

tattoo on the back of his neck. It was the Three Fates Mafia symbol, the one that seemed to haunt me.

It was everywhere, all the time.

He had other tattoos as well, ones I wanted to see more of.

Down girl, this fucker is your kidnapper. Not to mention, he's mafia.

Aaecus turned, holding up a string of diamonds. "Come here," he commanded.

Damn it. I was a sucker for sparkly things.

I walked over, stepping in front of him. He went around me, sweeping my hair to the side. I closed my eyes, heat rushing through me as I thought back to when he had me on the counter, his tongue thrusting inside of me.

And when his fingers were stroking me last night...

I felt his warm breath on my skin as he clasped the diamonds around my neck. "See, if you're a good girl, you get treated well," he whispered. "If you've figured that out, this week might not be so bad for you."

My throat burned as I swallowed. I didn't want to be some obedient bitch for them, but then again...

"Save Minos, talk Damon down, and I promise you will sleep well tonight," he purred.

"And if I fail?"

He pressed his hot lips over the bite mark Minos had left on me, drawing a helpless moan from me. It was like a hotline straight to my pussy, my cunt throbbing as he sucked my neck gently.

"Don't fail," he sighed. "I've already killed a few people in the last twenty-four hours, it gets exhausting."

"Charming," I muttered.

"When we're in the club, don't accept drinks from anyone," he warned. "Only from me, Damon, or Minos. And no one is allowed to touch you."

I fought the urge to be a smart ass. Just last night, he'd paraded me in public naked—and now, no one was allowed to even touch me.

Well, maybe I preferred it that way.

"Come on," he said. "I'm sure Minos is hating his life right now."

CHAPTER 12

BROKEN CONTRACTS

ASHLEY

The club was the exact kind I'd always avoided. It was loud, full of people, and smelled like alcohol, smoke, and sweat.

The crowd parted for Aaecus as he led me through. I looked around wildly, searching for any sign of Damon or Minos. I could feel eyes on me, the feeling of being watched making the hair stand up on the back of my neck.

Aaecus came to a set of stairs and gripped my hips. Leaning down, he growled in my ear. "Good luck." He gave me a light push, sending me forward and up the stairs.

I grabbed the hand rail before I tripped in these heels, cursing under my breath.

I went up the steps carefully, slipping between two men that were standing in the way, drinking. I felt their gazes follow me, but continued, looking for Minos or Damon.

The way their club was set up, the dance floor and bar were

on the first floor—and this second floor was very obviously for VIPs and...

Pleasure.

My cheeks heated as I passed a couple, a man in a chair, smoking a cigar, while a woman sucked his cock. He winked at me as I walked by, watching me like a godsdamned shark.

Suddenly, I remembered why Aaecus was a bastard.

I continued further, my eyes darting back and forth as I absorbed more information. I felt my instincts taking over, the ones that allowed me to blend in with any crowd.

Only, I wasn't dressed like someone trying to blend in. In fact, I could feel more heads turning, more gazes burning with lust as I went further into this part of the club.

There was a set of crimson velvet curtains covering a doorway and a buff man blocking it. I went up to him, offering a sweet smile.

"No," he said emphatically.

"I'm looking for Minos and Damon."

He snorted, shaking his head like I'd lost my mind simply by approaching him. "No."

I blinked at him, crossing my arms. "Are they behind this doorway?"

"Fuck off, lady, before you get yourself killed," he snarled.

"Aaecus sent me—"

He lunged, his hand swinging out. *Fuck.* I spun out of the way just in time and swung back, hitting him in the jaw.

The crack I heard wasn't normal. I felt the power behind my punch, power that had never been there before, even after the training I had done.

"Gods," I hissed, watching as he hit the floor like a ton of bricks.

That garnered me some gasps and movement, but I didn't

hang around to find out what would happen now that I'd KO'ed one of the fucking goons.

"Aaecus, you cunt," I breathed, pushing past the velvet curtains.

This part of the club was darker and more... intimate. I went through a dimly lit room, following a carpeted path that took me past gods knew what. I didn't look, doing my best to ignore the sounds of sex. Groans, growls, gasps, and squeals— all of them centered around pleasure.

My cheeks felt like someone had set irons to them, and now my knuckles were throbbing like I'd punched a brick wall.

I made it to another door and pushed it open, a cold draft making my nipples harden beneath the scarlet sequins. I stepped into another dark room, but I knew I'd finally found them.

They weren't alone, either.

There was an ominous silence over the room, heads suddenly turning to look at me. People I didn't know, all of them wearing masks. At the center was Damon and Minos.

I felt something strange, a tugging on my soul. Maybe it was the bond that Minos had spoken about—and yes, I had felt something strange earlier, but this?

This was hell.

I felt my pussy pulse, immediately wet even though I shouldn't have been turned on by what I was seeing.

Minos was at the center on his knees, in his wolven form. A muzzle had been drawn over his jaws and his massive clawed hands were bound by chains and pulled taut above him. The chains were attached to a rig on the ceiling. His cock was hard, his knot pulsing just like it had earlier.

I was drawn in, unable to stop myself. Like a moth to a flame, I went through the crowd until I was at the very front.

A low growl filled the room and I finally tore my gaze from Minos, looking past him.

Damon was standing a few feet back, a black whip gripped in his leather gloves. Blood speckled his face, his eyes burning with crazed anger.

Our gazes locked and he lifted his lips in a snarl. "Everyone leave. Now. Except *you*."

It wasn't a good sign when an entire crowd scattered the way everyone did. I stood still, frozen in place. Minos let out a low groan, tipping his head back.

I realized that there was a machine thrusting inside of him, a large dildo sliding in and out.

My own needs became more intense, lust rendering me breathless. This was the monster that had devoured me earlier. He'd fucked me, mated me, knotted me—and seeing him on his knees, helpless...

That turned me on in a way I'd never felt before.

The moment the door to the room shut, my attention snapped back up to Damon.

"You stole him from me."

"I didn't," I argued. "He wanted this. He's the one that bit me."

"You took my mate," Damon said.

His voice was eerily calm. My nerves were rattled and I winced, taking a step back.

"Run from me and die," he threatened. "I'm serious. And he will feel it. He should fucking feel it. He mated *you*!"

His last word was a roar, the kind that felt like it should make the earth quake.

"I'm sorry," I stammered. "I didn't know that biting him—"

"*You* bit him?"

Ah hell, I should have left that part out.

"You fucking whore."

I held up my hands, taking another step back—which did nothing but make him growl. Minos let out another moan, still caught up in the pleasure that was obviously keeping him unaware of us.

I could feel it though. I didn't have a cock filling me, didn't have someone touching me or kissing me, but the lust that rolled through me was undeniable.

This was not the right time to be this horny.

"Hercules sent you, didn't he?" Damon said. "He sent you for this. To seduce what belongs to me. He wanted you to steal them both from me. A master manipulator disguised in the body of a woman."

"Listen," I said, my heart pounding in my chest. "I didn't want this. I've tried to run away, Damon. Think about it. You're clearly not thinking straight."

Once again, I was not doing a great job of helping my case. Damon threw back his arm and swung forward. I watched, partly horrified and still partly turned on, as the end of the whip snapped—striking Minos' back.

Minos cried out and I gasped, my knees nearly buckling. It was as if I had been whipped too, the phantom pain tearing down my back followed by the lick of... wanting it to happen again.

"You're such a slut," Damon sneered. "You liked that, didn't you? Did the pain feel good, even though he's bleeding?"

"I'm not the one telling you to abuse him," I cried.

Damon threw his head back, letting out a howling laugh. The bastard had truly lost his mind, and it was apparent the creature I was negotiating with now was completely different from the one I'd struck a deal with.

He could deny it all he wanted to, but he was clearly upset —and of course wasn't handling his emotions the way he should.

"You need therapy," I said.

His response was to swing the whip again. I gasped, my ears ringing as it cracked against fur and flesh.

This time, my knees buckled. I hit the floor, catching myself before I face planted. The pain returned, followed by a wave of want. Of need.

"You bastard," I spat. "Fuck the gods and fuck the monsters."

Damon laughed again. "Neither gods or monsters made you love pain the way you do."

I looked up at him, blinking back tears. Minos groaned, his cock bobbing as the dildo thrusting inside of him became faster and faster. Cum dripped from the red head, the chains rattling as he pulled against them.

"Master," Minos groaned. "Let me come, please. Please!"

The machine suddenly stopped, and Minos groaned, denied his orgasm.

Damon came closer, walking around Minos to me. I looked up, trembling as he stopped in front of me.

Now, I was on my knees in front of him.

"Are you going to kill me?" I whispered.

I stared up at him, into those cruel cold eyes. I could feel his hatred, and could even see the pain hiding behind them.

"I didn't ask for this," I breathed. "I swear it , Damon."

"I know," he said. "But you took him anyways."

"He wanted me."

"I know," Damon sighed. "I know that, Ashley."

"I'm sorry."

My words burned in my throat and I blinked, tears sliding free. I looked down at his feet, at the polished tips of his shoes. I tried to hold back the sob, but couldn't.

I felt so broken. So fucking numb. I was tired of the hell that had followed me for so long.

"I just need to feel something," I whispered.

The soft leather of his gloved hand slid under my jaw, gripping me. He tipped my face up, forcing me to look at him.

"Hit me."

He froze, his brows drawing together.

"Do it. I need it. I need this. Punish me, Damon."

"Who removed your collar?"

Oh shit. "I did," I lied.

He snorted, leaning in so his face was directly in front of mine. "Try again."

"Am I really that bad of a liar?"

"Maybe not to mortals."

"Aaecus," I finally answered.

Damon's grip tightened, his eyes darkening.

"Hit me," I demanded again.

I wanted him to. I wanted to feel the pain. I wanted it more than I could explain. It was a salvation, a penance, a payment.

He let go and I gasped as his other hand came forward, slapping me across my right cheek. My head whipped to the side, the pain following.

Maybe I was a whore. My pussy throbbed, my chest heaving.

"Gods," Damon murmured. "They really made you just for us, didn't they?"

"What?" I asked.

He slapped me again. I cried out, the pain pairing with pleasure again.

"Open your mouth."

My ears were ringing as I looked up at him, tipping my head back in a daze. I parted my lips and he spat. I caught it on my tongue, swallowing it and never breaking his gaze.

I felt as if I could stay like this forever. On my knees in front of him, letting him slap me. Spit on me.

I was so wet.

"Just kill me, Damon," I groaned.

He spat again and then knelt, his hand sliding around my throat as I swallowed. "I won't kill you," he said. "I want you too much."

He squeezed my throat and leaned forward, his lips meeting mine. I didn't fight him, didn't resist.

It felt too good.

I groaned and leaned into him, gripping his clothes as our tongues fought. He took over the kiss, squeezing my throat until my brain felt like it had been dropped into the clouds.

He pulled back, his grip loosening just enough to let me breathe. I dragged in air, wondering if I could get high off kissing this monster.

He pressed his forehead to mine, breathing in my scent. "You are a demigod."

I nodded, swallowing hard. "I didn't want this."

More tears slipped free and he surprised me, wiping them away gently. "I know. The Fates are cruel, little thief."

With a heavy sigh, he pulled back, standing up. I looked up at him, wishing that he wouldn't have let go.

"Go home," he said. "Our contract is done. I'm terminating it early. Aaecus will give you the money. If you'd like to leave, then do so."

What? Was he serious?

The door to the room swung open, and I looked up, seeing Aaecus there.

"What if I want to stay?" I asked.

"No," Damon said. "Leave, Ashley. Get out before you can't."

I didn't know what to say.

Damon looked up at Aaecus, narrowing his eyes. "She's

free to leave. Give her the money and take her to wherever she needs to go. She's no longer under contract."

"Damon, *what?*" Aaecus snarled.

"Go," Damon demanded, looking down at me before turning to Minos. "I have other things to attend to here. Like taking care of him."

I felt an ache in my chest as I slowly stood. I was shaking now, but I turned and left, refusing to look back at Minos or Damon.

Aaecus' expression became stoic as I approached him. Unreadable. He straightened his shoulders, shaking his head before turning to lead me away.

"Let's go."

CHAPTER 13

FUCKING FATE

AAECUS

I drove her to the airport and handed her a first class ticket to the Bahamas, a bag with three million dollars, and a purse with her phone and wallet.

She took them silently. Her eyes were bloodshot from crying, her cheeks still red from where Damon had obviously slapped her.

I hated him.

I was bad. I'd always been bad. I did things that were considered terrible by human standards, but I at least did after-care. And even if he hadn't fucked her physically, he'd fucked her mentally, and sending her away like this pissed me off.

"I hope I never see you again," I said.

"Same," she muttered.

There was no heat to either of our words. Just a strange hollowness. We were standing on the sidewalk, people bustling around us.

"What if Hercules comes after me?"

"You're a demigod," I sighed. "Just remember that."

She nodded, tucking a strand of blonde behind her ear. Her hand came to rest on her neck, then slid to the base of her throat. "Oh," she said. "The diamonds."

"Keep them."

Ashley stared at me, her pretty blue eyes filling up with tears again. "Why is this so fucking hard?"

"Because we abused you. Gaslit you. Made you sign a contract that sold you to us," I growled. "*Go* before I change my mind."

She stared at me for another moment, holding back those tears.

I didn't want to see her cry. Not like this.

She sucked in a breath and grabbed her bags, turning and shuffling towards the airport doors. I watched her go.

My hands curled into fists as she was absorbed into the crowd of mortals, all looking for their flights, bags, or tickets.

I was unable to understand why I hated this so fucking much.

I was used to getting what I wanted, but that didn't mean I didn't know when to let go. Still...

I wanted her to stay.

She disappeared from my sight and it felt like someone had punched me in the gut.

None of this felt right. I'd sent her into the club earlier thinking she might have a chance of talking some sense into Damon, and she had talked *too much* sense into him. I'd never seen Damon back out of a deal before, especially one with a contract.

I should have gone in there with her.

I turned, ignoring the honks for me to get moving. I got into my car, lurching into the lanes of traffic.

My drive home was a blur, I was completely on autopilot. I pulled into the parking garage under the Helm, my mind still stuck on her. I kept replaying her face on repeat in my head like a movie reel, her words echoing through me.

Why is this so fucking hard?

I slammed my car door shut, not even remembering parking.

Damon's car was here too.

Great.

I stalked across the garage to the elevator and made my way up to our penthouse. The moment I stepped inside, I froze.

Her scent was still here, covering everything. Clinging to the rooms, to the walls, to the floors.

It would fade soon enough.

A low growl left me as I stalked into the living room. Damon was sitting on the couch, obviously waiting for me.

"Where's Minos?" I asked.

"In bed," Damon said. "He's asleep after..."

"After you fucked him up," I sneered.

Damon stared at me, his expression almost unreadable. If I hadn't known the fucker for centuries, I might have believed his ruse.

"I know you," I said, stalking closer. "I know you never cut out of deals. Why did you let her go?"

He sighed, sinking back into the cushion. "I was getting bored with the games."

"You're a liar," I whispered. "You were scared. Scared because of M. Scared because you don't think you could ever let a woman in again."

His mask cracked at the mention of her name. "I'm not talking about this."

"Yes you are," I demanded. "You are because one—she is

Minos' mate now. You can't just send her away. Does he know you did so?"

"Not yet," Damon said tightly. "He will find out tomorrow, and will thank me for it."

"Okay, well, two—I wanted to fuck her."

"Is that all you wanted?" he asked, standing up.

I could feel my control slipping and I did my best to hold on to it.

When Damon and Minos fought, they broke a few things. It was never a big deal.

But Damon and I?

Damon chuckled, leaning in closer. "You wanted more from her, didn't you? Maybe you wanted to mate her. But that would have been cruel of me to allow. You're a fucking mercenary. A murderer. You would hurt her."

"I'm a murderer?" I scoffed. "And you? What about you, Damon? Your hands aren't so clean, are they?"

"No," he said. "Which is why I refused to fucking touch her."

I shook my head, pressing my lips together. I hated him—hated that this was what the three of us had become. I had moved on from the old times. Yes, I was still fucked up. I was still a killer, a monster, a villain.

But I didn't hate myself the way he hated himself.

"How does it feel to hate yourself?" I seethed. "To know that you're the reason you can't be happy? That you'll never have what me or Minos could find? You get hurt by one person, and you let it rot you from the inside out. Ever since her, you've been cruel, Damon."

"I cursed us," he hissed.

"And? Do I seem like I'm still mad about that?"

"Both of you resent me for it."

"No we don't," I said. How stupid was he? "That's just what

you've told yourself. I did resent you for it, at first. Maybe for the first few hundred years. But I don't care now. We don't even live in the Underworld anymore. We live *here*, as heads of a mafia branch in the mortal world. We walk amongst humans, monsters in disguise, and have more freedom than we ever did before. I can do what I want, fuck who I want, kill who I want—and I dont have a god breathing down my neck treating me like a dog."

I shook my head, taking a step back from him.

"If we're going to fight, we need to take it out of here. I'd rather not destroy the penthouse," I said.

Damon growled, tensing. "Look at you, being so reasonable."

"You should try it some time," I snapped.

We stared at each other until he finally released a sigh, and plopped back down onto the couch. The tension melted enough for me to relax.

"Whiskey and talk?" I asked.

"Yes," he muttered.

I nodded and went to the small bar cart we had in the living room, pouring us two glasses. I brought the bottle with me, handing Damon his glass before I walked to the chair across from him, sitting down.

"This sucks," he finally said. He lifted his glass and then downed the alcohol, letting out a low hiss. "I found something."

"What did you find?" I asked.

"A letter. From the Fates. They sent it to the club, not here. It was on my desk. That fucking golden wax seal."

"They should really start an email at this point. An annual newsletter about how fucked everyone is."

Damon snorted, shrugging. He ran his fingers through his dark hair, his eyes becoming distant as he stared off into space. "They should. The letter was about Ashley. She's our mate.

They asked us to protect her. Not to hurt her. To keep her alive. So that's what I did. Sending her away from us was the only way, Aaecus."

Fuck. I stared at him for a few moments, then downed my own drink. If that was the case, then his actions made a lot more sense. "I want to see the letter."

He reached into his suit jacket and pulled out an envelope. We both leaned forward and I took it from him, trading him the bottle.

The envelope was black, the paper was the kind the mortals used to have to make by hand. The golden wax seal was cracked, a faint burnt scent clinging to it. I opened it, pulling the letter out.

Dear Damon, MINos, and ~~Aaaecus~~ Aaecus...

Congrats, your mate has been found. We have pulled the strings of fate and she will end up in your hands SOON.
Please **Don't HURT HER.**

Protect her.

Her name is Ashley and she is important. Good luck.

P.S. If a god asks, she doesn't exist.

Clotho, LacHESis, and Atropos
Three Fates Mafia

That was ominous.

"Another drink?"

"Yes," I said, swallowing hard.

My thoughts had already been jumbled before, and now they were even more so.

"Fuck," I muttered.

"Yep." Damon nodded, leaning forward with the whiskey bottle. I held out my glass and he poured it to the rim, sitting back with a grim expression. "She was just part of their plan."

"We all are," I said. "I hate it."

"I do too."

"That means we shouldn't have let her go."

Damon shook his head. "It means we *had* to let her go."

We both went silent and I sank back into the chair. If the Fates had known Ashley was ours, did that mean they had sent her? Had they really interfered that much?

Every time I dealt with these bitches, I had an existential crisis.

Did we even make our own choices?

"I have a question for you," Damon started. "It's... well. It's more out of curiosity, I suppose."

"Okay," I said. "Ask."

"You don't seem to care that Minos mated her, but you've never done anything with either of us. You've always been off-limits in a way. Why? And let's say that for some cosmic reason, we brought Ashley back and all wanted her. What then?"

I blew out a breath, pressing my lips together. "I have my reasons, but the biggest one is both of you have always been occupied with your relationship. And when M came around then left, you were so broken up over her. If Ashley were with all of us, I wouldn't mind. I wouldn't mind doing things in bed with her together as well. And to be honest, I wouldn't mind doing things with either one of you. So long as you're not bitches when we have to do our job."

Damon chuckled, regarding me thoughtfully.

"I also wouldn't mind parading her in front of the lobby again," I mumbled into my glass.

"I saw the video of that," he mused. "I'm too possessive, but I enjoyed watching it."

I smirked. "I'm sure our different tastes might feed off each other well, if we wanted."

Damon nodded, his eyes narrowing. "What about Minos?"

"He's a slut."

Damon barked out a laugh and downed the rest of his whiskey. "He is, and I love him for it. I'd never seen him act like this around someone before."

"Well, Minos was right, there was something about her." I felt miserable. "I wanted her. And sending her away tonight was harder than I thought possible."

"She should be safe now," Damon sighed. "Far away from us. Three million dollars in hand."

"Unless she tries to actually pay Hercules with that."

Damon and I were both quiet again.

"Surely not," Damon said, although he didn't sound convinced. "You put her on a plane."

"I did. Well, I took her to the airport."

"We really shouldn't interfere," Damon muttered.

"Right. A cosmic reason, you said earlier?" I inquired, raising a brow.

We stared at each other for a few moments.

"Honestly, I've always been one to say fuck cosmic reasons."

"Right." He leaned forward, running his hand over his face. "We should call Hercules then."

"Wouldn't that be odd?" We'd never helped a supposed mortal like this before.

"Gods damn it all," Damon muttered. "That would just make him go after her."

"I don't think we were followed. So at least there's that."

"He has people that work there," he grumbled.

True. He had people that worked everywhere though.

"Do you think he knew?" Damon asked. "Do you think he realized that she was one of them?"

"No," I said. "She bled red until Minos bit her. She didn't show any signs of anything except for terrible luck."

"And her scent."

"Sure, but that wasn't...a direct sign. But, she's definitely changing. Earlier tonight she put down one of our men with a single hit. His jaw was broken and he was out like a light. Gave me a fucking hard-on knowing she put him down like that."

Damon smirked. "Hmm."

We were both thinking the same thing, which was the exact opposite of what we should have been. But, she would be even more fun to play with now that she wasn't so fragile.

"I did wonder if she could take us in our full form," I admitted.

Damon's brows shot up. I could see that idea taking hold.

"We should get her back," he proclaimed.

"And try to win her over this time, perhaps. Instead of being assholes."

"We *are* assholes. But, yes."

It was true, we were. Damon had the right idea in sending her away, but I was too selfish. We were all too selfish.

"You were right to do what you did," I said. "But I don't care. She's ours, Damon. She's our demigod princess, Fates be damned."

"Fuck it," he agreed. "We'll bring her back and deal with everything else later."

"You'll also win you some points with Minos..."

Damon rolled his eyes, but didn't disagree.

I stood, looking out our massive windows at the city below.

I could see planes taking off in the distance and wondered if she'd already departed.

Damon stood and grabbed his suit jacket, pulling it on quickly. "Well, let's go get her," he huffed, his voice edged with excitement. "Before her luck runs out and we're not there to help."

"Or a god finds her."

What would happen then?

"I should have never listened to you," I muttered.

The two of us were already moving through the front door, slamming it behind us.

I could let some things go.

But she was not one of them.

We'd win her over, seduce her. Love her.

I hated the Fates, but conceded to the fact that I needed Ashley. Our four souls had been bound together the moment she had broken into our home, and our lives. Demigod or not, she belonged to us.

CHAPTER 14

GOD OF THIEVES

ASHLEY

My flight was delayed by three hours, which was not surprising. I sighed as I found a seat, wishing I had been able to just get on the plane and go, instead of being stuck at the airport. I was paranoid, tired, and confused. Everything that had happened over the last couple of days left me with feelings I didn't want to feel.

I wanted to stay. That had been the most fucked up thing of all. I'd wanted to go back to the penthouse and be with Aaecus tonight. I'd wanted to find out what it would be like.

I'd wanted Damon too.

Somehow, I'd ended up wanting three monsters who I should have hated.

I had a first class ticket, a bag with three million dollars, and a way out of this world that had ruined me. For so long, I'd been stealing and then ended up working for Hercules. I'd been trapped.

They'd given me a way out.

Not for free, of course. But everything still felt surreal.

"Mind if I sit?"

I looked up, seeing an older man who reminded me of a professor. He wore a tweed jacket and glasses, with shoulder-length dark brown hair that had a few strips of gray.

"Sure," I answered.

He sat next to me with a sigh. I pulled my bag a little closer, not wanting to risk anyone taking it.

"I heard they pushed the flight back," he said.

Damn it, I really didn't want to do small talk right now. I glanced around, noting there were literally rows of empty seats, then looked back at him. "Yeah," I sighed. "Bit of bad luck, I suppose."

"Right," he said. "Sorry about that. It's not fair to you, I know."

I blinked. "Do I know you?"

He gave me a lopsided smile, his bright blue eyes creasing. "No. And I didn't know of you until a few hours ago."

That didn't sit well with me. "Well, okay then." I tried remaining polite, standing up. "I'm going to move seats and I'd like you to leave me alone."

"Sorry, kid," he sighed. "Can't do that quite yet. You do want to talk to your dad, right?"

I froze and my heart skipped a beat. "I don't have a dad," I whispered. "You've lost your mind, man."

He raised a brow and grinned, reminding me of a fox. "Hermes," he introduced, holding out his hand.

"Fuck," I cursed. I shook my head, my mind now spinning. "Look, I've had a really long couple days. A long few years, really. I don't know who you are but—"

"I'm Hermes," he said, putting his hand down. "The god of thieves, travel, sleep, luck. And a few other things that are a little outdated now, but hey." He stood, grabbing my shoulders gently. I felt a zap, like an electric shock of knowing. "I had no idea," he whispered. "They hid you. A new demigod hasn't been born in ages because your grandfather is an asshole."

"Grandfather..." My voice sounded faraway, drowned out by the pounding of my heartbeat.

"Yeah, Zeus is like that. Has been like that. I have to ask—is your mother well?"

"Dead."

His face fell, his eyes darkening. "Oh," he muttered.

"If you were a god, I'd imagine you'd know that."

"You'd think," he said softly. "Well. I'm sorry about that."

"Sorry?" I hesitated, and then narrowed my eyes at him. He was *sorry* that my mother had killed herself? His words felt like a slap in the face, stinging enough to almost bring tears to my eyes. "You know what? Fuck you. I'm about to get out of this city and make my life better."

"You're right where you need to be," he said cryptically. "Listen, I am sorry for everything that has happened. But, everything happens for a—"

"No," I snapped, rage washing over me. "Don't finish that sentence. It's not true. Not everything happens for a reason. You can't tell me there is a cosmic answer to all the pain and suffering!"

"I mean, Oizys is not my favorite goddess—"

I scoffed and snatched up my bags. As I turned to walk away from him, I stopped in my tracks. The world around us was frozen and I saw Hercules across the terminal. No one was moving. The yellow airport lighting bounced off the glossy tile floors and the screens showing flights had stopped blinking. Everything was silent and felt eerie, stuck in this moment.

Hercules looked pissed, and he wasn't alone either. He was

wearing a black suit, a menacing look stuck on his ugly face. There were three men on either side of him, all holding guns.

Man, fuck the mafia. I was over this already.

"What the hell is happening?" I whispered to myself.

"Ashley."

I turned back to look at Hermes. He gave me a sad smile and spread his hands. "I have a gift for you before I have to leave. And this has to be our little secret. The others can't know about you yet. They will all come after you."

He reached into his pocket and pulled out what looked like a hotel key card. A cheap piece of blue plastic with an image of wings on it.

"You're joking," I said, my voice flat.

"This key will unlock any door," he explained. "*Any* door. Only you can use it and you can't lose it. It'll always find its way back to you."

"Sounds too good to be true," I quipped. We stared at each other for a few awkward moments until I caved. "If I take it, what happens next?" I asked.

"The world starts spinning again," Hermes said. "And you'll have to deal with Hercules."

"You can't help me out with him, *Dad*?" I asked bitterly.

Hermes smirked and stepped up to me, handing me the card. "Good luck, kid. I can only interfere so much before I draw attention."

I snatched it from him, cursing under my breath. He winked at me, snapped his fingers, and disappeared in a blink.

Everything started moving again, the bustle of people and machines returning. I heard a shout, followed by a gunshot. A bullet sailed past me.

"FUCK!" I yelled, kicking off my heels.

I took off running, along with everyone else in the godsdamned airport. I glanced over my shoulder, which was a mistake.

Hercules was close.

This motherfucker.

I dodged to the right, squeezing between a group of people. Adrenaline fully kicked in as I ran, the sound of another shot sending panic into the crowds.

People bumped into me, screams and cries echoing around me. I managed to veer to the side and ran towards one of the gates, heading straight for the door.

I had the key card clutched in one hand and waved it, hoping I hadn't just been screwed over by a god. I heard the lock click and grinned, yanking open the door and hauling ass down the ramp.

I heard the door rattling behind me, but didn't stop. I came to the end of the boarding ramp and went through the small door on the right.

What's the plan here?

I paused at the top of the metal staircase, sucking in deep breaths. It was dark outside and I didn't want to run out in the middle of a runway.

"Where do you think you're going?"

The hair on the back of my neck stood up, a chill working up my spine. I felt the cold nose of a gun press against my back and I stiffened.

"Hercules," I spoke as calmly as possible. "Funny meeting you here. Took you more for a private jet kind of guy."

"Very funny," he said drily.

His hand clamped down on my shoulder and he spun me to face him. I looked up at him, scowling.

The fact that people had written kind things about him was ironic. He was a bastard, and gods—I really would take Damon, Aaecus, or Minos any day over dealing with him.

Hercules glared at me. His nose was slightly crooked, his mouth pulled into a sneer, and his eyes burned with malice.

"I sent you to steal a painting from them and—"

I held up the bag with three million dollars in it, shoving it at him. "Here's your money," I interrupted. "We're done, Hercules. That pays off my debt. I'm flying out of this fucking hellhole and I'm never coming back again."

He took the bag and set it on the ground, leaning over to unzip it. He snorted, and as my eyes fell down to it, I cursed.

It was filled with game money. Like, fake money from a board game.

"Very, very funny," Hercules seethed, the vein in his forehead ticking.

I thought back to earlier, back to Hermes.

That bastard had taken my fucking cash.

If I ever saw my father again, I was going to kick him in the nuts.

In one swift move, I knocked the gun out of Hercules' hands and ran down the steps, into the dark. Lights from the runway flashed in the distance.

"Come back you little bitch!"

I ignored him and ran faster, mentally cursing everything.

Part of me wished Damon had never sent me away.

My lungs burned as I ran faster. I could hear Hercules catching up.

The world turned upside down as I was suddenly tackled to the ground, Hercules growling as he slammed me to the asphalt. I rolled over, shoving and kicking against him.

I threw a punch and managed to land it. I watched as his head snapped back. His expression was priceless.

"*Yeah*," I gloated. "You're not the only demigod, you bastard."

He leaned back, staring at me like I'd lost my mind—which

was the exact reaction I'd been going for. I leaned up and shoved him back, managing to slip out from under him.

His massive hand clamped around my ankle and I hit the ground again, the impact rattling me.

"Fuck," I growled, trying to kick at him.

"You aren't a demigod," Hercules snarled. "There haven't been any for a long time. You've lost your mind, thief."

"I am one," I said, using my other foot to kick his hand still gripping my ankle. "Let me go!"

"If you were, then I wouldn't be able to—"

I kicked him hard again, managing to break his grip. I heard several shouts, but didn't look up as I kicked the bastard in the face.

His nose crunched, and he reeled back with a howl.

"There you are, princess."

Strong hands gripped my arms and pulled me up to stand. I felt a wave of relief at the familiar voice. I immediately turned, throwing my arms around the chest of Damon. I didn't look up at him, instead burying my face against him. His arms slid around me, tightening as he let out a low rumble.

"Hercules," Damon snarled. "Why are you attacking my mate?"

"Mate?"

I wasn't going to argue with him at this point. I turned my head slightly, looking back at Hercules. Gold dripped from his broken nose, his dark brows pulling into a malicious glower.

Damon's arms tightened around me. I never thought I would find comfort in being held by him, but I felt happy to see him.

"She's with me," Damon said. "And if you take one step closer, Aaecus is going to put a bullet through your brain. I know that won't kill you, but it won't be very fun."

I could hear other men shouting and knew that his goons were catching up.

Hercules turned and looked at the roof of the airport. I snorted as a red beam followed his movements.

I couldn't see Aaecus but knew he had Hercules in his crosshairs.

They'd come back for me.

I drew in a shaky breath. I'd spent the last couple days fighting them so damn hard. Hating them. Wishing them death, wanting to escape.

But right now, more than anything, I was happy that the monsters had come for me again.

I glared at Hercules, holding up my hand and giving him the bird."Fuck you, Hercules," I sneered. "Our contract is done."

Damon let out the softest chuckle as my arm slipped back around him.

"You didn't pay me, you bitch," Hercules snarled.

"Where's the money?" Damon asked, his voice malicious.

I winced, looking up at him. That was the Damon I thought I'd known until he'd broken our contract at the club. There had been a moment between us, one where I had realized that he wasn't as evil as he acted. He wasn't just a mafia boss or a monster.

I swallowed hard as Damon looked down at me, thinking about the money. All three million dollars. "About that," I said. "It... I'll explain later. It's gone."

Damon gave me a very slow blink, and then shook his head. "I'll send you the three million," Damon said. "She's no longer in your debt."

"Six for the hassle," Hercules sneered.

"Three and you don't get a bullet through your ugly demigod head."

"You're fucking someone that'll do the same to you," Hercules snarled at me. "Mortal or demigod."

"No, I'm fucking someone that'll pay off a debt to a cunt that will never live up to his name."

Hercules growled, taking a step forward.

That was the wrong move.

Damon yanked me close right as a bullet struck Hercules. I didn't see most of it, as I was already being hoisted over his shoulder like a damsel in distress, but I still yelped as blood sprayed everywhere.

Damn, they really had meant it. I let out a startled giggle as shock settled in again. I clung to Damon as he carried me to the car waiting for us, the scent of him offering comfort. He opened the back door and put me in, coming in after and pulling me into his lap.

"Go," he barked at the driver.

The car lurched forward, the wheels peeling over the asphalt.

I looked out the window, watching as the airport began to disappear. My heart thrummed in my chest and I realized I was breathing hard. I swallowed, closing my eyes for a moment.

"What about Aaecus?" I asked.

"He'll catch up," Damon said, his voice gentle. "Don't worry about him, princess. He'll meet us at home."

Home.

His hands slid around my waist as the car went over speed bumps, holding me in place. I became very aware of the fact that I was in his lap, being held by the man that had made my life hell.

I also became aware of the fact that he was hard, his cock pressing against me.

"Damon," I gasped.

He was silent for a moment. My back faced him, his fingertips pressing into my body. He drew in a short breath, his words surprising me.

"I can't let you go, Ashley," he whispered.

I curled my hands into fists, my thoughts spinning. The truth was, I hadn't wanted him to let me go either. As fucked up as it was, him telling me to leave the club had hurt more than the slaps I'd asked for.

Aaecus dropping me off at the airport had been more torture than being paraded around naked in the lobby.

And knowing that the contract had been severed had left a very strange hole in my heart.

These three men were bad. They had done terrible things to me. They had done even worse to others. But underneath their monstrous exterior, there was good. I had seen glimpses of it, the cracks in the walls they all so desperately tried to keep up.

"I didn't want you to," I finally admitted.

I felt a weight lift off my shoulders.

"Even after everything that you've done and said to me, I didn't want you to send me away," I said.

He leaned forward, his forehead pressing against my back. We stayed like that, in silence, him holding me.

"I've hurt you," he murmured. "Over and over again. I don't expect you to forgive me. If you truly want to leave, I will let you go. But I want a second chance. I don't deserve one, but I'm asking for one anyways."

A second chance.

It was a choice. A choice that both of us were making, for me to stay with them, to know them. The contract was up and the three monsters I had sold myself to wanted me to stay.

He was right. He didn't deserve a second chance.

But I was going to give him one.

"If I asked to leave, you would let me?" I asked, my thoughts spinning.

"Yes, but I would follow you wherever you went."

My heart skipped a beat. "What about the mafia?"

Damon's fingertips pressing a little harder into my skin. "Aaecus or Minos could run it. I'll live my life as your shadow making up for everything wrong that I've done."

I smiled and turned in his lap until I was straddling him. His head fell back against the seat, his eyes widening as I braced my hands on his shoulders. "What if I wanted them to come with us?"

"Then we quit the mafia and run away forever," Damon said, slowly smiling at me. "Minos can make us Pina Coladas. I can fuck you endlessly, making you come over and over again."

"And Aaecus?"

"He can sprinkle rose petals on us while I breed you," Damon teased.

I snorted and grinned like an idiot. Was this how he could be? Stupid and silly and sweet?

I wanted to find out.

I cupped his face and leaned in. "You don't deserve a second chance, but I'm willing to give it a shot. But if any of you ever do the shit you've done the last couple days, I'm going to rob you of every last penny and then disappear for the rest of my life."

He narrowed his eyes. "You wouldn't be able to take all our money."

"I'm sure your passwords are either your birthdays or something to do with Cerberus."

He pressed his lips together, but didn't disagree. "What if I said all my money is yours anyways."

I raised a brow. "You drive a hard bargain."

He snorted, his hand sliding up to the back of my neck. He

pulled me in, our lips meeting in a soft kiss. It was gentle for a few moments, and then he let out a low growl, deepening it. His cock throbbed in his pants, my entire body lighting up like fireworks.

I drew back from him, breathless. "So where are we going now?" I asked.

"Home," Damon said, tucking a strand of my hair behind my ear. "And you're going to sleep, princess."

I pouted at him, my body still aching to be with him. "You don't want to..."

"Oh, I want to," he whispered. He leaned in, nipping the soft skin of my neck. I groaned, my blood starting to rush. "I want to do everything to you. But I need you well rested before I destroy your pussy."

I swallowed hard and rocked my hips, rubbing my pussy over his hard length. He let out a low growl.

"Ashley," he grunted. "If you don't listen to me, I'm going to bend you over and spank your bare ass."

"We're not alone, you wouldn't do that." I knew damn well he would.

I ground against his cock, letting out a throaty whimper that set him off. In one swift motion, I found myself face down in the back seat, my ass balanced on his thighs. He hiked up my dress and yanked down my panties, his palm striking me hard enough to make me cry out.

"If you want something, maybe ask nicely," he growled, spanking me again.

I cried out again and then burst out laughing, the sting of his hand sending a wave of euphoria through me.

"You're not supposed to laugh at the pain," he snorted.

I looked over my shoulder at him, the laughter melting into pure need. "Daddy," I whispered. "Will you please fuck me when we get home?"

The noise he made was priceless.

"Brat," he muttered. "You want my knot, princess?"

"Yes," I said. "I want everything. Please, Daddy."

"Fine. The only reason I'm saying yes is because we've put you through hell this week."

I smirked. Based on how hard his cock was, I knew that wasn't the only reason.

Chapter 15

Princess

Damon

I carried her to the penthouse like she was a princess, ignoring the looks of surprise we got from some of the men stationed throughout the Helm. My cock was throbbing as I kicked open our front door and then closed it behind us.

"Aaecus will be home later," I said. I'd managed to text him on the way to the penthouse and let him know the plan.

He'd been right earlier when he said our tastes might align in ways.

I let her feet touch the floor, then slammed her against the wall hard enough for it to rattle. She gasped and reached up, her fingers gripping my hair as she dragged me down for a kiss.

The taste of her had been haunting me since our kiss at the club, and now, I fully intended to do everything I wanted. Fates or no Fates, I *needed* her.

"Daddy." Her voice was breathy, her hands sliding down to my cock. "I want your cock in my mouth. I want to taste you."

All the blood left my brain. I was entranced by her. Enchanted.

Snap out of it, I mentally shook myself.

Finally, I regained control, the trance dispersing into pure lust.

This demigod would be mine for eternity now, starting tonight. She asked me if I'd ever let her leave, and I would. But I'd never let her go.

I partially shifted, my claws lengthening and sharpening. I curled them around her heart-shaped jaw, tipping her face up to look at me.

"Kneel then," I growled.

Ashley sucked in a breath before slowly lowering in front of me, her eyes never leaving my own. They burned with that same defiance I had seen when we'd first met.

Fuck. I knew she didn't hate me, but I loved that look. I loved that fiery passion, the desire to see me suffer while giving herself to me.

She was submitting and it was a gift.

One that I would hold.

One that I would use for both of us.

"You're going to suck my cock until you choke on it," I demanded. "For pissing me off earlier this week."

Those eyes flashed again, her brows drawing together. "You're the one that—"

I snarled, cutting her off. "Talk back and we'll skip the pleasure and go for just pain."

She smiled like she'd won. Her hands slid up my thighs, and she unbuttoned my pants, tugging on the zipper. Her fingertips grazed over my shaft and I fought the urge to bend her over and breed her now.

"I bet you can't even take it in my mortal form," I challenged, planting my hands against the wall.

"I bet I can," she said, her voice dark and sultry. "If I win, then you get to lick my pussy."

Fuck. She was perfect in every way possible.

"I've already won, princess. I get whatever I want," I hummed, curling my fingers in her blonde hair. "You're going to suck my cock like you love it. You're going to suck it like it's the only thing in the world you want."

"And then you're going to make me see fucking stars, or I'm going to bite it off," she quipped.

That just made me harder.

"You'd like to try," I snapped. "Wouldn't you? Eat the rich, as they say."

That pissed her off.

She yanked my pants down, my cock released now. I was already starting to harden when she leaned back, giving me a fake pout.

"Only one knot?" she asked. "That's it?"

My self-control snapped.

Originally, I was just going to have her suck my cock, but now, I was going to make her cry too.

I grabbed her jaw with one hand and the back of her head with the other, forcing the tip of my cock between her sweet lips.

"Remember your safe word," I snarled. "If you can't speak because you're choking on my dick, then tap me three times. And I swear to the gods, woman," I said, fighting a groan. "If you fucking bite me, I *will* kill you."

Ashley gasped right as I forced more of my cock into her mouth. I hit the back of her throat, choking her, and her groan went straight to my balls.

I was going to fuck the remaining hatred out of both of us. Because gods knew, she was fucking mine. All the pent up frustration had broken free.

She wouldn't escape me for the rest of her life.

Villain or not, monster or not, demigod or not—none of those things mattered anymore.

There was no place in heaven, hell, or on earth that she could hide from me.

"Fucking take it," I snarled.

Her nails raked down my thighs, her moan turning me on. I held her head still as I drew my hips back, thrusting forward again.

She couldn't take every inch, but gods did she try. I groaned, my head falling back as I began to thrust in and out of her mouth, the wet sounds making me even more hard.

I wanted to shift, I realized. I wanted her to see me in my full, monstrous glory.

I wanted her to worship me as I truly was.

I pulled back from her mouth, looking down at her. Her saliva dripped from her mouth, tears streaking her cheeks—but that burning light was still in her eyes.

Determination. Lust. Need.

I growled, my form shifting right in front of her. My bones cracked, my skin sprouting night-black fur. I knew my eyes turned bright red, my claws now sharp enough to end her if I wasn't gentle.

I leaned down, snarling at her.

She only grinned at me like a fucking lunatic.

"You don't scare me," she whispered, kissing my nose.

My growl faltered. My chest warmed, a feeling of...

What was this feeling? It was warm and kind of hurt but felt good too. It flooded me, overcoming me.

She leaned forward, her mouth opening. Welcoming me.

I kissed her, gripping her hair and pulling her up to stand. She leaned against me, her hands exploring my hard muscles as she took my searching tongue.

I drew back for a moment, huffing.

"Bedroom," I whispered. "Run to my bedroom. Now."

She hesitated for a moment, but then I gave her a push.

"Run, little thief, before I devour you."

"I *want* you to devour me," she said.

"*Run.*"

She stared for a beat longer, then turned and took off down the hall. The primal part of me watched with glee, desperate to hunt her. I wanted to chase her, pin her down, and breed her perfect little cunt.

Part of me wished that Minos wasn't passed the fuck out because I wanted him to see me claim his other mate.

Seeing her hips sway as she disappeared down the hall was enough to recenter my thoughts on her. I waited a few moments, wanting to let her anticipation build up.

I wanted her to think she'd escaped me. Maybe she'd outsmarted me, maybe I wasn't going to hunt her. I wanted her to wonder all of these things before I made it known that she was my prey.

I stalked after her, letting out a low and deep warning growl. A possessive one.

"You think you can handle monsters, little thief?" I snarled.

I heard her breaths, her heart beating loud enough that I could hear it. The tremor in her veins, the buzz of adrenaline in her blood.

I would taste her soon and that was enough to make my cock even harder.

I crept down the hall to my bedroom, shoving the door open.

She was trying to climb up onto my bed, but she could barely get on top of the mattress without gripping the blankets.

"Why the fuck is your bed so tall?!" she huffed.

She turned as I stalked towards her. I lunged and she ducked, another giggle leaving her. She attempted to take off again, but I snagged her arm and dragged her back.

She squealed as I lifted her and tossed her onto the bed.

"I have a cage under the bed for when Minos is being bad," I confessed, forcing her onto her back, then gripping her thighs and tugging her closer.

I reached down and grabbed the fabric of her dress. She gasped as I ripped it straight down the front. I dragged the tip of my claw between her breasts and down her stomach, to the piece of cloth around her pussy.

Her chest was heaving, her nipples hard as I pressed my claw against her clit. She cried out, a throaty moan as I yanked those down, letting them fall to the floor.

I pushed her legs apart, staring down at my prize. The woman that had crashed into our lives, the thief that had stolen all of my sanity and will.

I leaned down, my eyes lifting to hers over the curve of her body. I let my tongue run over her clit, and she arched against the blankets with a breathy squeal.

Just a taste. It took every ounce of self control to pull back.

"You have to tell me before we continue," I rasped. "What are you willing to try? What kind of things do you enjoy?"

"I..." she trailed off, her words faltering. "Fuck, I can barely think."

It threw her off for me to ask her this now, with her legs spread and my cock pulsing. I liked the way her brows drew together, her lips pressed in a tight line.

"I've always wanted to be collared," she confessed. "But not with an electric collar, thanks."

I chuckled. "That wasn't a real shock collar, but yes. I do love collars."

"What?" she hissed.

I leaned down again, running the tip of my tongue over her pussy.

"Fuck you," she moaned.

I would collar her. I'd fucking walk her around on a leash, keeping her close to me. My mind went into a frenzy as I thought of all the things I could do to her.

I drew her legs up, placing them against my chest so I could lick her calves. I dragged my claws back and forth over her skin, enjoying the red streaks that bloomed.

"Fuck." She shivered, biting her bottom lip. "Why is that so hot?"

"What else?" I asked, holding her gaze. "You can't tell me that's the only thing you want to do."

"I like being spanked. Bitten...."

"Worshiped," I said. "Punished. Both. I can do that, princess, if that's what you wish."

"Please," she whispered.

I smirked. "We have all night to figure out if there's anything else you want, too. I'm going to collar you, fuck you, and then you're going to stay under my bed until Minos wakes up. You're going to listen to me claiming him, fucking him....then the two of us are going to take you together...." I leaned in closer, her legs wrapping around my waist.

I planted my hands on either side of her head, drawing in her sweet scent with a deep inhale.

"Please," she begged. "I want all of that."

"Will you be a good girl for me?" I asked. "Especially when you're under the bed."

"Yes," she promised. "I like the idea of being caged by you."

"I know," I said softly. "And I like the idea of locking you up. You've given me so many ideas, princess."

"I need you inside of me," she rasped. "Please. I want to feel your cock in me."

I moved my hips forward just enough to tease her entrance with the head of it. She was so fucking wet.

"I want you to knot me," she demanded. "To claim me and collar me."

"With pleasure, little thief."

CHAPTER 16

TAKEN BY THE MAFIA BOSS

ASHLEY

I had asked Damon for things I'd never asked anyone before in my life, and it felt good. I stared up at him, taking in every monstrous part of him.

The head of his cock pressed against me, his muscles trembling as he fought to restrain himself from thrusting inside of me. I was so desperate for him to fill me, for him to shove his knot inside of me.

"Look me in the eyes," he commanded. "I want to see your face as you take me, princess."

"Your little demigod whore," I breathed out.

His eyes lit like embers, a low growl leaving him. "No. My demigod *princess*."

He thrust forward and all I could do was breathe. His cock speared me, tears filling my eyes as intense pleasure spread through me. He stretched me, making me moan helplessly.

"You're not a whore to me," he grunted. "You're mine,

Ashley. I'm going to fuck you," -thrust- "mate you," -thrust- "breed you," -thrust- "worship you."

I cried out with each movement, every sound louder than the one before.

"But don't worry, princess," he rasped, his monstrous expression enrapturing me. "I may worship you, but I can still fuck you like you *are* a whore."

He began to pump into me, picking up a brutal rhythm that had me screaming. The bed groaned beneath us as he took me, the two of us lost to each other.

He changed the angle ever so slightly and I moaned, my brain feeling like it was going to combust.

"Right there," I panted. "Fuck! Right there!"

"I hear you, princess," he rumbled. "Now shut the fuck up and take that monster dick like a good girl."

I cried out as he kept fucking me, hitting that spot over and over until I clamped my hands on his shoulders and arched under him—an orgasm tearing into me.

"Good girl," Damon crooned. "Just like that, princess. I can feel you coming so hard."

I could barely understand him, my entire body feeling like I'd been pummeled with pleasure. I melted under him, still panting.

"Good girl," he praised again. "Did that feel good?"

I nodded, holding up my hand and giving him a thumbs up.

Fuck, I did *not* just do that.

He laughed, clearly amused. "I fucked you stupid, hmm?"

"Fuck you," I whispered, closing my eyes.

I realized that he'd stopped thrusting into me, but his cock was still hard and buried inside of me. He leaned in, his sharp teeth gleaming.

He moved his hips ever so slightly, and I cried out. Every touch and movement felt like so *much*.

He slowly pulled out and I whimpered. "Where are you going?"

"Don't worry, love, we're not done yet," he said softly.

He left the bed for a few moments and I just let my head fall back into the blankets, wondering what he was doing. I heard movement, then the bed rocked as he came back.

"Sit up."

I opened one eye, wondering if it was worth sitting up for. In his clawed hands, he held a soft black leather collar with a leash. I reached out in awe, running my fingertips over the buttery material.

"I'll have one made for you," he said. "But this will do for now."

"Okay," I mumbled, my voice shaky.

He leaned forward as I swept my long blonde waves to the side. He clasped the soft leather collar around my throat, tugging on the little lock with a possessive growl.

An orgasm like he'd just given me wasn't good because now I just wanted more. I was still wet for him, desperate to take his cock again. He leaned forward and I parted my lips, our tongues meeting. Kissing a monster wasn't easy, but it lit every nerve ending in my body on fire. Every touch, every kiss, every lick. All of it made me hot, made my blood boil. All of the tension between us had turned into the kind of lust you dreamed about.

Damon pulled me off the bed and forced me to my knees on the floor in front of him. His cock was hard and while it didn't have as many knots as Minos—it was beyond glorious.

It was perfect.

I reached up, running my hand over his slick shaft, all the way down to where I cupped his knot.

"Thieves and monsters," he said, forcing me to look up at him. "Who would have ever thought, huh? A pretty little thief begging for me to fuck her sweet cunt. Are you sure you want my knot, or do you want to sleep?"

"How can I sleep now?" I asked.

He looped a claw beneath the collar, scraping my skin as he jerked me forward.

"Why do you have to be so perfect for me, little thief?"

Heat flooded me, his words an arrow straight to my pussy. His eyes burned with need, his claw tugging me again.

"Beg," he whispered.

"I'm not begging you," I retorted. I had to put up some sort of fight, right? I couldn't just swoon on command, even though that was exactly what I wanted.

"Beg," he snarled.

I stayed still.

He let out a frustrated noise and gripped the collar, dragging me to stand. Excitement rushed through me as he bent me over the bed, pinning my wrists. I could feel his cock pulsing, the tip rubbing against me. His body was warm, his strength domineering.

"Beg, little thief," he demanded.

"No," I breathed.

I said no even though I wanted to say yes more than anything. I wanted to feel his cock inside of me again, was desperate for it even.

Still, I liked the way it felt to push him to the edge, to know that both of us were falling down this rabbit hole at the same speed.

He lowered his bared teeth to my face, his growl growing louder and darker. His chest vibrated against my back, and I gasped as the tip of his cock slowly spread me.

His hand smacked my ass cheek, drawing a cry from me.

"*Beg me for this cock.*"

"Beg to fuck me," I snapped back, wanting him to spank me again.

His hand smacked my ass again, his cock edging a bit further.

He growled and I moaned. A moment of silence fell between us before he chuckled, his cock easing in a little more. I hissed, my nipples hardening as his breath warmed me.

I needed him. Fuck. I needed him so badly, but I wouldn't dare utter that to him. He'd just given me one of the most mind shattering orgasms, but I wouldn't beg.

Not when I'd been so good at telling him no.

His growl twisted into a groan for a moment.

I flexed my hips, gasping.

"You're going to break me," he finally snarled. "Will you let me knot your cunt, princess?"

I grinned into the blankets, feeling victorious. "Beg."

That earned me another snarl, but he didn't spank me again. "Remember what I said? You're *mine.*"

His hips thrust forward, his cock filling me. I cried out, his shaft hot and pulsing. Every inch after number eight made me scream until I felt his knot against me.

He chuckled before drawing his hips back and thrusting back in.

"You're mine," he growled. "Making me beg for this sweet cunt. I'll beg if that means you'll let me breed you until you can't walk anymore."

I moaned, pleasure searing me as he took me. Every thrust drew out another groan, every touch another cry. I gripped the sheets, groaning with pure delight.

"*Mine,*" he panted. "Gods, you feel fucking good."

"Please don't stop."

He grunted, his arms wrapping around me and lifting me. I

sat against his chest, his claws digging into my thighs as he began to bounce me up and down. I gripped his fur, crying out.

"Look in the mirror," he rasped.

I looked up, realizing we were in front of one. My pussy was spread wide, glistening as he slid in and out of me. His knot had darkened in color, ready to swell within me.

Damon was in his monster form, holding me like I was nothing.

I was so turned on already, but seeing him take me...

Watching him fuck me...

"Come again for me, baby," he groaned, his tone melting me. "I want to feel you come on my cock before you take my knot."

I felt the build-up, the rise of desire as he fucked me. I gasped, I was so close...I wasn't even sure I could come again after the last one, but he seemed to know.

"You're mine, baby," he moaned, his head tipping back.

I was his. Heart, body, soul. I cried out as my orgasm crashed into me, finally tumbling over the edge.

I watched our reflection through slanted eyes, my chest heaving with pants. His clawed hand slid up my body, covering my mouth, offering me the softer part of his palm. I knew what he wanted—and fuck. I wanted it too.

I sank my teeth into him as hard as I could, feeling the rise of our connection. He growled, giving me one last thrust and then opening his jaws.

I knew what was going to happen, and I didn't realize how much I would enjoy watching until now. I let go of his hand and cried out as his teeth sank into me, the snap and sizzle of being bonded to him engulfing me. There was the soft pain of it and then the heady waves of pleasure that followed.

He groaned and I felt his knot shove into me, the heat of his cum filling me.

The two of us moaned, and I felt something click. Like the lock of a massive secret vault finally being opened, all of the gears inside my soul turning as my second mate claimed me as his.

I had given myself to three monsters who shared one form, and they had given themselves to me.

Damon still held me against his chest with my legs spread and his knot buried inside of me.

"Mine," he murmured, nuzzling me.

"I'm yours," I confirmed, swallowing hard as I slowly began to drift back down from cloud nine. "It's like I can feel that something has been unlocked...."

"You were meant to be ours," he murmured, almost reverently. "They made you for us, princess."

Normally, I'd shrug off a comment like that, but I wasn't in the normal world. "Who?"

"The Fates," he explained. "They made you for us. They sent a letter."

"A letter?" I whispered.

"I'll show it to you later."

I nodded, my mind spinning. Still, it was hard to focus when his cock was knotted inside of me. I let out a moan, all of my muscles relaxing.

I looked back up at him and studied his face, trying to memorize every detail. "What happened to your eyebrow?" I asked sleepily, reaching up.

I ran the tip of my finger over the scar that dashed his left eyebrow.

He let out a low hum. "A long time ago, I was dating someone called M. She was...bad for me. I was bad for her too, I'm sure."

"Was she a mortal?"

"No. She was Hades' daughter."

"A demigod?"

"No... a minor goddess."

"You dated a goddess?" I asked, raising up to look at him closer.

He snorted and dragged me even closer to him. "Jealous, princess?"

Maybe just a little.

He chuckled again and I gasped as I felt his knot pulse. "I like the idea of you being a little jealous, but you have no reason to be."

Damon gave a little groan and then stood, taking the two of us to his bed. He managed to roll us to the center, my body splayed over his. His cock still pulsed inside of me, filling me with every last drop of his hot cum.

"Anyways, the story is, she and I had a bad breakup that led to me, Aaecus, and Minos, being cursed by Hades to form Cerberus. We were also forced to guard the gates of the Underworld because Melinoe whined about it."

"Whoa, whoa, whoa, cowboy," I snorted. "That was a lot to just cram in there, and I'm basically high from how hard I came."

"I'm never letting you go," he whispered, staring up at me with a happy monstrous smile.

"I don't want you to," I said. "But let's go back to that story maybe?"

"What about it?"

I raised a brow. "Come on. So that's the entire story then?"

"Yes," Damon said. "That's how I got that scar. And that's all I'll tell you, princess. It was a dark time."

I nodded, knowing that it would take some time for him to completely open up. He had built careful walls around himself, and being able to finally see more of him felt good.

"I didn't want you to send me away earlier. I'm sorry about the money…"

"Don't worry about it," he said. "Three million is nothing."

I shook my head, his words bewildering.

Damon stroked my body as his knot loosened, slowly going down until I was popped free. Before I could roll to the side, I was lifted up and deposited straight onto his face—his tongue lapping up every drop.

"Daddy," I cried, planting my hands on his chest.

His tongue lapped at me, cleaning me until I was ready for him to fuck me all over again.

No, I didn't want him to ever let me go.

THREE FATES MAFIA

DAMON

CHAPTER 17

LONGING

MINOS

I woke up slowly, blinking away the dreams I'd had of taking Ashley. My cock was hard, which was no surprise, and my body was fully worn out.

I blinked, remembering everything that had happened.

Damon had been pissed. I'd known that he would be, but he'd never given me such a brutal punishment. Still, he'd cared for me after, promising that I didn't need to worry about Ashley because Aaecus was taking care of her.

I closed my eyes again, fighting the urge to fall back asleep, when I heard the sound of my bedroom door.

I caught Damon's scent before I felt him sliding into bed against me.

"Hey," I whispered hoarsely.

"Hey," he replied softly.

I frowned, rolling over beneath the blankets to look at him. His scent was...

"Your scent..."

"A lot happened while you were asleep," Damon explained. "I broke Ashley's contract, gave her the money, and sent her to the airport to get her out of Moirai."

"What?!" I shot up, but Damon growled and pulled me back down into bed. I tried to shove against him, but he pinned me in place.

"Listen," he snapped. "Before you fight me, Aaecus made me see reason. We went back to the airport to get her, but Hercules had found and attacked her."

"Oh gods," I whispered, panic tightening my throat. "Damon, if she's hurt—"

"So, I rescued her and brought her home, while Aaecus took care of other things. Then I fucked her. I knotted her. And...I mated her."

I stared at him, completely stunned.

He raised a dark brow, relaxing now that he had told me everything. In his mortal form, he looked like a cocky son of a bitch.

"What the fuck is wrong with you?" I hissed.

"Wrong? Did you not hear what I said?"

"Yes—that you *mated* her! Did she even want you—"

"Yes, she did," Damon growled, sitting up. "You really think I would mate someone if they didn't want me?"

I went silent, my thoughts still spinning. "I thought you were furious earlier. When I mated her."

"I was," Damon said. "But I punished you the way I did because you didn't trust me enough to just tell me—"

"I tried telling you," I snapped. "In fact, I did tell you. From the beginning, I told you that I wanted her."

"Wanting and mating are two different things, and you know that," he chastised. "And don't tell me you didn't enjoy the punishment you got."

True. I had.

I scowled. "You're a bastard."

"I can be," Damon chuckled. He then leaned up, stealing a kiss from me.

I could taste her on him.

Fuck. I felt every instinct kick into gear, delight spreading through me. My mate was mated to my other mate, and I could feel the web of bonds forming.

He deepened the kiss, groaning as our tongues met.

I pulled back and swallowed hard, letting out a breath. "Where's our little demigod mate?"

"In her cage," he said, smirking. "Come with me."

Fuck. Damon gave me a dark smile before dragging me out of bed and down the hall to his bedroom. He pulled me inside and I swallowed a moan as he gripped me.

He shoved me back onto the bed with a growl. "Shift."

"Shift?" I asked, my mouth watering.

He was being so rough, so demanding. His eyes burned with need, with an erotic fury that made me want to come here and now.

Then, there was the sound of Ashley's heartbeat, her soft whimper.

He must have told her to be quiet. As if I didn't know she was there.

As if the scent of her being mated wasn't strong enough that I could taste it.

Damon stepped forward, our lips meeting hungrily. I felt his hands shift, his claws ripping through my clothes. They scraped against my skin, drawing out a low moan from me.

Ashley let out a little pant from beneath the bed.

Fuck.

Damon chuckled now, knowing full well that I was aware

she was here and listening. That she was about to hear me be dominated by our mate.

Our mate.

Fuck. My cock hardened.

Damon's eyes flashed as his teeth scraped against my skin. He kissed me for a moment before turning me around and bending me over the edge of the bed.

"Do you think Aaecus will finally fuck you?" Damon growled. "Maybe he can fuck your ass after I use you."

"Aaecus?" I whispered.

I'd thought about it a thousand fucking times, but Damon had never brought him up in this way before.

"Would you let him?" Damon asked carefully.

"Yes," I responded immediately. "I've wanted him for a long fucking time."

"Because you're a slut," Damon said. "Our little man whore."

I sucked in a breath, groaning. Heat filled me, a mixture of pleasure and humiliation. I liked how it made me feel. I liked submitting to him, knowing that my own little sub was under the bed, listening helplessly.

The sound of footsteps had my head lifting. Aaecus entered the doorway, leaning against the frame. He was wearing nothing but gray sweatpants, the kind that left little to the imagination. Tattoos covered his muscled body, his gaze locking with mine.

I could see the bulge in his pants and was surprised to hear Damon laugh.

"I got a text from our boss," Aaecus said, smirking. "He said you needed some help."

I let out a helpless whine, shocked by how much harder my cock felt now.

We'd never crossed that line with Aaecus.

But here we were.

And fuck, I wanted him. I'd wanted him for so long. I'd known him for ages—he was more than a best friend.

"Where's Ashley?" Aaecus asked playfully, as he winked at me.

He knew. All of us knew.

We all fought stupid grins as we heard her suck in a sharp breath. Her scent of arousal was getting stronger with every passing second.

"She's resting," Damon smirked, his hand sliding down my back. "Sleeping in her bed like a good princess."

He slapped my ass, drawing a grunt from me as the pain stung. I couldn't help laughing, though, enjoying it a little too much.

"I told you to fucking shift."

"Fine," I caved, letting my human form start to slip away.

The bed groaned as my muscles began to change, my bones cracking and blood pumping as I turned into a monster. A low growl came from behind me as Damon followed suit, his monster even bigger than mine. His fur was darker, his rows of teeth glinting with hunger.

"I'm going to breed you like I bred her," Damon growled. "And then Aaecus is finally going to have his way with you. After all this fucking time."

"Please," I groaned, my claws ripping into his blankets.

Damon smacked me again, spreading my ass. I felt his spit drip down, and I groaned, my cock aching. It was fully hard, my knots pulsing with need.

My ears perked up at the sound of Ashley rubbing her eager pussy. I could hear how wet she was and could almost taste her arousal from here.

"Fuck," Damon and I both groaned, pausing for a moment.

Damon closed his eyes and shook his head, a low growl leaving him. "Gods help us."

Aaecus grunted, leaving the doorway. He leaned over the foot of the bed, cupping my jaws. We stared at each other and I couldn't help but crack a sly smile.

"I don't know why we've waited so long," Aaecus said.

"I've always wanted you," I admitted. "For a long, long time."

"I know," Aaecus chuckled, arching a brow. "Open your mouth, slut."

I obeyed him, parting my jaws. Aaecus spit in my mouth and I groaned, swallowing what he gave me.

Damon rubbed the tip of his cock against my ass, his precum and spit mixing together. It smelled like us, like them. I pressed my face into the blankets, smelling Ashley's cum.

Fuck. This was going to be my undoing.

Aaecus leaned down, gripping the fur on the back of my head. I looked up at him as Damon began to slowly ease into me, his cock filling me. I panted and groaned, only for Aaecus' mouth to meet mine.

I took his kiss, feeling my cock react like it was being stroked. It was too much, and no one was even sucking me off yet.

I was going to come just from Damon fucking me, Aaecus kissing me, and Ashley pleasuring herself to us. It was erotic, a dream, and everything I could ever want.

Aaecus grunted, his body starting to shift right as Damon completely slammed into me.

I cried out, the bed creaking. Damon let out a growl, his claws raking down my back to my hips. He gripped them as he began to thrust in and out, owning me. Taking me.

Aaecus climbed onto the bed.

I'd seen his cock before. I'd seen his cock many times, but

I couldn't resist reaching for it as he sprawled out in front of me. I gripped his shaft, still crying out with every pump from Damon.

"Suck his cock, Minos," Damon commanded. "Let him fuck your throat. Then we'll bring our princess out."

"Fuck," I rasped, parting my jaws.

Aaecus groaned as I took the head of his cock into my mouth. I licked him, the flavor of his precum driving me crazy. Every touch, every movement... Fuck. His three knots pulsed, his breaths shortening.

"Fuck. Minos, I didn't know you'd be this fucking good," Aaecus groaned.

"He's had practice," Damon growled, fucking me harder. "He's a fucking slut. My slut. *Our slut.*"

Aaecus' cock thrust into my throat just as Damon started to come, his groans of pleasure echoing through the room. His cum filled me with heat, his knot popping inside of me and swelling immediately.

I choked as Aaecus hit the back of my throat, his hips moving.

"Maybe you can knot him once I'm done, and he can knot our little princess," Damon breathed.

I would have answered yes, but I was too busy sucking. Aaecus wasn't gentle, knowing I could take his brutality.

Fuck, centuries of pent-up needs were behind every movement.

All the while, I could hear Ashley getting closer and closer to climaxing. Right as her little voice echoed through the room, Aaecus grunted and started to come down my throat.

I swallowed every drop, my head spinning.

He kept coming until finally, he slowly pulled out, panting as he melted into the bed.

"Fuck," he sighed. "Fuck. I've been missing out."

I nodded, my head falling on the blankets. Damon gave me a gentler rub, a soft lick with a moan.

I grinned, even though my cock was still hard and dripping. I could feel the drops coming from the tip, hitting the floor.

"Little princess," Damon called softly. "Did you come from listening to us?"

There was silence for a couple of moments, followed by a breathless whisper. "Yes."

Damon pressed his face against my back and I could feel his monstrous smile. He was just as smitten as Aaecus and I were.

"Come out and see us, baby girl," Aaecus called.

I listened to the cage unlatch. All three of us looked up as a very flushed Ashley stood, her face glowing with lust.

Her lips parted, her eyes widening. "Wow. All three of you...."

I chuckled. "Come join us, little thief."

Ashley stared for a moment, then her lips pulled into a sensuous smile. She climbed up on the bed, pausing to kiss my snout and ruffle the top of my head.

"You look good knotted," she whispered to me.

Damon barked out a laugh, his knot swelling even more.

"Oh, really?" I teased, as she climbed up onto Aaecus' massive body.

I lifted my head, amused, as she sat on his chest. He gripped her calves, smirking.

"Can I help you, little thief?" he asked.

"Do you think you can get hard again?" she asked. "So you can knot Minos next and he can knot me. And maybe Damon can fuck my throat? I've had so many thoughts running through my head."

"I'm already fucking hard again, baby girl," Aaecus growled. "Just knowing you have such dirty thoughts in that pretty head turns me on. I like knowing we're all you can think about."

It was true. His three knots were already filling again, his shaft getting harder and lengthening.

Damon slowly began to pull out of me, and I gasped as his knot popped free, his cum dripping from me.

He chuckled, patting me. "Your turn. I want to watch."

CHAPTER 18

TOGETHER

DAMON

I sat in the plush leather chair in the corner of my room, my hand sliding to my cock as I watched. Ashley was pinned under Minos, their mouths fused together as they kissed. Aaecus was behind him, stroking Minos' cock while he played with his own too.

My blood burned as I watched them, lust filling me in a way it never had before. I'd always enjoyed being a voyeur, but this was special.

Ashley let out a low moan as Minos pressed his fingers inside of her, stroking her in a way that had her arching gracefully against the mattress.

I gripped my cock and groaned, watching the three of them between narrowed eyes as pleasure worked through me. Ashley's little cries were almost enough to make me come, but I held onto my self control.

Our little princess. The thief that had stolen our hearts. I'd fallen so fast that I couldn't even be angry at the Fates.

Ashley gasped beneath Minos as his tongue found her clit, lapping away all the cum from when she pleasured herself. Listening to her was like listening to the sweetest music, her breaths and moans a chorus of lust and need.

Minos' cock was hard, but he wouldn't take her yet. Not until she was begging.

Aaecus looked up at me, our gazes locking. We'd never done anything like this. Hell, we'd never even fucked someone in the same room. I was turned on, curious, and wanting him more than I had ever thought.

I'd told him that I'd need a cosmic reason to bring Ashley back, but that had been a lie and he had known it.

He slowly smiled, then winked, and refocused on Ashley and Minos.

I cursed under my breath, closing my eyes for a moment to find my restraint again. I could feel my balls turning blue the longer I kept myself from coming again, but it was worth it. I wanted to come the same moment all of them did, as that would be the most satisfying release.

Minos grunted, drawing back. His tongue was coated with her juices, his gaze burning with hunger. He looked up at me for a brief second, a shared look I knew all too well.

Fuck. Watching the three of them was going to be the best form of torture. Just as listening to the three of us had been for our little thief.

She had come just listening to me fuck our mate.

"Mmm," I hummed to myself, stroking my cock faster.

Minos kissed up Ashley's body, pausing to bite her nipples. She cried out, her cheeks bright pink. I slowed my strokes , sucking in a breath as her legs wrapped around his hips.

I watched as Minos began to shift, his form shimmering as

his mortal body gave way to the monster. I felt the excitement of seeing him shift with Aaecus and I present, knowing that the three of us could come together at any moment as Cerberus.

Would she be able to take us in our full monster form? I wanted to pin her down beneath our massive claws and watch as she tried to take just one of our cocks in her little hole.

Aaecus growled and shifted again too. My bed groaned beneath the weight of two snarling beasts and a sexy demigod.

Both of them were so giant compared to her, their monstrous bodies at least three times her size. She was swamped by Minos, but that didn't stop her from kissing him. I watched as our princess opened her mouth for his long tongue, sucking on it as the head of his cock rubbed against her.

She accepted us as we were. Monsters, villains, mafia.

Aaecus rubbed the tip of his cock against Minos, running his claws down his back. "Fuck. Get inside her, Minos. I want to bury myself in you. I want her to feel me fucking her through you."

I growled, gripping my knot.

We would have to do this every fucking day from here on out. All of the wicked ideas I had just watching the three of them...

"Fuck her," I commanded Minos.

Both of them groaned as he began to spread her pink pussy, his cock slowly easing inside of her. She cried out, her little fingers gripping the blankets, her body writhing.

Aaecus watched the two of them, rubbing Minos. "Look at how good she is," he said. "Taking your two knots. Our little princess. Mmm, baby girl, you're doing so good."

"Fuck," I cursed, unable to take my eyes off them.

The way he called her baby girl...Mmm. I'd started calling her princess, but baby girl had a nice ring to it too...

"I bet that feels so good," Aaecus said, chuckling. "Does it?"

"Yes," Ashley cried. "Fuck. Yes. It feels so good. So fucking good. I needed this."

"Awww," Aaecus said, positioning his cock now. "You needed one of our monster cocks to fill you and breed you?"

"Fuck, Aaecus," Minos gasped.

Aaecus' words had captivated all three of us. Hearing him talk like this was new and exciting for all of us.

I began to pump my cock faster and faster.

"I'm going to breed your mate," Aaecus said. "I'm going to fuck his ass while he fucks you. I want you to remember that every thrust from him is one from me too. That we're taking you together."

"Yes," she rasped. "Fuck, I'm already so close again."

"We're not stopping even if you come, baby girl. We have to make sure you're filled with as much cum as possible."

Minos groaned, finally inside of her. Ashley screamed, her voice hoarse.

"Please," she begged.

"Fucking hell," Minos murmured. "I can feel her pulsing around me."

"Good," Aaecus said.

He looked up at me again, his eyes going from my cock to my piercing gaze.

I'm going to breed both of your mates, he told me.

I'm going to make you my mate, I quipped back, arching a brow. *Enjoy it while you can. I'm going to fuck you so hard you'll be asking yourself why it took you so godsdamned long to cave.*

Aaecus snorted, but he didn't disagree. Which only gave me more thoughts about what it would be like to fuck with him, to take the two of them with him.

Maybe I liked sharing more than I thought possible.

Minos groaned as Aaecus began to slowly ease into him, his

eyes never leaving mine. I could feel my mates' pleasures echoing through our bonds, Ashley and Minos groaning in sync.

I knew exactly how fucking good it felt, and it made me want to come all over them.

Aaecus grunted before pushing all the way into Minos, hunching over him. Ashley was buried under muscles, fur, teeth, and claws—her pants reminding me that she was okay.

More than okay.

"Oh gods," she cried. Her voice was ragged, her moans desperate.

Aaecus began to pump into Minos, and he into Ashley. The three of them fell into a beautiful, erotic rhythm—one that was driving me back to the edge all over again.

"Your knots, Aaecus," Minos groaned. "Fuck. All three of them are fucking perfect."

Aaecus gripped his hips, thrusting into him over and over again. I watched as my mate took the first of Aaecus' knots, before it popped back out.

I snarled as they kept going. My senses were being driven crazy by the chorus of cries and slaps, their scents making my mouth water.

Ashley wrapped her arms around Minos' neck, holding on to him. He was so close, and so was she. So was Aaecus.

I stood from my seat, stroking my cock as I went to the edge of the bed.

Minos looked up at me, his jaws parting on a pant. He had that stupid look, the one I loved. The one that told me he was about to fill up our mate with all of his seed and then knot her.

"You wanted this," I groaned, stroking harder.

"I did," he moaned. "Fuck. I'm about to come inside you, little thief."

"Please," she groaned.

Aaecus began to fuck into him harder, only a few moments before losing his control.

"Your knots better keep every fucking drop inside of her, or you'll be pushing it back in with your tongue," I growled.

"Fuck," he gasped.

His eyes fluttered as he drove into our mate one last time, the two of them crying out. Aaecus was right behind them, his head tipping back as he started to come inside Minos.

I watched the three of them, their orgy finally tipping me over the edge.

Chapter 19

Sweet Dreams

Ashley

I was dreaming about the beach. I stood on the sand, the waves lapping at the shore. The water was pristine, the sky baby blue with fluffy white clouds. I could feel the sun on my skin, warming me.

Pleasure suddenly interrupted the dream and I looked down at myself. I felt something, the vision of the beach wavering in and out.

"You're so tight, baby girl, but you're doing so good at keeping my cock warm."

I groaned in my dream, the visions melting into something else. Suddenly, I was laying on a bed, Aaecus hovering over me in his full monster form.

"That's right, baby girl, keep dreaming. I wonder if you're thinking of me now that my cock is in you."

I groaned and looked down, the dream flickering in and out again.

My eyes flew open and I gasped as arms circled me. My pussy throbbed so intensely I groaned, moving my ass back and realizing I was being spooned by someone.

"Good morning, baby," Aaecus' low voice came. "Thank you for keeping me warm this morning."

His hips moved and I cried out, realizing that his cock was inside of me. I could feel him starting to harden too, and realized that he'd just been in me like I was his own fleshlight.

"Aaecus! *Fuck*," I gasped.

"Shhh," he hushed, his hand slipping over my mouth. "I don't want to disturb anyone. Stay quiet for me."

"*Aaecus*," I growled against his hand, my voice muffled.

"My perfect little cocksleeve," he whispered into my ear. "Go ahead, baby girl, be angry at me. Bite me with those cute little teeth. I can feel your hot pussy clenching around my cock as you do."

Fuck. I was so turned on that it was impossible to be mad at him. He had put his cock inside me while I'd been asleep, and that was a secret desire I'd never asked for.

I bit his hand, but that only made the both of us groan.

"You've been craving this cock," he breathed. "And I've been craving this pussy. I love just lying here, soaking in your wet cunt. You were ready for me too."

I nodded, letting out a soft whimper as I bit into his hand harder. He chuckled, kissing my neck. "Does it feel good?"

"Yes," I rasped.

"Good," he murmured. "Squeeze my cock, baby."

My pussy pulsed in response, the two of us gasping together.

"I'm going to shift while inside you," he groaned.

I closed my eyes, reaching down to grip his hand on my waist as he began to slowly change. I moaned softly as his cock began to stretch me, growing thicker and longer. His body became bigger, his lips becoming jaws with rows of sharp teeth. I cried out as he kept stretching my pussy, until he stopped.

I'd never been this full before. I sucked in small breaths as I adjusted to his hot cock, and then cursed as I remembered he had not one knot, not two—but three.

How was I going to take every part of him?

"Good girl," he growled. "You feel so fucking good."

I whimpered as he slowly pulled back, before thrusting up inside of me. I felt his first knot bump against me and cried out, his cock throbbing with heat as he began to fuck me.

He felt *so* fucking good.

"Harder," I whined.

He chuckled. "Mm, are you sure, princess?"

"*Harder*," I groaned again.

He growled and rolled me onto my stomach, pinning me down beneath him as he thrust his cock inside of me. I cried out, the twinge of pain as the head of his cock bumped my cervix turning me on even more.

He grabbed my arms and pinned them to the blankets as he fucked me. I pressed my face into the pillows as I screamed, my voice muffled. The sound of his cock filling me over and over echoed around us, my wet pussy taking him.

Sunlight filled the bedroom, covering the two of us as he fucked me. I could feel my orgasm creeping up and groaned, desperate for it.

He released one of my arms. "Rub your clit, baby girl."

I groaned as I slid my hand beneath me, my fingers finding my clit as he pumped into me.

"Atta girl," he rasped. "Fuck, I can feel you squeezing me so tight, baby. Look at you, taking my monster cock so well."

I groaned as I took him over and over, his massive body pressing against me. I rubbed my clit faster, my voice becoming louder even as I buried my face into the pillows.

"I'm going to come!" I wailed.

"I am too," he groaned.

Finally, an orgasm ripped into me and every muscle in my body tensed. I felt his hot seed spill inside me as he cried out, his cock bursting. I screamed as his first knot slipped in, the wave of pleasure never ending as he loaded me with his cum.

"That's right, baby girl," he huffed, groaning as he gave another gentle thrust.

Tears filled my eyes as the next knot pushed inside of me, his movements slowing. I clenched around him and he grunted, our breaths softening.

His knots swelled, locking him to me. He leaned down and chuckled. "Can't fit any more," he said.

I shook my head, closing my eyes and basking in the dreamy state I was in. "I want you to mate me," I whispered.

Minos had, Damon had. And now, I wanted him to as well.

This entire week had turned my life into a circus, but it had been worth it. I was falling for these three idiots. I wanted to know more about them, to explore what they were each like. What were their favorite colors, their favorite foods?

"Mate me and then take me on a date," I requested, smirking.

He let out a deep hum, his arms circling me. "I think you have that backwards." His hips moved ever so slightly, drawing a long groan from me. " I can do that," he said. "But I'll take you on a date first. I'd love for the whole world to know you belong to me, sweetheart."

"Clothed," I mumbled.

He laughed. "Yes, clothed. Although, I wouldn't mind ripping those clothes off in front of an entire crowd. Their jealousy would make me happy."

I smiled and turned my head, giving him a side eye. "Clothed."

He snickered again, nipping my shoulder playfully. "Fine," he conceded. "But I pick out what you wear."

"Fine," I said. "Deal."

The deal had backfired.

Of course, Aaecus chose to dress me in something that made me question...well, everything about myself.

He'd fit me in a very short—*a very, very short*—black cocktail dress with a slit up my left thigh, and v-neck that dipped low. The slit and neck were both connected by a sheer fabric. It was hot and evocative, and the exact type of dress I would have eyed on the rack but would've never dared to wear.

He'd also chosen black heels, emerald earrings, and a necklace with an emerald pendant.

After lying in bed this morning, we'd spent the day in the penthouse. Aaecus had deposited me on their couch for awhile and I'd cozied up with the three of them to watch a couple movies before Minos had to head out.

About an hour ago, Aaecus had told me to go change into the items that had been brought to our front door. The thief in me practically drooled over what he had picked out because of price alone, but I also felt strange wearing it.

Strange, but also hot.

"She's not leaving here without her collar," Damon called.

Aaecus and I were both almost to the door, but I turned to meet him. My hair was swept back, leaving my neck exposed. Damon pulled out a box and handed it to me.

"Oh," I breathed, pulling the lid off.

Inside was a thin black leather collar with a silver pendant. The pendant was Cerberus, which made me suck in a breath, fighting back tears.

"Where did you get this?" I asked, smiling.

"I had it made while you were sleeping," Damon said. "Don't cry, princess. If your makeup is going to run, it'll be because you're taking our cocks." He lifted it out of the box and placed it around my neck, and it fit perfectly.

He let out a noise of appreciation as he clasped it, trailing a kiss along the curve of my neck.

"Mmm," he hummed. "You smell delicious."

I shivered, my breath hitching. His words were a bolt straight to my pussy. He took a step back, his eyes darkening. He then looked up at Aaecus, arching a dark brow.

"I hope you're ready to fight off every man and woman in the city. She's stunning."

"She is," Aaecus agreed. "Don't worry, I'll bring her home."

Damon nodded, although I saw a flicker of concern. "Minos is already out in the city checking on some things. Night is coming soon, and just... be careful. I'll be out running errands too, there are some things I need to check on."

I bit my lower lip, wondering what *things* he meant. That was one of the questions I'd ask Aaecus tonight.

I knew what kind of businesses they ran, but I wanted to know more about the mafia. More about their world. I had only known the side of it that involved me being a thief, not every-thing else. Their sleep schedules were insane, and aside from the disruption I had caused in their lives, they seemed to work all the time.

"Come on," Aaecus said.

I leaned up and kissed Damon on the cheek and then grinned at the lipstick mark it left behind on his face. I turned and went to Aaecus.

It was hard to take my eyes off him as he led me to the elevator. There was an aura around him, one that drew me in. He was wearing a charcoal gray jacket, pants, and a soft shirt.

There was a sense of power that dripped from him, and even though he was dressed well—you could still see the scrappier edge to him. The side that was the tattooed killer, the part that left me wondering if I knew what I was doing, wanting someone like him.

I couldn't stop myself though.

I could have left at any moment, but I didn't want to. The longer I knew the three of them, the more I wanted to stay by their side. They called me their princess, but I wanted to be their queen.

Aaecus surprised me by hitting the up button on the elevator panel.

"I thought the penthouse was the highest we could go," I said.

"This takes us to the helicopter pad," Aaecus answered.

I looked up at him, startled. "The what?"

He smirked but didn't say anything. Instead, the doors slid open and we were met with a cold breeze. The sun was setting over the city, the sky the same colors as mimosas and berries. He led me out onto a concrete pad where a black helicopter waited, the blades already whirring.

"Fuck," I gasped.

He laughed and we both moved quickly for it. I found myself ducking like an idiot even though I was nowhere near tall enough to get whacked by the blades .

I squeaked as he grabbed my waist and lifted, placing me inside. A man I'd never met before handed me a set of headphones, then I noted the bodyguard I'd met the first night was in the pilot seat.

Aaecus slid in next to me and shut the door. I turned towards him. "Where are we going?"

"You'll see," Aaecus said loudly, his voice carrying over the sounds of the helicopter.

This was wild. I nodded and sank back into my seat, ignoring the lurch in my stomach as we began to lift up. I sucked in a breath, leaning to the left so I could look out at the city.

Aaecus' hand settled on my bare thigh, giving me a squeeze. I bit my bottom lip and shook my head, leaning back against him. He was warm and smelled good, but part of me wished that he didn't have to pretend to be human for the sake of others. I'd started to enjoy his monster self more than I cared to admit.

His fingers crept further up my thigh and I hissed at him. He let out a laugh, smirking as I pushed his hand back down.

"Behave," I said.

He only grinned, his sharp teeth glinting.

The helicopter carried us over the city. The setting sun turned my skin bronze and I looked down, studying his hand. There was the tattoo of the Three Fates eye again over the top. I traced it absentmindedly, wondering about what the future would bring us now.

It wasn't long before the helicopter began to descend. I looked out again and realized that we were at the bay, the ocean glittering like jewels. We landed on a pad and the engine turned off, the blades slowing. The doors opened and Aecus got out first, then helped me not stumble and face plant in these heels.

"Shit," I whispered.

I recognized where we were now. We were at a restaurant I'd seen in all the magazines, Kalopsia.

Aaecus pulled me close, tucking a loose strand behind my ear. "You look lovely," he said.

"Thanks," I whispered, my voice hoarse. This was not my type of crowd, not my type of people. We weren't even inside yet and I felt nervous. "Are you sure you don't want to just get burgers?"

He raised a brow. "Are you scared?"

"Not scared, just... What if Hercules shows up?"

"He has nothing to do with you anymore," Aaecus said. "We own this city too, love, which means now you do. You're ours. You belong to one of the most feared monsters in all of history. Hercules isn't that stupid."

Part of me wanted to bring up that Hercules also had a bullet put through his head last night because of us, but I bit my tongue.

Aaecus led me towards a set of glass doors. My stomach twisted as I saw inside. The luxury was almost too much, but I didn't have time to think too much about it.

The doors opened, a woman giving us a nod. "Welcome to Kalopsia. I will seat you now."

Aaecus' hand slid to my lower back and he guided me. The two of us followed and I did my best to focus on her, and not the murmurs and looks that followed us the moment we stepped inside.

The interior of the restaurant was luxe, with black marble pillars and gold decor. We were led to a table for two that was set against massive windows, giving us a view of the sea and the rest of the restaurant.

I took my seat, entirely flustered.

"Would you like anything to drink to start with, madam?" The woman asked.

Aaecus took his seat, giving me a curious look.

"Water," I said. "With a lemon if you have any."

"Yes, madam. And you, sir?"

"Water and can we have a bottle of the Domaine d'Au-venay white?" Aaecus asked. "Well, assuming you like white wine."

I was a beer drinker through and through. "Sure," I said.

He scrutinized me for a moment. "Actually, we'll take two whiskey and cokes."

"Yes, sir," she said.

I blew out a breath and felt his shoe bump me under the table. "Baby girl," he crooned. "You look like you're going to throw up. What's wrong?"

"I don't know anything about any of this," I hissed. "I grew up with an uncle who liked Bud Light, Aaecus."

"And? We could have ordered that."

"Not in this type of place," I exclaimed.

He snorted and leaned forward. "Look at me."

I looked around the room for a couple seconds before refocusing on him. He had an easy going expression, although he couldn't hide the hint of amusement.

"You think I'm ridiculous," I mumbled.

"No," he said. "I think you don't understand that I don't care if you order a two dollar burger while we're here. They'll go get it for you, and I wouldn't give a shit."

I stared at him like he'd grown a second head for a moment, then relaxed a little. "Right. I steal from people like this. I have been for five or six years now."

He nodded and over the room. "It would be funny if you've taken something from someone here."

I grinned now, relaxing even more. He'd thrown me off this evening by bringing me here via helicopter, but I was still with the same guy I'd gotten to know this week.

This week.

Our waters and cocktails were brought and I fought off a laugh as I was presented with three wedges of lemon on a silver filigree plate.

"We need some time to look over the menu," Aaecus said.

The waitress nodded, leaving us again.

"So, what questions do you have?" he asked. "A question for a question."

"You want to ask me questions?" I inquired, amused.

"Always," he said.

"Alright," I said as I squeezed the lemon into my water. "How does the whole Cerberus thing work?"

"Damon, Minos, and I can form the bigger monster."

"And you used to live in the Underworld?"

"Yes," Aaecus said. "We served Hades. Initially we were just hell hounds, but eventually became Cerberus."

"Does it hurt when you shift?"

"No, but it does feel strange. It's like...the three of us are suddenly living in each other's minds. And sharing the same body."

"Interesting..." I trailed off, wondering what Cerberus looked like.

"Now, it's my turn. Tell me about your uncle."

"He died," I replied, pressing my lips together. "He was good. He taught me everything I know. I went to art school for a while, to try and get away from being a criminal like him, but the world always pulls you back in. Plus, it only made me a better art thief. I know how to spot originals and fakes. I know how to break into systems and secure items. He taught me a lot of that."

Aaecus nodded, regarding me thoughtfully. "I'm sorry he died."

I shrugged, ignoring the way I felt like I was being choked now. "Everyone does," I whispered.

He leaned forward, his hand sliding over mine. "Not us," Aaecus said. "And not you. You're a demigod. You'll live until someone kills you, and you're damn hard to kill. Hercules, Jason, Perseus, Theseus, and Orion have all hung around a lot longer than anyone would like."

That hadn't crossed my mind yet. "So what you're saying is that I'm dating three old men."

Aaecus laughed, arching a brow. "Yes, very old. Ancient even."

I wrinkled my nose at him and picked up the menu. "Jesus fucking Christ," I mumbled.

The appetizers alone started in the triple digits.

"Will you pick for me?" I asked.

"Yes," Aaecus answered. "Always, baby girl."

CHAPTER 20

JASON AND THE ARGONAUTS

ASHLEY

Aaecus picked out our food from the menu, which helped me relax more. We were waiting on it to come to the table, so now was the right time to break away for a few minutes.

"I'm going to run to the restroom real quick," I let him know.

"Okay," he said, his gaze turning to the rest of the restaurant. He narrowed his eyes, letting out a growl as I stood. "Come back to me soon."

"I'm just going to pee," I whispered, my cheeks turning hot again.

I shouldn't be embarrassed by that, I reminded myself. I crossed the restaurant, ignoring others' gazes on me again. I didn't like drawing attention. I was used to blending into the shadows, especially around crowds like this.

The restaurant was huge, but I eventually found my way past a faux wall covered in foliage that blocked an open doorway with two halls going in opposite directions. I went to the right, slowing as my gaze roamed over the decorations. Statues and massive paintings of—surprise, surprise—greek myth scenes practically covered every inch of the place.

I went into the ladies' room and scowled at the couch in the center.

"Ridiculous," I sighed.

I used the restroom quickly, but when I came out, a woman was standing in front of the sink. She leaned against the counter, facing me. She wore a long crimson dress with her dark hair pulled up.

She was gorgeous, but there was something about her that made me feel uneasy.

Not to mention, she was looking right at me.

"Uh, hi," I greeted awkwardly, going to the other sink.

"Hello, child," she said, her voice silky smooth despite how ominous she sounded.

I squeezed my eyes shut for a moment, trying to gather my composure. Great. That wasn't a great thing to hear.

I washed my hands then turned towards her. "What do you want?"

She grinned, and her smile was every bit as stunning as she was. "Do you know who I am?"

"Nope. A goddess, maybe?" My long lost aunt?

"No," she mused, letting out a feminine chuckle. "My name is Clotho. I'm one of the Fates."

Oh.

Oh fuck.

My stomach immediately twisted, my nerves making sweat spring to my palms.

"Don't worry," she soothed. "I'm not here to kill you or anything."

"Comforting," I said weakly.

"I came here to tell you a couple of things," Clotho said. "Starting with this—you must kill Hercules."

"*What?*" I hissed.

She nodded, her expression never changing from all-knowing and slightly amused. "When the moment presents itself, you must kill him."

"But how?" I asked. "He's twice my size and he's been around forever. I may be a demigod, but he has thousands of years of fighting behind him. I'm not even thirty yet."

"We know this," Clotho said. "But as I said, you must kill him, Ashley. The other thing is this—there will be a cage with a lock. And even if you are warned not to open it, you must use the gift from your father to open it. This action will bring no harm to you or Cerberus."

"Will it bring harm to others?" I asked.

"Yes," she answered. "But that is their Fate."

"Okay then," I mumbled. "This is... how do I know you're not lying?"

"My sweet child," she crooned, offering me a soft smile. "Do you really think I'd lie about who I am?"

"No," I sighed. Which was the truth. She was already giving off an aura of power that made me want to throw up. "I don't understand this world. I don't understand why it is the way it is. Why demigods haven't been allowed, why ancient beings are running a fucking mafia instead of doing something good."

"I can't answer those questions, child," she said sadly. "But, I can tell you this. You were the first, but you won't be the last. You will be a helping hand to the others, and part of the new era."

That was very cryptic.

"I may or may not see you again," Clotho said. "Good luck, and may my sisters guide you."

Her body began to glow. I looked away right as the whole room turned white and she disappeared as if she'd never been there.

I let out a breath and leaned against the marble counter. I should have said other things to her, called her names or something, but instead I'd found myself being drawn in.

I heard a growl echo from outside the bathroom and cursed, heading for the door. I'd been away from Aaecus longer than I had planned—

A gunshot popped, followed by screams.

"Gods damn it," I hissed.

I heard more screams, followed by more gun fire, and stood at the door for a moment, torn between running out there or staying in here to hide.

"*Find the demigod!*"

Well, stay in here it was. I kicked off my heels and grabbed them both, ready to jab the stiletto into anyone that came through the door.

I heard more gunshots, more growls, and then a low laugh.

"*She'll come out,*" a voice called. "We have her mate."

Fuck. My heart was beating so hard I could barely focus, my blood rushing. Aaecus wouldn't get caught, right?

Fuck, fuck, fuck.

If they hurt him...

"Get the fuck out of here!" I heard Aaecus bellow.

I couldn't, I was trapped. And I couldn't leave him even if there was a way out. What if they killed him? Could monsters be killed?

I heard movement outside the bathroom getting closer and gripped my heel harder. I pressed my body to the wall, ready to lunge around the corner.

I'm a demigod, I'm a demigod. And a thief. I know how to fight. I know how to escape.

My thoughts were going a thousand miles per hour. This was a kill or be killed situation, but I felt myself fighting the idea that I might have to murder anyone that came through the door.

I didn't have time to think anymore.

The door to the bathroom burst open. A burly man with a gun shoved in and I lunged, driving my heel straight into the fleshy spot of his shoulder. He screamed, grabbing me and slamming me against the wall, but I brought my knee straight up into his balls.

Bingo. The sound he made told me I'd landed my blow. I grabbed his gun and hit him in the head, taking a step back as he collapsed to the floor. I fought the urge to giggle, delighted by my demigod strength.

My adrenaline was pumping now. I looked down at the gun and then turned it towards the couch, pulling the trigger. A bullet burst out, the gun lurching in my hands.

Great, it was ready to go.

More shouts sounded and I heard more footsteps heading towards the bathroom—but now I had the upper hand.

I aimed the gun at the door, muttered a wish for good luck, and pulled the trigger as two men piled in. They shot their guns too, but the bullets flew past me, putting holes into the pretty luxe bathroom.

My ears were ringing as they both went down and I moved quickly, stepping over their bodies and out the bathroom door. I moved down the hall swiftly, crouching down lower as I came to the doorway.

The men's bathroom was down the opposite hall, and the door was barely cracked. I could see a couple of regular people looking out, their eyes wide.

This was the first time that I really thought about how I was a demigod and they weren't. I stared at them for a moment, feeling the adrenaline flowing through me, the power in my veins.

"Get the fucking woman!" A shout came. "Go! Now!"

I ducked down and came out of the opening, going to the faux wall with the plants. I moved silently, listening for which direction the footsteps were coming from.

Right side.

I went left, keeping myself low as I turned the corner and sawthree more men going towards the bathrooms.

Thank the gods this place was like a maze.

I listened again, staying where I was as I tried to figure out what the hell I would do next.

Aaecus' voice carried through the restaurant. "You've gone too fucking far, Jason."

"Well, the same could be said for you three idiots. You fucking shot Hercules."

"And? This isn't the first time we've spilled each other's blood."

"Yes, but I've heard it's because you have a demigod , and we can't have that. She will need to come with me, or you will die."

Pffft, not a chance in hell.

I pressed my lips together, taking in my surroundings again. There was a table a few feet away, one I could hide under for a few moments if needed.

Or I could spring up and go Rambo on these motherfuckers.

I liked option two more.

"Well, here goes nothing."

I jumped up, and for a split second felt the immense satisfaction seeing the looks of surprise I got from at least six men.

But then they held up their guns.

Bullets began to fly as I pulled the trigger on the one in my hands. I ran forward, aiming at each man on either side of Aaecus—and laughed maniacally as they hit home.

"Everyone fucking stop!"

All the men froze, and even I paused.

A man stood over Aaecus, a knife pressed to his throat. He gave me a menacing glare, his eyes burning gold.

Oh, so this was a demigod.

Unlike Hercules, he actually exuded the energy of a god. He had salt and pepper hair, dark brows, and a beard that was also streaked with gray.

"I'm guessing you're Ashley," he said coldly. "I'm Jason."

"I heard," I snapped, turning my gun towards him. "Let Aaecus go."

"Why? Is he your pet?" Jason asked, giving me a dry smile. "Your dog? Is that why you're staying with them and not us?"

"Them, as in monsters? I'm staying with them because Hercules fucked me over, and because they're my mates."

Aaecus' eyes widened, his face telling me that was something I should maybe not have said.

Jason tipped his head back and let out a boisterous laugh. It echoed around me, sending a shiver down my spine.

"Your name is Ashley, right?" he asked.

"Yes," I said.

"Daughter of....?"

"Hermes."

He raised a dark brow, studying me. "Interesting. I think that makes us cousins or something."

"I'm pretty sure everyone is someone's cousin amongst gods and monsters," I sneered.

"How about this, *Cousin*," Jason chuckled. "I'll let your dog go if you sit and talk with me, alone. I won't hurt him, and I'll let you both leave without any trouble after we talk."

Aaecus' gaze burned with rage, and I met it—feeling it all the way down to my bones.

He could be mad at me, I didn't care. I just needed him to be safe.

"Deal," I said.

Jason nodded and let go of Aaecus. He held up his hand. "Everyone out. Get the bodies from the bathroom. I will speak with her alone. That includes you, *dog*."

Aaecus stood and looking as if he was about to jump Jason, but I called out. "Aaecus!"

I ran around towards the two of them, avoiding broken glass and toppled tables.

He let out a low growl as I threw myself at him. He lifted me up, holding me to him for a moment. "Don't let him trick you," Aaecus warned. "The two of you have ten minutes before I have Damon and Minos burn down every business you own, Jason."

"Fine," Jason sighed, obviously annoyed. "Not one hair on her pretty head will be harmed."

Aaecus held onto me for a few more moments. "I'll be close by," he said.

I nodded, feeling a wave of nerves and worry. I'd already run into one of the Fates in the bathroom, and now I was dealing with yet another demigod.

I watched Aaecus and the other men go, leaving me alone with Jason.

"Sit with me," Jason said. "If you'd like."

No, I really don't like anything about this. I went to a table with food on it and, despite the fact that this was not the most ideal situation, grabbed one of the rolls from a basket at the center.

"Hungry?" Jason asked.

"Yes, my dinner date got interrupted," I said.

We sat down across from each other.

"So," I said. "Jason. And the Argonauts."

"So you've heard the myths," Jason chuckled.

"I have. I don't know why you're interested in me," I said. "Or why you're coming after Cerberus."

"I'm certain you know more about our mafia than that," he said, as if this was the most pleasant conversation in the world. He cocked his head, studying me carefully. "Or have they kept you locked up?"

"What do you want?" I asked.

"Straight to the point. I like it."

"I'm serious," I said. "I'm not playing these games."

"Honey, you are the game," Jason chuckled. He picked up an abandoned glass of wine and swirled it before taking a sip. "Based on the little bit of gold dripping from a cut on your face, I'm going to bet you are, in fact, a demigod. Which means *you* are a prize that everyone—gods, monsters, mortals, and demigods alike—will be after. There hasn't been another one of us in ages. You are the forbidden fruit."

Gross. I couldn't hide my annoyance or disgust. "I'm not some prize."

"You are," he insisted. "And a prize that cannot be mated to mutts."

I glared at him, feeling a prick of my temper. "They aren't mutts."

"They're monsters, honey."

"If you call me *honey* again, I'm going to shoot you in the balls," I growled.

He held up his hands, giving me an admonishing look. "Apologies. All I am saying is that this *mafia* has rules. You're in my city, and you have to play by them."

"Says who?" I asked. "Last time I checked, the Three Fates were the rulers of this mafia. You're no better than me. You're only like what—one quarter demigod? Your grandfather is my daddy, *honey*, so you can bend your knee to me."

The stem of the wine glass snapped, his eyes lighting up like mini suns. He didn't raise his voice, though, despite his obvious rage. "Listen here, you little bitch. You will be leaving with me. You are a demigod, and your place is with *demigods*."

That was it, I was done. I was sick of everything. I had been through enough this week, and having some snotty bastard try to tell me what to do wasn't going to fly.

I leaned forward, enunciating every word as clearly as I could. "My *place* is with monsters. I will not help you. I will not work with you. If you come near me again, I will kill you. Tell Hercules I hope he has a migraine for a century, and leaves me the fuck alone."

I stood up, the table rocking back. Jason glared at me, golden blood dripping down his hands like ink from the wine glass that had cut him.

"You will regret this," he whispered.

I leaned down, my face hovering right in front of his. I held up one finger, my middle finger. "You can kiss my demigod ass," I said, and then turned, leaving him sitting at the table, alone.

CHAPTER 21

PIZZA NEST

AAECUS

I was silent on the way home, and so was Ashley. The moment we stepped inside the penthouse, she turned and shoved me against the wall, shocking me and making me growl.

"You could have died," she said. "And you told me to fucking *leave*. As if I was going to leave you when I heard gunshots!"

"*You* could have died," I snapped. "You should have trusted me!"

"Where the fuck was I supposed to go? I was in the bathroom! How come any time I'm with you, we get into trouble?"

I snorted now, my hands falling down to her waist. In one swift motion, I threw her over my shoulder and carried her to the living room. "Damon and Minos are on their way home, of course. Panicking."

As if on cue, the door crashed open, the walls rattling. "Ashley?!"

"I'm here!" she called.

I put her down and turned as Minos barreled in, scooping her into his arms. He gave me a dark look over her shoulder, one that told me there was a lot more going on than I knew at the moment.

"Where's Damon?" I asked.

"He'll be here soon," Minos said quickly.

He pressed his face against the top of Ashley's head for a minute, breathing in her scent before leaning down to kiss her. I watched them, trying to keep my thoughts from going elsewhere.

"Hey, I'm okay," Ashley said, cupping his face. "I shot people."

Minos drew back, studying her with surprise. "You did? You? Our moral princess who would never, ever break the law?"

"Shut up," she hissed. "I did. They were trying to kill me, so..."

"Well, it's a good thing you shot them," he said tightly.

I fought the urge to say anything. While she'd been having her little meeting with Jason the Arrogant, I'd been snapping pictures of every bastard that had been there.

Every man that shot at her tonight and still lived would be dead by morning.

I *felt* Damon before I heard him. The front door shut as he came in, blood and dirt marring his face and suit.

"What the hell happened?" I asked.

"Some problems have come up," Damon growled. "But first —are both of you okay?"

"Yes," Ashley said. She looked at me, her eyes showing concern. "I think so."

I took a deep breath, but nodded. "I'm fine. Pissed. Murderous. Ready to kill. But, both of us are okay."

Damon nodded. The vein in his forehead was ticking, which was not a good sign. He went to Ashley, giving her a kiss on the top of her head. "Let me go rinse off," Damon sighed. "Maybe pour some drinks, Minos."

"And order some food," I said. "We got fucked over on dinner."

Minos pulled Ashley close, letting out a low noise that reminded me of a purr. "You order food, I'll pour drinks, and if we have time for dessert..."

Ashley raised a brow, smirking at him. "You'd like that, wouldn't you?"

He growled, his grip on her tightening. "I should make you strip and serve us drinks."

"Maybe just ask," she quipped, sticking her tongue out.

Minos chuckled. "Will you please strip for us and pour us drinks, little thief?"

"If all of you strip too," she countered.

"Deal," I growled.

"We're not fucking until we all talk!" Damon called from his room.

The three of us all grinned like idiots, and I pulled out my phone. "Pizza?"

"Yes," Ashley said, her eyes widening. "Pepperoni and pineapple."

Minos and I both wrinkled our noses. "Alright, baby girl," I sighed.

"And ranch sauce on the side."

I made a face. "Are you sure you're not already pregnant?"

She flipped me off and I grinned.

"I have an idea," Minos said. "I'm going to bring one of the mattresses in here for the floor."

"We need a bigger couch," I said.

"We do," Minos sighed. "Much bigger."

Ashley grabbed the hem of her dress, lifting it up. I froze, letting out a low growl as my brain short circuited. Where was I? Who was I? All I could see were her magnificent tits jiggling as she stripped for us.

Minos moaned, his cock hardening in his pants. "Fucking hell, love. I'll get the mattress and blankets."

Within the hour, the four of us had managed to create a chaotic and cozy space. Four pizza boxes spread around us along with a myriad of different drinks. Ashley was sandwiched between me and Minos, and Damon was on the other side of him.

Damon sighed, falling back against the mattress. Minos leaned back next to him.

"I met Clotho," Ashley blurted.

The three of us erupted in a series of *what the fuck* variations.

"She was in the bathroom," Ashley said quickly. "That's why I was in there for so long."

I cursed under my breath and reached for her, my hand sliding into hers, our fingers interlocking. "Honestly, I'm glad you were in there because they would have shot you. It worked out."

"Almost like it was—"

"*Minos,*" Damon and I growled.

He grinned like the cheshire cat, sinking into the blankets. Ashley leaned back too, dragging me with her.

"We can say it," Minos said. "It's not like they listen to every single thing we say."

None of us were sure about that. As far as I was concerned, the Fates knew all.

"Jason attacked because Hercules called him like a little bitch," I said. I hated that prick. "The moment he caught wind that we were at the restaurant, he brought his men in. Ashley was in the bathroom when they flooded the place. There were too many of them to fend off alone." I hated that more than anything. What if we were attacked like that again?

I'd failed tonight.

I felt the weight of that on my shoulders. It was a punch to the gut knowing Ashley could have been taken tonight because of me.

"You should have brought more men with you," Damon sighed. He didn't sound angry as I had expected, but concerned.

"I should have," I mumbled, my mood souring some.

Ashley turned towards me, her hand sliding over my bare chest. "It worked out," she murmured softly. "I got a gun, shot those guys, and snuck out. For once, I actually had a bit of luck."

"You did," I said, tugging her close so I could nuzzle the top of her head. Her warmth felt like the sun chasing away my storm clouds.

"It wasn't your fault," she protested. "You can't blame yourself for Jason's actions."

"What did Clotho say?" Damon asked.

"She was very cryptic," Ashley sighed. "Which makes sense. She told me there will be a moment where I'll be presented with a lock that is holding something or someone, and I must unlock it. Oh, and I need to kill Hercules."

The silence that settled over us spoke volumes. Damon was the one to disrupt it.

"Are you fucking kidding me?" he snarled. "You can't kill Hercules, princess."

Ashley raised her head, looking over at him. "Because I shouldn't kill someone or because it's Hercules?"

"Because he's impossible to kill," Minos explained. "Demigods in general are almost impossible to murder, unless a god does it. Sometimes monsters succeed, but it's not that easy. Are you certain it was Clotho? Truly one of the Fates?"

"Yes," she said, annoyed. "She was definitely one of them. I thought she'd look older…"

"Baby girl," I sighed. "You are a demigod, yes, but I don't think you'll be able to fight off Hercules."

"Your faith in me is heartwarming."

The three of us groaned and I reached for her, pulling her into a straddle over my body. Naked talks were possibly my new favorite thing.

Her skin flushed, her eyes widening. "Damn it. What were we talking about?"

I ran my hands up her thighs, reaching for her breasts. She sucked in a breath as I teased her nipples, rolling them between my fingers. "I think Damon and Minos had some things to tell us."

Damon let out a low growl. Minos softly moaned.

"This evening was shit," Damon huffed. "Some of Hercules' men attacked our clubs, so there were some turf wars. Minos and I had to divide and conquer."

"And conquer we did," Minos added.

"Right," I whispered.

My cock was starting to throb, all the blood from my head rushing down to it. Ashley bit her lower lip, her cheeks flushing as she ran her hands down my body.

"I like your mortal form," she confided. "I like the tattoos and how fucking hot you are. But I like the monster side better. The real you."

Fuck. Her words poured fire into my veins, lust rushing over me. "Do you want the monster, baby girl?"

"I do," she said. "Please."

Damon snorted now. "She says please so easily for you. I feel like we're intruding."

I looked over at him sharply. "So join us, *Daddy*. Or do you just want to sit there and watch?"

"I want to sit here and watch," Minos said. "Because this is gonna be good."

Damon's eyes lit up. I drew in the scent of Ashley's arousal, knowing she was already turned on by the thought of taking us both.

"Please, Daddy," she said in a breathy whisper, giving him the sweetest look.

No man or monster could say no to that.

Damon moved onto his knees, reaching for Ashley. He grabbed her hair with a growl, all while her hot pussy continued to grind against me.

My cock was so fucking hard. I needed to be inside her, to give her all of my knots until she couldn't take anymore, but not before making her scream with Damon.

She squeaked, her eyes widening as he dragged her into a kiss. I continued to play with her nipples, teasing her breasts as Damon took her mouth. Their lips remained fused as he got to his feet, and then he pulled back to stand up, his cock now fully hard.

He slapped her face with it and she gasped. I watched her melt into her submissive space, the one that I loved.

"Baby girl," I crooned. "Ask Daddy to slap your face with his cock again."

"Yes, Sir," she immediately responded.

Fuck. I groaned as she looked up at him, all while her hand slid around to my cock and gripped me.

"Daddy? Will you slap my face with your cock?"

"Yes, princess," he said. "But you gotta keep stroking his cock. Okay?"

"Yes, Daddy," she whispered.

Damon swept all of her hair back, gripping it with one

hand as he held his cock with the other. Her hand worked up and down my cock as he slapped her face again with his.

"Open up," Damon growled.

She parted her lips, taking the head of his cock between them. She groaned in surprise as he thrust forward, hitting the back of her throat.

"Fucking hell," Minos groaned.

I stole a quick look. He was stroking his cock, precum dripping from the head. Both of his knots were swollen with need, his hand moving up and down.

"You're such a whore," I said to him.

Minos grinned, his breath hitching. "Yeah, and I like it."

"Why don't you eat me out while I fuck our mate?"

Minos' expression became feral, the hunger apparent. "Is that a command?"

"Eat my ass, slut," I growled.

"Yes, Sir."

Minos crawled down as I gripped Ashley's hips. Damon drew back and I lifted her, pulling her back down against my cock. She cried out as the head pushed against her pussy.

"Fuck," I groaned. "You're so fucking wet."

I felt Minos between my legs now, his tongue running over my knots.

"Fuck," I hissed.

Ashley cried out as Minos' fingers dipped inside her, all while he began to suck my knots. I groaned, my fingertips digging into her skin.

"She can take you," Minos groaned. "But, let me get more lube anyways."

"Please," I mumbled.

Minos disappeared for a moment and then came back. I heard the cap of the bottle and watched as her eyes widened.

Minos gripped my cock too, pouring lube over it and rubbing it up and down.

"I can take you," she gasped.

"Keep your head down there," I growled at Minos.

He chuckled and I heard him put the bottle down, his head moving between my legs.

I pulled Ashley down and thrust up at the same time, filling her tight little hole with my cock. She cried out, and Damon stepped over my chest, his cock slipping into her open mouth again.

Fucking perfect. My cock throbbed inside her sweet heat, the view of both of them turning me on in ways that I'd never experienced before. I watched as Damon's balls moved, his hips pumping forward as she sucked his cock over and over.

Minos' tongue moved down to my ass and I nearly came inside Ashley right then. I gasped as he shoved his tongue inside of me, plunging it deeper. Pleasure curled through me, my entire body humming with need.

Her pussy clenched my shaft life a fist, her muffled moans perfect. I held her hips and moved mine up, impaling her further.

"You're taking him so well, princess," Damon growled. "You're going to take me too once you finish sucking my cock. Do you want that?"

She made a noise, her head bobbing up and down in a *yes*.

"Maybe I'll take your little ass," Damon said. "Hell, maybe we'll let Minos shove his cock inside you too. Our own little fuck hole. Do you think you could take us?"

She tensed around me as she kept sucking his cock. I groaned as Minos kept fucking my ass with his tongue, all while her sweet pussy took my cock over and over again.

"I don't know if you can fit both our cocks inside your little mortal form, baby girl," I said.

Damon pulled free from her mouth and stepped to the side. She groaned and her torso slid forward, her swollen lips wet with her saliva. I pulled her down and lifted my hips just slightly before pumping into her hard.

She cried out, her nails raking down my chest.

"We're going to get our cocks in and then shift," Damon said. "If you need us to stop, you'll use your safeword, princess."

"Yes, Daddy," she said, her voice ragged. "Please take me, I need to be more full."

"Anything for you, princess."

Chapter 22

Mated to the Monsters

Ashley

I cried out as I felt the tip of Damon's cock press against my pussy. I was already full with Aaecus', but I needed more.

I needed them both inside of me.

Would it be wrong to pray to the gods to make my pussy able to take both of them with ease?

Probably, but I didn't care. I sent up a prayer to whatever god was listening, and then gasped as I felt Damon push in further.

"You're so fucking tight," he groaned, gripping my ass cheeks.

He slapped one of them, drawing out a sharp cry from me.

Aaecus leaned up, taking one of my nipples into his mouth and sucking. Pleasure and lust had me moaning, my body shivering as Damon shoved his cock inside of me next to Aaecus'.

"Oh fuck," I groaned.

Aaecus sucked harder, his sharp teeth tugging. My bonds to

Minos and Damon were alive, but I found myself wanting him to make his mark too.

"Mate me," I begged. "Please, Aaecus. *Please.*"

He growled as I planted my hands in the pillow on either side of his head. I pushed back, forcing more of Damon's thick cock inside.

Damon grunted, slapping my ass again. I looked up and realized that Minos was standing over us, stroking his cock as he watched.

Aaecus groaned and then I felt his teeth finally pierce me. A cry was torn from me as the pain of being bitten was replaced by the pleasure of a mating bond taking root between us. He sucked and swallowed my blood, his cock starting to swell inside of me.

"Bite me," he growled, holding his wrist to my mouth.

I felt feral, desperate for the bond with him to be complete. I sank my teeth as hard as I could, the taste of him on my tongue as the tie between our souls was knotted.

He pulled back and I licked my lips, basking in our new concoction. I could feel his control slipping. "I'm going to shift," he grunted.

My eyes widened as he growled, his body starting to change beneath me. Damon cursed, and then thrust forward, driving more of his cock inside of me as Aaecus began to turn into a monster.

I cried out as he stretched my pussy, heat flooding my entire body. I had three mating bonds now, and I could feel the power in them. The strength and connection.

"Fucking hell," Damon gasped. "How are you doing princess?"

"Good," I moaned.

Aaecus growled again as he finished shifting. A massive beast now beneath me, his cock buried deep inside of me. He pulsed and throbbed, Damon's cock pressed together with his.

Aaecus leaned up, taking my entire breast between his massive jaws. I gasped as the tip of his tongue began to tease my nipple, his breath hot.

"I feel like I'm going to come," I whimpered.

I was so fucking close just from being filled like this. Stretched as far as I had ever been, two cocks inside of me.

Damon began to slowly pull back, making the three of us moan, before slamming back inside me. I cried out, pleasure following every movement.

"Take her ass, Minos."

What? There was no way. I whimpered, looking over my shoulder at Damon. His eyes met mine, his lips pulling into a dark smile. "Do you want to try, princess, or no?"

Minos slid his fingers in my hair, offering me a comforting touch. "If you don't want to, that's okay. I'll come just from watching you, princess."

My heart beat a little faster and I let out a moan. "We can try. I want to try."

And that was the truth.

Would I be able to take him, though?

"Please breed me," I said. "I want all of you inside of me."

Minos groaned. "Fuck, keep begging, little thief."

"Please put your cock in me," I whined. "I need it. I need you."

Aaecus and Damon both growled. Damon gave a small thrust, one that had me making all sorts of noises.

Minos stepped behind me. I looked over my shoulder as Damon spread my ass cheeks, pouring lube onto me. I gasped as he circled his fingers around my hole, and then slid them inside.

"We've never taken you here, have we?" Damon asked.

"No," I whimpered.

Aaecus chuckled and I looked down at him. I moved my hands to his shoulders, gripping his dark fur. His fangs glistened in the low lighting of the living room, the shadows engulfing all of us.

"You feel so good, baby girl," Aaecus growled.

Minos let out a low moan and I felt him push two fingers inside of me, joining Damon. The two of them began to work my ass as Damon slid his cock back and then thrust forward.

I squealed, closing my eyes as they pulled their fingers free.

"Are you ready for my cock, princess?" Minos asked.

"Yes," I groaned. "*Please*, please, please."

"You're being so good for us," Aaecus praised. "Our good little monster whore."

"Yes," I gasped. "Fuck. Put it in me, Minos!"

He chuckled and leaned forward. I felt the head of his cock press against me and sucked in a breath right as he began to ease forward.

Fuck, fuck, fuck. I'd never been filled like this before. I felt like I was being torn apart, but there was no pain. Only pleasure. Only lust and need and *fuck*—

Minos thrust his cock inside of me. All three of my mates were now buried in me, their cocks stretching me, filling me.

"Breed me." It was the only thing I could say. "*Please.*"

"Are you sure?" Minos asked.

"You want all of our cum, baby girl?"

"Yes," I gasped.

"As you wish, princess," Damon groaned.

Damon pumped his cock forward, thrusting inside of me. I could feel all of their knots bumping against me as they began to fuck me. Minos would thrust in and pull back, then Damon would thrust in and pull back. Aaecus held onto me, letting

Damon do most of the thrusting as he made sure I didn't lose my balance.

"Good girl," Aaecus groaned. "You're so full, baby girl."

All I could do was whimper.

I slid one of my hands down to my clit. The moment my fingers touched myself, I cried out—an orgasm crashing into me. My mates groaned as I came, my body squeezing all three of them.

"I'm going to come," Aaecus groaned.

"Come then," Damon growled.

Aaecus' claws dug into my skin, his hips lifting as he thrust into me repeatedly.

"Oh, fuck," Damon grunted. "Me too."

My mind was still spinning from coming so hard, when Aaecus and Damon both growled. Their hot cum began to fill me, both of their cocks throbbing with their release. I moaned as I felt it start to drip out of me.

Damon slowly pulled back, his cock sliding free.

"Fuck," Minos groaned, pumping into my ass harder.

"Fill her up," Damon growled at him.

The sound of his skin slapping against mine echoed through the living room until he finally let out a long groan. I gasped as he came, his hot seed filling me too.

He pulled out and Aaecus lifted me, rolling me onto my back.

"Shift and clean her up, Minos," he growled.

"Yes, Daddy," Minos said.

He had that devilish smirk, the one that I had come to enjoy so much. He started to shift into his monster form, his body changing in front of me from man to beast. I barely had time to make a sound before his jaws were large enough to snap me in half. His long hot tongue found my pussy and I cried out as he drove it inside of me, lapping out all of their cum.

Aaecus groaned and moved to his knees. His cock was hard all over again and he began to stroke it over me.

Damon let out a low growl and began to shift too.

"Gods, yes," I gasped. "Right there, Minos!"

His tongue was working its magic, stroking me in a way that had my toes curling and pussy melting.

"Fuck," Aaecus huffed.

Damon moved to hover right above my head, his thighs to either side of my shoulders. His cock was hard again, and I now had the perfect view of both him and Aaecus. Damon started to stroke his cock too, both of them leaning over me. I opened my mouth, sticking out my tongue ready to catch their hot cum.

"That's right, princess," Damon growled. "Keep that pretty little mouth wide open. We gotta fill every hole."

"Yes, Daddy," I moaned.

Minos pushed his tongue deeper, making me scream as ecstasy rolled through me. I arched my back as I started to come, groaning as every muscle in my body stiffened and then released.

He pulled his tongue free with a satisfied growl and then moved opposite of Aaecus, grabbing his own cock too. I reached up with a moan, gripping his knot and making him howl.

"Come all over me," I pleaded.

Aaecus leaned down, gripping my breast with his sharp claws as he stroked his cock faster. All three of them made grunts and growls, and I kept my mouth open.

"Open wide, princess," Damon huffed.

I stuck my tongue out right as he started to come. It splashed onto my tongue, filling my mouth before dripping onto my face and neck. Minos groaned as his cock burst too, more cum spilling all over me.

"Fuck," Aaecus snarled.

He gave himself one last stroke, and started to come. Their

hot seed covered me and I squeezed my eyes shut, swallowing as much as I could.

Finally, the three of them stopped coming, the sound of their pants surrounding me.

I wiped away their seed from my eyes and carefully opened them. I was completely covered in their cum.

"I think we all deserve a hot shower," Minos said.

"Me too," Aaecus grunted. "Hmm... maybe a hot bath?"

"Yes, please," I said.

Minos scooped me up, holding me like a princess. "My precious little cum dump."

"You say it so romantically," I giggled.

The four of us smiled like idiots, and he took me down the hall towards Damon's bathroom—all of us ready to wash off.

CHAPTER 23

OUR FUTURE WIFE

DAMON

Aaecus, Ashley, and Minos were all snuggled up in the living room, sleeping—but I hadn't been able to fall asleep next to them. Not knowing what Clotho had said to Ashley and that Jason was after her now.

Even after all of our activities, my mind wouldn't rest.

Jason and Hercules. Two fucking demigods, both of them the types that got what they wanted. They were bastards who fought dirty, and now that the secret was out about my mate...

I worried. I worried that something bad would happen. That we wouldn't be there to stop it.

I'd seen the same concern in Aaecus and Minos.

The three of us had lived for so long. First we had lived to serve Hades, until we'd been cursed and had lived to get revenge. Then the Three Fates gave monsters a chance in the mortal world, and we'd lived for them. We'd done their bidding while building up our own kingdom.

We'd lived for others, but we'd always been able to care for ourselves. I trusted Minos and Aaecus more than anything.

But now?

Now, we'd mated Ashley, and it wasn't just us anymore.

I'd do anything for her. She didn't understand the power t she had over the three of us already. I would kill for her, murder for her. Not even Hades ever had this much power over me.

She was the reason our world would spin from now on.

There had been a time when I thought I'd found this kind of love, but looking back, it wasn't even a tenth of what this was. But then, the things I'd done for that woman...

What would I do for Ashley?

I made my way down the hall to the room where we'd first caught her. I kept some of my favorite art I'd collected over the years in there, along with some of my best whiskey. I slipped inside and poured myself a drink, taking a seat in my chair and just staring.

What was next? What could I do to protect her? What would convince the rest of our mafia to let her live in peace? Our mafia wasn't exactly like the *Bratva* or *Cosa Nostra,* but there were still some similarities. Marriages and alliances were respected, and...

Marriage.

I downed my glass, the alcohol stinging my throat.

Marriage.

Fuck.

I'd never in a million years believed that I would like the sound of being a married man, but the more I thought about it, the more it made sense.

Jason was after her.

Hercules would be after her.

The gods might be after her too. She'd met Hermes, and

gods knew that fucker spilled secrets. He was the whole reason the *telephone* game had been invented.

Marriage would at least disband most attacks against her. There might still be other problems that came up, but it would give me time.

It would give us time to protect her, to guard her, to ready her for a life with us.

Did she want a life with us?

"You're thinking really hard about something."

I looked up, startled to see Minos leaning against the door frame. He was wearing a pair of gray sweatpants, his dark hair pulled back into a bun.

"Come here," I requested softly.

He gave me a little smile and crossed the room, coming to me. I set my drink down and pulled him into my lap, pressing my face against his chest.

"Mmm. It's not often I see this side of you," Minos said, wrapping his arms around me.

I breathed in his scent and closed my eyes, my thoughts going a thousand miles per hour, until he cupped my face and tilted it back, forcing me to look up at him.

"What is it?"

"All of them will want to kill her," I whispered. "She is our mate. She was meant to be with us. It's only been a few days, but our entire lives have changed. It's no longer just us. It's her and us."

"You're scared," Minos accurately guessed.

"Yes." I was never scared. Not like this. "Jason knows she's a demigod. Hercules knows. Hermes knows about her now too. What will he think of his daughter being mated to us?"

Minos pressed his lips together. "Would the Fates really send her to us only to die?"

"Are tragedies not what our history is known for?"

Minos was silent until he let out a sigh. "It will be okay. What's your plan? You always have a plan."

"Marriage."

He stiffened in my lap and scowled. "Marriage?"

"Marriage," I repeated.

"Hmmm." Minos was quiet for a few more moments, his brows drawn together as he contemplated my proposal. "I like the idea of her being our wife, but I think that if we are to marry her, it should be because we all want it."

"We're mated to her already," I pointed out.

"Yes, true," Minos sighed. "You know this is different. What if she doesn't want to be married? Maybe she doesn't want three monster husbands. And how would that help us all?"

"If we are married, then the gods will not interfere. And it will help prevent any external attacks. We need the support of the other branches as well."

"We should have kept her a secret," Minos murmured.

"Am I interrupting?"

Minos and I both looked up, unsurprised to see Aaecus.

"Damon thinks we need to marry Ashley," Minos blurted.

I rolled my eyes at him, but didn't disagree. Aaecus raised a brow for a moment and stepped in, shutting the door behind him carefully. "She's passed out," he said softly. "Our future wife."

I grinned, looking back at Minos.

"It does have a nice ring to it," Minos teased. "I can call her wifey. Little wife."

Aaecus and I both snorted, but Minos was right. It sounded... right.

"I don't know if *she'll* go for it so soon," Aaecus said.

"We should just ask," I suggested. "That's all we can do. It's the logical move, but I won't make her sign herself away to us again, not unless she wants to. That would be a contract I would never break."

Minos planted a kiss on my lips then slid from my lap, standing up and stretching. "I'd have to stop being such a man whore."

"You have three of us," Aaecus noted. "I think you'd be fine."

"True," Minos said, giving him a devious smile. "Maybe the two of you can tag team me in our shifted forms."

Fuck.

Aaecus and I both looked at each other—another silent agreement that yes, that needed to happen—and I swallowed hard. "Yes, but let's put a pin in that."

"We need to get her a ring," Aaecus said excitedly. "For the proposal."

"Can I pick it out?" I asked. "Unless one of you are dead set on doing so."

"No, you can choose," Minos said.

"You can pick, but it better be good, Damon, or I'm disowning you."

"It'll be good," I murmured thoughtfully. "It'll be the best."

"She likes shiny things," Minos chuckled.

I smiled, thinking about the woman that had truly stolen our hearts. "It'll be perfect."

"Well. How about you pick out the ring and I go murder the cunts that shot at our future wife?" Aaecus asked. "And Minos stays home with her."

"Like a good malewife," Minos teased.

"That sounds like a plan," I agreed. "Which jewelry stores do we own again?"

"All of them," Aaecus said.

"Excellent."

"What if she says no?" Minos asked. "Maybe I could talk to

her first... get a read on her thoughts about us. What if... What if we all go on a little date in the morning? It would be good to take her out, and we can go from there."

I narrowed my eyes, thinking it over. Would she say no?

The more and more rooted the idea of her being our wife became, the more I needed her to say yes.

I nodded. "Yes. We can do that," I said to Minos. "We'll go on a date tomorrow, and then tomorrow night, we can pop the question. No one will attack us if we're all together during the day, unless they are fucking idiots. And if she says no, then we make a new plan."

CHAPTER 24

ICE CREAM

Ashley

"Where are we going?" I asked, feeling excited.

This morning, I woke up and was thoroughly pampered. Minos made everyone breakfast, Damon and Aaecus swore off any work, and we'd all woken up together. Aaecus had massaged all of my sore muscles until I'd been as limp as a spaghetti noodle, then I'd been told to get ready for a day trip.

They had a surprise for me, which made me nervous.

Damon was driving all of us in his fancy car. I ran my fingertips over the leather seats, watching as Moirai passed us by. I craned my head as we left the city, driving only gods knew where.

After everything that had happened last night, it felt refreshing to get out of the apartment and city. It was easier to put stress out of my mind, and to forget about what Clotho and Jason had said.

I really wanted to forget about demigods, monsters, and the Fates for a little while and spend time with my men.

My men.

I'd really grabbed onto the idea that I belonged with them, and they belonged with me, fast. But it felt right.

Minos was sitting next to me, his arm around the top of my seat. I was wearing a cherry red dress with Aaecus' leather jacket, giving me a bombshell motorcyclist look that I was feeling good in.

"There's a farm outside of Moirai that grows fresh fruit," Damon said. "They also happen to make fresh ice cream with that fruit."

"What?" I squealed. "That sounds amazing." My mouth instantly watered at the thought of ice cream.

Damon smirked and hit the gas pedal hard as we hit a long stretch of road. "Roll down the top," he instructed.

Aaecus leaned forward in the front seat and I squealed as the roof to the car began to roll back, the wind whipping my golden hair. Minos leaned forward between the seats and turned on the radio, blasting music as the four of us sped down the highway.

I laughed. Truly laughed for the first time in what felt like forever. I felt free and happy.

The song blasting through the speakers was one we all knew and Aaecus surprised me by singing. Minos joined him, followed by me—and by the time we got to the chorus, even Damon was singing along.

Minos leaned back, grabbing my face and stealing a kiss. I grinned against his lips, melting into him as the car slowed.

"We're here," Damon said, turning down the radio.

He pulled off down a small road that was framed by beautiful trees. They arched over us, light dappled with shadows. There was a sign with an ice cream cone painted on it along with some fruit, and we pulled into a gravel parking area next to a small house.

I wasn't sure what I was expecting, but the three of them bringing me to a quaint ice cream shop on a fruit farm was not it.

I ran my fingers through my hair, trying to tame the mess it had become from our topless drive. Aaecus opened the car door for me and I slid out, leaning up on my tiptoes to kiss him.

He groaned, pushing me against the car and deepening the kiss until I felt like I was burning up.

"Hey," I squeaked.

"Later," he teased, pulling away with a wink.

"What kind of ice cream do you want?" Damon asked. "You and Minos can go pick out a table."

"Surprise me," I said.

Damon smirked, then he and Aaecus headed for the small house. Minos slipped his hand into mine, leading me towards a grove of fruit trees where some tables were.

"It's better in the Spring," Minos said. "When all the fruit is growing. But still, everything they make here is fresh."

"That just means we'll have to come back," I said.

Minos chuckled and then surprised me by lifting me up. I gasped, grabbing onto his shoulders as my legs wrapped around his hips and he carried me over to one of the tables.

"Hey," I squealed as he laid me back. "We're in public!"

"Damon booked the whole farm with explicit instructions," Minos teased. "Starting with—don't watch whatever we do to the pretty blonde woman."

He pushed me back onto the table and sat down on one of the chairs. I propped myself up on my elbows just as he pushed my legs apart, the two of us both groaning.

"Minos," I said, still nervous about being in public.

"No panties," he noted, his eyes darkening. "Mmm, you're a naughty girl, princess."

I smirked and glanced around us, making sure no one was near.

But even if they were, did it matter? Maybe, I realized, I liked being watched. Maybe I wanted the whole world to know I liked getting fucked by monsters. By my monsters, my mates.

A growl carried towards us and I looked up to see Damon and Aaecus coming towards us, both of them carrying two ice cream cones.

"No fucking until we have our date," Damon barked. He grinned as he approached the table, arching a dark brow. "Both of you little sluts behave."

"Fine," Minos sighed longingly.

It was true, I was a slut for them. They'd turned me into one.

"Your ice cream," Aaecus said, handing me a waffle cone.

It had two scoops of ice cream, one a bright pink with bits of strawberry and the other sunshine orange with bits of mango.

"This looks delicious," I said.

I licked the first scoop, letting out a low moan. It *was* delicious. I closed my eyes, letting out a satisfied hum.

If being part of the Three Fates Mafia meant renting out fruit farms instead of being murderous monsters, then perhaps I could get used to it.

I opened my eyes and realized that all three of them were staring at me, entranced. Hungry.

I licked again, taking my time. Savoring it.

And fought the urge to laugh as I could suddenly see the outline of all their cocks in their pants.

"Maybe ice cream was a bad idea," Minos whispered, his voice hoarse.

"I think it's a great idea," I teased as a drop of strawberry cream fell on my hand.

I lapped it up, feeling like a goddess.

"Fuck," Damon muttered. His ice cream dripped onto his shirt and pants.

"Do you want me to clean it up for you, Daddy?" I asked.

"Fuck the date," Aaecus growled. "I want her, Damon."

"No," he growled. "We have plans for her later."

"There's nothing wrong with eating dessert first," Minos suggested.

Damon hissed between clenched teeth, but ultimately relinquished. "Come here, princess."

I slid to the edge of the table and took another bite of my ice cream before handing the cone to Aaecus. He watched me with a feral hunger that had the hair on the back of my neck standing up. I moved off the table, falling to my knees in front of Damon.

"Good girl," he praised. "I'm going to eat this and you're going to lick up anything that falls."

"Yes, Daddy," I moaned.

I leaned in, running my fingertips down his thighs as I lowered my lips to the drop of cream. I lapped up the bead, humming happily.

"You got pomegranate ice cream," I said.

"With some chocolate," he said. He took a bite, another drop rolling free. "Such a mess," he whispered.

I licked it up, my eyes locking with his. His cock strained against his pants, his breath hitching as a drop of ice cream fell right over the zipper.

"Let me get that for you," I offered, tracing the zipper with the tip of my tongue.

He groaned, his head tilting back. "I feel like I could come without you even taking me in your mouth."

I smiled, wanting to make that happen.

Challenge accepted.

I continued to tease him, waiting eagerly for another drop to fall. Another did and I caught it with my tongue, swallowing before kissing his cock through his pants.

"Fuck," he muttered.

I moved lower, tracing his knot with my tongue. He sucked in a breath as he ate more ice cream, finally getting to the cone.

I hit the right movement with my tongue over his cock, because his hips suddenly bucked and the cone slipped from his hands and tumbled to the ground. He growled, his fingers curling into my hair.

"Fuck you," he moaned.

I grinned as he came, his cum wetting his pants. He dragged in a couple breaths before looking down at me with narrowed eyes. "We're going to finish our treat and then take you home and breed you until you beg us to stop."

"At least I'm not the one with cum in my pants," I said.

Minos and Aaecus both laughed, but I knew what I'd done. I'd just signed the rest of my day over to get fucked by my three monstrous boyfriends.

Chapter 25

Rope

Minos

We barely made it home without pulling over to fuck Ashley. The only reason we didn't was because we knew that none of us had the will power to fuck her quickly. It was all or nothing.

By the time we got her to the penthouse, my cock was aching to be inside her. My knots pulsed, a growl leaving me as Aaecus shut the door behind us.

Ice cream dates might have been my new favorite activity.

"Tie her up," Damon growled.

Aaecus moved past us quickly, disappearing down the hall to his room to retrieve rope. I shoved Ashley against the wall, our lips meeting in a passionate kiss. She tasted sweet and sinful, and I couldn't wait to fit my cock in her pretty mouth while she took Aaecus or Damon. Or both.

She moaned, wrapping her arms around me. I grabbed her ass and lifted, bringing her legs around my hips and carrying her to the living room.

We'd left the mattress at the center from the night before, which was perfect.

"Get her naked," Damon commanded.

I pulled the jacket off her, tossing it to the floor.

"Fuck," she groaned as I lifted her dress, tearing it away.

She was so perfect. Fucking hell, I loved her.

"Little thief," I whispered.

Fuck. The words got caught in my throat. So instead of telling her that I loved her, I ripped her bra off.

She let out a giggle as the fabric tore. "Hey, I need those."

"I'll buy you more," I said. "All the bras in the whole world. Better yet, I'll follow you around and hold your tits up for you."

Now she laughed. I grabbed them, running my thumbs over her nipples. Her laughter faltered, her breath hitching.

"That's my girl," I teased.

"Slut," she mumbled.

"Me?" I said, feigning innocence.

"Yes, you," Damon said. "Get naked, Minos. And move so Aaecus can tie her up."

Ashley's bright blue eyes lit with curiosity. She sat up as I slid off her, Aaecus returning to the living room with three colorful bundles of rope. She bit her bottom lip, eyeing him suspiciously.

"You're going to tie me up?" she asked.

Aaecus smirked, raising a brow. "I am, baby girl. I'm going to tie you up, suspend you in the air, and then we're going to take turns fucking you. How does that sound to you?"

"Good," she blushed.

Aaecus gave me a knowing look and I smiled, stripping off my clothes. My cock was so fucking hard, but I had to focus on helping him bind her up first.

The rope he'd chosen was different shades of blue and it

was beautiful. I couldn't wait to see how she looked wrapped up like our own little fuck toy.

"How are you going to suspend me?" Ashley asked.

All three of us pointed up.

Had we installed a rigging system into the ceiling at 5am this morning while she'd slept?

Yes. Yes we had.

Sometimes we made plans and they actually worked out.

I reached above her, grabbing a carabiner for Aaecus. He came over to us, tipping her chin up and kissing her.

"Wrists together, baby girl," he said gently.

I'd never get over seeing how soft he could be with her.

Damon stripped off his clothes, watching the three of us closely as he went to his favorite chair and took a seat. His cock was hard again, precum dripping at the tip.

I licked my lips but he shook his head. "Get her tied up, slut, then we'll see about letting you taste my cock."

Fucking hell. I nodded and turned back around, helping Aaecus.

Ashley held out her wrists, pushing them together. Aaecus started the knot, looping everything in a way that would be safe for her. Demigod or not, none of us wanted to actually harm her.

She closed her eyes, her heart beating a little louder in her chest. "I like how the rope feels," she confessed. "The vibrations..."

I knew the tie that Aaecus was planning on and fought the urge to laugh.

She'd be feeling those vibrations everywhere soon enough.

"You should be able to feel everything. If at any point you feel numb or tingly, you need to let me know. And I'll go easy since it's your first time," Aaecus said. "Okay?"

"Okay," she breathed.

She opened her eyes, and I watched the mischief return. The brat was coming out to play, and all of us were ready for her.

"You kidnapped me," she started. "Forced me to sign a contract."

"Indeed," Aaecus growled, unable to fight off his smirk. "Changed all your perfect plans."

"You *ruined* my life."

I leaned in, nipping her earlobe. "You ruined ours, little thief."

She sucked in a breath, making a soft noise. "Fuck you," she growled.

"What's your safeword?" Damon asked.

"Lock," she answered.

"If we're going to play like this and you're going to say these things, then we have to know that you don't actually mean them," Damon said. "And you have to know that we don't actually mean what we say. Or maybe we do..."

Ashley nodded as Aaecus continued to bind her arms and then lifted them above her head. I attached the rope to another piece, and Aaecus double checked the knots, making sure that she was secured to the rigging point.

Now she could tug on that if she wanted, and her arms would still be bound above her head.

Her nipples hardened, her head tipping back so she could look up. He looped more rope around her, creating diamond shapes. Slowly, methodically, ensuring that the ropes rubbed her skin.

"Yes," she rasped.

"You will use your safeword if needed. Understood?" Damon asked.

"Yes," she said.

"Good." Damon rose from his seat, coming over to us. "And as Aaecus said, you will alert us if the rope feels wrong. Yes?"

"Yes."

Aaecus stepped behind her, and now our little demigod was sandwiched between the three of us.

I felt the shift. The dynamic became darker, edgier. The tension was like a razor's edge over my cock, turning me on.

Ashley hadn't truly met the Damon I knew, but she would now. The monster that turned pain into pleasure and pleasure into pain. He would control us, use us, abuse us, but in the best type of way.

And we'd fucking want it.

He growled and brought his hand up, gripping her face. I watched as she melted into the act—becoming the girl who was being tied up against her will. Even though she wanted this as much as the rest of us.

"Let me go," she rasped. "I don't want this. I hate you!"

"Fucking liar," he snarled, gripping her harder. "I can smell your cunt. You're dripping for us."

"I'll never be with monsters!" she shouted.

That roused all of us up. We each growled and I leaned it, taking a strand of her hair and looping it around my fist. I tugged on it, breathing in her scent.

"You're disgusting," she said, attempting to push against me.

Damon snarled and slapped her face, drawing out a low giggle from her.

"You're just as crazy as we are," Aaecus grunted.

He continued to work the ropes until she gasped, realizing what was about to happen. He looped a piece of rope between her legs, placing it right over her clit and pulling it through, knotting it to a piece on her back.

"Oh," she grunted. "Fuck you."

"You like it," I said.

Aaecus worked down her legs and she gasped every time he pulled the rope.

"Lift her," he said.

Damon gripped her waist and did just that. I grabbed her thigh and helped Aaecus secure another suspension point, repeating the same process with her other leg.

Now she was completely suspended in the air, unable to escape. Her legs were parted for us, her arms bound above her head.

"Oh, fuck," she moaned, her head tipping back.

"Bind her hair," Damon said. "So if she moves her head, it pulls. I want it to hurt just a little bit."

I could see her pussy now, the sweet pink begging to be licked. The blue rope crossed over her pussy, strapped against her clit but still gave us what we wanted—which was the ability to fuck both holes.

Gods. My mouth watered, and I swallowed, fighting for patience.

"This feels good," she whispered.

Aaecus fisted her hair, yanking hard enough to make her cry out. I grinned as he wrapped the rope, pulling harder so that tears sprang to her eyes. Her scent of arousal grew stronger, her nipples hard and pussy glistening with need.

He tied off the last point, and now she was ready.

Damon was already between her legs. In one swift motion, he thrust forward and filled her with his cock. Ashley cried out, the ropes pulled taut as she realized the predicament we'd put her in.

She was a trapped little lamb, and the wolves were hungry.

"Damon!" she moaned.

"Are we still *disgusting*, you little monster whore?" Damon snarled.

He began to shift while buried knot deep inside her. She gasped, her eyes widening as his cock began to grow, his muscles becoming larger, claws growing. He raked them down her body, leaving angry red marks that had her howling in pain and pleasure.

My cock pulsed, cum dripping from the tip. I wanted to see her take every inch of it.

Fuck, I wanted to see her take every inch of *Cerberus*.

The idea of bending her over and fucking her in our form was....

I groaned as I watched Damon start to fuck her as a monster. I would come just at the thought of trying to shove our cocks inside of her.

He slammed into her harder and harder until he released a wild howl, coming inside her. I watched as some of the cum dripped to the blankets below, his cock pulling free before his knot could lock her.

"Your turn," he said to Aaecus.

Aaecus growled and came around, still in his human form, and did the same thing that Damon had done. Cum dripped from her pussy, the rope rubbing her clit as he squared his hips between her thighs and drove his hard cock inside her.

She moaned, her head yanked tight by the rope. Tears streamed down her cheeks, but her cries were not ones of pain.

Aaecus fucked her as he started to shift, thrusting in and out of her tight pussy as he turned into a wolven monster.

I felt the call of our bond, and knew that they both did too. The urge to become one, to breed her in our massive monstrous form.

We'd fucking destroy her. There was no way. Not now. Not yet.

Aaecus groaned, fucking her over and over. His knots popped in and out of her as he shoved all the way in. Her body arched like a bow, her cry ringing through the penthouse as she came hard.

"Fuck I can feel you squeezing me," Aaecus grunted. "Fuck."

He gave one more hard thrust and started to come, pulling out just like Damon had before.

I groaned, reaching down to stroke my already hard cock. More cum dripped out of her, and she moaned as Aaecus stepped back. He winked at me, his breaths hard as we switched out.

"Little thief," I taunted. "I hope this gets you pregnant."

"Fuck you," she moaned, but her lips tugged into a smile.

I pressed the head of my cock against her, feeling Damon and Aaecus' cum already making her so slick. I licked my lips, gripping her thighs and thrust forward.

Fuck she felt like heaven.

I filled her completely and then let myself shift just like Damon and Aaecus had. I grunted, my cock expanding in her tight pussy. She gasped as I became a monster, my claws digging into her skin as I thrust into her.

"Minos," she moaned.

I dragged my cock out and then thrust forward again, falling into a brutal rhythm.

Her pussy gripped me tighter and she moaned. I leaned forward, taking her nipple between my sharp teeth and teasing her as I pumped my hard cock into her.

Within a few seconds, both of us cried out together, coming at the same time. I filled her with every drop of my hot seed, her body shivering as her orgasm rushed over her.

I pulled out, watching as it dripped from her.

Damon let out a low growl, stepping up again. His cock was already hard and ready.

"Again," he rasped.

So all three of us fucked her again, taking turns, filling her with more and more cum.

And again.

And again.

Fucking her until the sun set over Moirai.

I went between her thighs again. Her body was trembling, her breaths ragged. She was covered in our seed and claw marks and bite marks, completely ravaged and thoroughly bred.

"Are you ready to come down, princess?" Damon said softly.

She let out a breath, the three of us surrounding her.

"You did so good," he praised.

"Yes," she whispered, her voice hoarse.

Aaecus and I began to untie her. Within a few minutes, we had her unraveled, and I caught her before she could collapse into the mattress. My perfect little princess.

She wrapped her arms around me and I held her.

"I think it's time for a hot shower, cuddles, a movie, and dinner baby girl," Aaecus said.

"Yes please," she sighed happily.

The three of us had worked together as a team to care for her after what we'd all done. I showered with her and rubbed out her shoulders, Aaecus got fresh blankets and pillows for what was becoming our permanent living room nest, and Damon ordered food and picked out a movie

As we settled onto the mattress to watch the movie, I knew we all wondered the same thing.

Should we propose to her now?

We couldn't. Not after how intense our sex had been. She was soft and vulnerable right now, and we wanted to protect her and love her until she was back to her sassy, bratty self.

So we didn't propose.

"How are you feeling, princess?" Damon whispered, tucking a strand of hair behind her ear.

"Good," she said with a yawn. "Sleepy. Happy."

The three of us smiled like absolute idiots.

Damon waited until she started snoring before he spoke.

"Tomorrow," he whispered. "I'm going to pick out the ring."

"I can talk to her in the morning," I murmured. "I'll make her breakfast."

"And I will make sure our empire hasn't burned down," Aaecus said.

For the first time in forever, it finally felt like we all fit together.

Ashley had been the missing piece.

CHAPTER 26

DIAMONDS AND DICKS

ASHLEY

I woke up to the smell of bacon, eggs, and pancakes. I sat up slowly, yawning as my brain fought to get working. Morning light poured into the penthouse and I was in the living room on the mattress the boys had dragged in last night.

I was sore as hell, but it was a good kind of sore. Last night was incredible. Hell, the last two days had been amazing.

"How do you like your coffee, my love?" Minos called.

Minos was cooking? I grinned sleepily and grabbed a blanket, pulling it around my shoulders and going to the kitchen. Minos was in gray sweatpants, which were quite possibly my Achilles heel. My body felt like a train wreck, but I'd do it all again, here and now, just because of those fuckers.

"Hey sexy," he said, winking at me. "Coffee?"

"Hi," I said sheepishly. "Yes, please. If you have cream and sugar, I'd love some in it."

"I had groceries bought," Minos said, going to the fridge. "Groceries and some pans because we didn't have any."

I eyed the stove top suspiciously where the bacon and eggs were sizzling. Three pancakes were starting to bubble up, so I grabbed the spatula and flipped them as he made my coffee.

"I slept through you getting groceries and starting breakfast?" I asked, yawning again.

"You did," he confirmed, stepping up behind me. He leaned down and snuck a kiss before patting my ass. "I got this. Drink your coffee, little thief."

He gave me a gentle push, handing me a mug filled with coffee. I hummed happily, sipping it as I grabbed one of the bar stools and perched on it.

This wasn't a bad view. A man cooking breakfast for me after fucking me senseless last night.

"How are you feeling?" Minos asked as he scooped the pancakes onto a plate.

"A little sore," I said. "But I'm okay."

"Are you sure?" he asked. "Do you need some pain medicine?"

I stared at him for a moment, unsure what to say. It had been a long time since I'd been cared for like this, and I wasn't sure what to do. "Sure... some ibuprofen maybe?"

Minos nodded, plated the eggs and bacon, turned off the stove, then opened up a cabinet where there were different medicine bottles. I raised a brow at the box of tampons in there too.

"Did you have them buy tampons?" I asked.

"Yeah, although none of us were sure what kind," Minos sighed. "Or if you prefer something else. I meant to ask you."

Tears sprang to my eyes and I swallowed hard, fighting to keep them from falling.

He turned around, his eyes widening. "Why are you crying, princess?"

"Why are you caring for me?" I asked, the first tears slipping free.

"What do you mean, baby? Of course I'm going to care for you," he said, rushing over to me.

All my words failed, so I just made a noise, my thoughts becoming jumbled. Minos turned me around on the stool, cupping my face and thumbing away a tear gently.

"I've fallen for you," he whispered softly. "So damn hard, Ashley. All of us have. Of course I'm going to care for you. I might need pointers every now and then, but I want you to have everything you need and want."

That just made me cry harder.

He winced, wiping away every tear that fell. "Ashley, I need to ask you something. What do you want?"

"What do you mean?" I hiccuped, trying to hold back more tears.

"What do you want with us? Because we want you forever, little thief. Forever with us. Ours. Damon is picking out a ring right now."

"A ring?" I whispered.

Minos only nodded, wiping away more tears.

"A ring," I said again. "*Oh.*"

The meaning of his words hit me and I just stared at him.

I hadn't thought about the future. I hadn't thought about what I wanted or what it would mean now that I was mated to three monsters. Hell, I had barely come to terms with the fact that I wasn't a regular mortal. I was the daughter of Hermes, and that only made me wonder what the hell my mother had been thinking.

Did my aunt and uncle know? Or did they just believe my mom had been knocked up by accident?

I'd never been the most traditional girl, but a ring on my finger would mean something. Marriage to the three of them would change my life.

We were already mated, yes, but this would be putting everything on paper.

That scared the hell out of me.

"Open up," Minos requested softly.

I parted my lips and he popped two pain pills on my tongue, handing me a glass of water seemingly out of nowhere. I grabbed it and took a sip.

"You don't have to answer me right now," Minos said. "But, I just want you to think about what you need. I don't know when Damon or Aaecus will be home. And I feel I need to tell you why marriage would be a good idea, besides the simple fact that all three of us want you to be our wife."

I raised a brow, sniffling. "Go on."

"The gods will come for you. Jason and Hercules will come for you too. If you're married to us, it formalizes our relationship and will help protect you."

"So, it's a business move?" I asked.

"No," Minos said, pressing his lips together. "Yes, but no. A business move would be us forcing you to."

I snorted, my mood starting to sour. "How gracious of you not to force me to do something against my will."

Minos grimaced. "I'm sorry. You know what I meant. The proposal is because we've fallen in love with you and want to protect you."

"And because you want to call me *wife*," I said, glaring at him. "Like three cavemen."

"We're not cavemen," he said, his eyes hardening. "We want you."

How could I be sure they wanted me and not the shiny new toy their entire mafia would be after? I felt an ache in my chest and looked away from him, my thoughts blurring. "I need time," I muttered.

"Ashley—"

"You just told me that the three of you are already getting a ring. You didn't even ask me if I wanted to marry you," I said. "You *warned* me about it."

"I asked what you wanted," he said tightly.

"I want time to think," I returned. "And if you can't even give me that, without throwing a fit, then the answer is no."

Minos went quiet. I could feel his fiery gaze on me and knew that I was hitting a different nerve, but I wouldn't take back what I said.

This week had been the most fucked up and amazing week of my life. It was hard to tell what was real and what was just another mirage. I'd been deceived by a demigod before, and now I had run straight into the arms of these three monsters.

Minos plated my food quietly. He put it in front of me and then left the kitchen. I sighed, watching him go down the hall to his room.

"Shout if you need anything," he called back, his tone unreadable.

I pressed my lips together. Fine, he could go pout. I'd probably hurt his pride and ego, but godsdamnit—marriage?

I stared down at the pancakes and let out a short laugh. I wasn't sure if he'd had real pancakes before. They reminded me of burnt hockey pucks.

He'd tried though.

That's all we could ask for right?

I wanted them. Everything had moved so fast, but would I want it any other way? Would I want someone to spend forever courting me if I knew it was right?

No. I did things fast, I always had. I dove into situations

and always managed to land on my feet, no matter how crazy it was.

I'd seen the dark parts of Damon, Minos, and Aaecus. I'd seen the wild side that would kill, that would hurt. The controlling mafia bosses that demanded things be exactly as they wanted. They'd taken me in and had made me sign a contract, making me their sex slave for seven days in exchange for my life.

Yes, Damon had nullified the contract.

But if the four of us were really going to build a future, then I needed to know there was more to our relationships than that.

We'd done everything backwards. I'd mated them—and now they wanted to marry me, but did we love each other? Could we love each other?

"Minos," I called.

His head immediately poked around the corner of the doorway to his room.

"I want a meeting with all of you," I said. "All four of us. And not a naked meeting."

Minos nodded. "I'll let them know."

"I also want some alone time."

Minos came out of his room, crossing his arms. "I'm not leaving, princess. Sorry. Those are the rules."

I glared at him. "I was told I could leave if I wanted to. So, how about I just go?"

"No," he said immediately. "It's not safe for you to leave."

That only pissed me off more. I slid off the stool, marching towards him. I stopped once I was toe to toe, looking up at him. "Was that a lie then?"

"Why are you so angry this morning?"

Wrong question.

"Why aren't you listening to me?" I volleyed back. "How in

the hell am I supposed to marry you if you act like this when I say I want to be left alone?"

"If you want alone time, then go to your room," he growled.

"Damon ripped the motherfucking door off the hinges," I snarled.

"Then I'll put it back on!"

"I don't want you to solve every problem!" I yelled. "I want you to *listen* to me!"

"Then I will go," Minos said, glowering at me. His eyes had darkened, his temper right on the edge. "I will go, princess, and you will stay up here. Locked away in the tower, safe from everyone that wants to murder you. But you have to promise me you will stay here. *Please.*"

I held his gaze as his words softened.

"Please," he repeated. "I have to keep you safe."

"Fine," I whispered. "I will stay. I just need some space to think about everything."

"Okay," he said. He closed his eyes for a moment, releasing a deep breath before looking at me again. "I am new to this. We all are. Even you. I will be back in a couple hours, okay?"

I nodded. Minos went back to his room and put on a black shirt and leather jacket before coming back out.

Stay strong, I reminded myself, trying not to ogle him.

He paused, cupping my face for a moment. "Swear to me that you won't leave."

"I swear that I wont leave," I whispered. "Do you want me to sign a contract?"

His eyes flashed with hurt and he swallowed hard. "I'm going to go," he said softly. "I put all of our phone numbers in your phone, in case you need us."

I nodded, trying to ignore the wave of guilt.

He held my gaze for a few seconds, then kissed my forehead, heading out towards the door. I pulled the blanket around me tighter, listening to the front door shut.

I blew out a breath, my shoulders relaxing. Fucking hell, emotions were messy. I was messy. *They* were messy.

I went back to the kitchen and sat down, picking up a piece of bacon to eat.

This entire week had really turned me upside down. I needed to clear my head and think.

I had sworn up and down that after this heist, I was done. Done with the mafia, done with crime. No more stealing. I had been set on finding a beach and retiring. I wanted peace. I wanted to be able to wake up each day and determine how it would go. To see a sunrise over the ocean and go on runs and *live.* I wanted to live.

But now, it was hard to imagine that sunrise without Damon, Minos, and Aaecus there with me.

"Fuck," I mumbled.

I had it bad. I'd never felt like this before about anyone. The three of them turned me on in ways that were unheard of. Then there was the fact that they were full of surprises, like Aaecus on our date or Minos making breakfast.

If that was what our lives would be like together, then I wanted it.

I wanted them.

I would take the mess of being involved with the mafia. I would take everything that would come with being a demigod in this world.

I just had to be honest with them.

Fuck.

"Damn it," I growled, almost planting my face on the bar.

I was in love with them.

Minos had said they'd already fallen for me, and damn the fucking Fates—I had fallen for them too.

My heart knew. Gods knew that my pussy knew. It was just my head that was caught up in this mess.

Still, if they wanted to marry me, it wasn't going to be about diamonds and fancy dates. It was about listening and supporting, helping and caring. It meant that if one of these bastards had the shits, we'd be there to wipe their ass—and still be turned on once they were better.

My aunt and uncle had that kind of love. Tears filled my eyes as I thought about the two of them. When my aunt died, my uncle hadn't been the same.

Their marriage had ups and downs, of course. There had been days where my aunt wouldn't speak to him, or he'd be a grumbly bastard over stupid things. But they worked it out.

I hadn't known her long enough, but I still remembered. I remembered everything.

I wiped away a couple tears and sighed. I'd gone the last few years believing I'd never find actual love, but here it was.

The sound of the front door opening had me smiling. "Minos, I'm feeling better—"

"Ah yes. Honey, I'm home."

I froze.

Fuck. *Fuck, fuck, fuck.*

"Did you miss me, sugar?"

I slowly turned around, seeing the ugly mug of none other than Hercules. Five men with guns filed in after him, all of them filling the hallway.

I pointed my bacon at him. "You don't look well," I said blandly, despite the fact that my heart was in my throat. "Almost like you were shot in the head by my mate."

Hercules gave me a cruel smile. I could still see the bullet wound on his forehead and it looked like his head was still reforming. He did not look happy.

"Did it hurt?" I asked, popping the last bit of bacon in my

mouth and sliding off the stool. "Did you pray to your daddy and have him kiss it better?"

His face turned scarlet. He raised a hand, making a signal. All the guns pointed at me, cocked and ready to shoot.

Perhaps taunting him had been a bad idea. I could see the last thread of his temper snapping right before my eyes.

Hercules marched across the penthouse, letting out a roar. "You ruined everything, you little bitch!"

He lunged for me and I dove to the side, rolling as bullets began to fly. I sprang to my feet, taking off down the hall to Damon's room.

I slammed the door and locked it, ignoring Hercules' taunting laugh.

He was such a cunt.

Fuck. I was fucked.

I ran to Damon's closet and grabbed one of his shirts, pulling it on quickly, followed by a pair of pants that were too big. I dug further in, looking for any type of weapon. *Something.*

The door was kicked in, Hercules stepping through. "How about we fight—demigod to demigod? Or were you just lying about that?"

Gods, where the fuck were all the sex toys? Some of those could be weapons, right?

Hercules ran towards me and I cursed, moving out of the way. He reached for me, his hand gripping my arm and slamming me back against the wall full force.

The breath was knocked from my lungs and I growled, bringing my knee up. He grunted as I landed my blow straight into his balls, giving me the time I needed to shove him back.

There was a lot more oomph behind my movements, and for a moment, I was flying high on that feeling.

Then I felt his hand wrap around my ankle and he yanked me down to the floor.

"You're coming with me, you stupid bitch," he snarled.

I yelped as he slammed my head back on the floor, pain immediately following. My vision began to blur, and he did it again.

"I'm going to kill you," he growled. "But I'm going to make it slow. I haven't had a demigod to play with in a long time. And to think, I saved you from the *Bratva*."

He laughed, pinning me to the floor beneath him.

"They'll find you," I rasped. "My mates. They'll find you and kill you."

"They might find me, but they won't kill me. No. But they will get to watch me kill you."

"Fuck you," I choked out.

"Night night."

My world went dark.

CHAPTER 27

RAGE

MINOS

I finally tracked down which jewelry store Damon was hiding out at. I parked my car and stretched, glancing up at the clouds in the sky. I wasn't used to being out in the daytime like this.

I felt my stomach twist again and stood there for a moment, contemplating turning back.

I had fucked up. The way I had said things to Ashley this morning hadn't gone over well, and I could understand why. This week had already been a whirlwind, and throwing marriage into the mix might not have been the right decision.

Her making me leave had hurt, though. I had seen her coming apart at the seams, but instead of allowing me to help pull her back together, she'd turned me away.

I wanted to be there for her. I wanted to show her just how much I had come to love her. The heart knew what the heart knew, even if it was only a matter of days.

The fact was, the three of us had been waiting for centuries for someone like her. Even if it was all designed by the Fates, I didn't care. We all still had our choices, and I had chosen her.

I spotted Aaecus' car and raised a brow. He must have come here too. Hell, of course we were interested in what had held Damon up at a jewelry store for so long, but knowing him —he was being very picky about what ring we'd give to Ashley.

If she even took it.

Fuck, they weren't going to be happy.

I reached into my car and withdrew a gun from the glove compartment, tucking it into my waistband and heading inside. The clerk gave me a frightened nod, because even in gray sweatpants and a leather jacket, he knew I was the boss.

"Where are they?" I asked.

"In the back, sir. They are being very particular about the jewels. Our master jeweler is assisting them."

I nodded and weaved through the glass cases, my eyes wandering over all of the gems. This was the kind of shop Ashley might have snuck into for fun, right?

I couldn't stop thinking about her.

I pushed through the back door and pulled out my phone, checking for any messages. There were none.

Damn it.

"What the fuck are you doing here?"

I looked up, seeing Damon hunched over a platter of jewels with weird goggles on. A man stood next to him, a very nervous man and undoubtedly our master jeweler. He gave me a stiff nod.

Aaecus was sitting, his tattooed arms crossed. There was blood speckling his face, and he had the same look that a lion did after it devoured it's prey.

"She wanted alone time," I said, holding up my hands. "Actually, she demanded it. I brought up marriage, and she wanted to think about it."

"She wanted to think about it," Damon hissed, tearing off his goggles.

"What the hell did you say?" Aaecus asked.

"Leave us," Damon said, looking up at the man.

"Yes, sir," he said, giving us an awkward bow or curtsey–I don't know what it was—before fleeing from the room.

We waited until we heard the door shut.

"I talked to her. I cooked breakfast when she woke up, and I talked to her about the benefits of getting married, the protection it could provide. She said I made it sound like it was just a business deal, and that didn't make her happy."

"Of course that didn't make her happy," Damon exclaimed. He rubbed his temples, glaring at me. "Now she's just going to think we're trying to make her sign another contract."

"Are we not?" I snapped. "Do you love her? Do you both love her? Would you give up the empire we've built for her? Would you give up everything for her?"

I went to the table, my temper finally igniting. I was always Mr. Easy Going, the nice guy that was able to woo anyone into doing what he wanted. But the pressure of everything from this week was getting to me.

"I fucking love her," I growled. "*Love* her, love her. I would leave this mafia behind if she wanted me to. I would do anything for her, and I've only known her for a week. There's so much more for me to learn about her. Like her favorite foods, her favorite colors, her likes and dislikes. Is that what you both think too?"

"Yes, godsdamnit," Aaecus growled. "I bought her flowers." He threw out his hand, gesturing to a bouquet of roses resting on a chair in the corner of the room. "I bought her flowers after I gutted ten men for trying to attack her. I should have bought white ones so I could turn them red with their blood, but I decided she might not find that quite as romantic as I did. I've got it bad, Minos."

I snorted in frustration, but he was right. "And you?" I asked Damon.

Damon glared at me, drumming his fingers on the table. He stood up, coming around to me. "You're really asking me this?" he whispered. "You know how I feel."

"That's not enough," I said. "I'm okay with you not being expressive, but she might need to hear it."

Damon stopped right in front of me, his lips hovering in front of mine. There was that tension between us, the one that drove me wild and made me weak.

But not right now.

"Say it," I hissed. "Is she just another hole for you, Damon?"

He snarled and grabbed me by my jacket, slamming me against the wall. "How fucking dare you?"

"Say it," I growled again. "Tell us why you deserve her."

"I don't deserve her," Damon growled. "I don't fucking deserve her. I never will. But I plan on spending the rest of my life doing every single fucking thing I can to deserve her, even if it will never be enough. I like the way she smiles. I like the way she laughs. I like the way she'll tell us all to go to hell if we need to hear it."

I relaxed against the wall, holding his burning gaze. "Do you really think you don't deserve love? After all the love I've given you?"

His temper cooled off and he blew out a breath, leaning forward and pressing his forehead against mine. "I don't deserve you either, even when you're a fucking brat."

I smiled, sliding my hands over his chest. "I think that's your biggest flaw, my love."

"What is?"

"Thinking that you don't deserve us," I sighed. "You do. And you deserve her too."

Damon swallowed hard and pulled back, rolling his shoulders. We both looked up at Aaecus, who was watching us with an unwavering gaze. Damon raised a questioning brow.

"What?" Aaecus grunted. "Don't look at me like that. You already know that he's right."

Damon snorted and then shrugged. "Okay, well. Minos, I left you there for a reason, revelations or no. We can't leave her alone. What if something happens?"

"They would be insane to attack us in our own home," I said. "She was adamant. What should I have done?"

"Tell her no?" Aaecus suggested. "Fuck her to distract her? Go put yourself in a corner and stare at the wall?"

"She wasn't having it," I sighed. "She was pissed, and I only made it worse. I can go back, though. She hasn't messaged me, and I was certain that she would by now."

"Call her," Damon said, his tone worrying me.

Surely no one would be stupid enough to go to our penthouse. We were Cerberus, three crime bosses that would literally raze the city if someone messed with us like this. Even with there being other branches, no one would dare go to our home.

Then again, Hercules had been sending thieves towards us for some time now. That's what started all of this. It was unreasonable that Aaecus literally shooting him might make him lose it.

I felt a streak of nerves as I reached into my pocket and fished out my phone. The screen lit up as if on cue, Ashley's name flashing over the screen. I let out a breath of relief. "See, she's calling me," I said. I smirked, hitting the answer button. "Hey, princess."

"Is that what you call this stupid whore?"

My blood went cold. Damon and Aaecus immediately

came to me, both growling at the sound of that demigod asshole's voice.

"*Hercules,*" I snarled. "What are you doing with her phone?"

"You mean my thief's phone? The whore that I contracted to work for me? You know I practically bought her from the *Bratva*. They were ready to gut her, then I swooped in and saved her."

"If you lay one fucking hand on her—"

"Let me talk to your daddy," he said, his voice dripping with a sickening sweetness that made me want to vomit.

Rage burned through me, but Damon snatched the phone before I could react. I sank against the wall as I listened, my heart pounding in my chest.

This was all my fault.

If she was hurt, I would never forgive myself. I had left her alone.

"What the fuck are you doing, Hercules?" Damon asked, his voice calm and collected.

"I'm giving you a courtesy call," I heard Hercules sneer. "The three of you were stupid enough to leave your mate alone, and now I have her. Say hi, *princess.*"

"*Fuck you, you asshole.*" That was undoubtedly our mate.

Aaecus' hands curled into fists, his breaths quickening. I could feel the monstrous bonds that tied us fighting the urge to go completely feral.

I closed my eyes, trying to focus on what was being said. My mind immediately began to spin with darker images of everything Hercules could do to her.

I felt Damon's hand on my shoulder, jarring me out of it.

"See," Hercules said. "Your little demigod, who you thought you'd be able to keep all to yourselves, is here with me.

That three million you sent me wasn't worth it and I decided to reclaim what was mine to begin with."

"We paid you," Damon said. "We bought her contract. She stopped belonging to you the moment the money went through."

"I sent it back," Hercules said happily. "Would you like to know something? I know exactly how to kill a demigod... and I know how to do it slowly."

I heard a cry from Ashley and my knees weakened, my vision spotting as my adrenaline picked up.

Damon's expression was unreadable. "This will start a war between us," Damon said, his voice carrying a soft rage that sent a chill through the room. "Are you prepared for those consequences, Hercules?"

I heard Ashley cry out again, followed by a sick laugh from Hercules. "You should have never touched a demigod," Hercules said. "Monsters like you aren't worthy."

"Answer my question, Hercules," Damon seethed, the vein in his temple pulsing.

"What consequences will a mutt from the Underworld have for someone like me?"

Damon smiled, the energy in the room becoming increasingly violent. "If you have spilled a drop of her blood, I will kill you. No one will stop me. Not the gods, not the demigods, and not the Fates."

"Good luck," Hercules laughed. "Don't worry, I'll take my time with her. Oh, and in case you were wondering... I brought her home with me. To my bedroom. Got her all tied up on my bed, she's so pretty and unmarked. But she won't be that way much longer."

The line cut out and Damon put the phone in his pocket, the silence settling over us becoming volatile.

"This is my fault," I whispered.

Damon shook his head, a low growl rumbling in his chest. "No, Minos. Don't think about that. We have to act."

"I'm going to lose it," Aaecus said, his voice trembling. "I'm going to snap."

"Snap when we have to fight his men," Damon said. "No mercy. No lives spared. We call our men, we call our resources. We find our mate, and we rid our world of a demigod. Agreed?"

"Okay," Aecus and I both agreed.

"Let's go," Damon said. "I don't know how much time we have, but I do know it isn't much."

CHAPTER 28

DEMIGODS AND MONSTERS

AAECUS

The three of us moved with the fluidity of brothers who had fought countless battles together.

Hercules lived in a mansion with white marble pillars that glistened in the sun. There were steps that led to the grand front doors, and blood flowed down them like a lazy crimson river. Bodies surrounded us—casualties that I might have liked to avoid, only they wouldn't stop shooting at me.

Their blood was on Hercules' hands, not mine.

We moved up to the front doors, our men surrounding the massive home. Figures moved behind the windows, but anyone that might have been up on the roof fell like swatted flies as our men shot them.

It was bloody. It was ruthless.

He had stolen her from us, right out from our noses. We had known that something might happen, but now that it had, it was hard not to think of everything he might do to hurt her.

Damon rushed ahead in his monstrous form, slamming into the front door. Wood splintered and the doors broke open quickly.

I barely had time to blink before three men lunged for me. Out of the corner of my eye, I could see others fighting Damon and Minos. Bullets began to fly again, some of our men hitting the ground and joining the trail of corpses.

I raked my claws over the three men who had jumped me, tearing straight through the bulletproof vests they wore. Blood sprayed over my fur, the scent filing my nostrils.

Pop, pop, pop.

Bullets hit the walls, taking out more men. Pain tore through my shoulder, but the bullet that had struck me had only grazed me.

I grabbed a gun from one of the fallen men, turning and aiming.

One, two, three. Pop, pop, pop.

Dead, dead, dead.

They were quick deaths. No screaming, no agony. Just more blood pooling over Hercules' perfect marble floors.

The inside of the manor was luxuriously eerie. At the center there was a fountain of Zeus, a lightning bolt clutched in one hand while the other covered what would have been his cock. There were two long hallways on both sides.

"Go," Damon snarled.

I nodded, breathing in the scent of our mate.

I could feel her close by.

I could smell her, taste her.

What if she's dead?

Pain tore through my chest, my thoughts self-inflicted wounds

They'd dragged her through these halls, and my mind was

fucking with me, repeatedly showing me images of her screaming. Of her being in pain.

Killing a demigod was almost impossible, but tonight? I'd send that heroic cunt back to the underworld, and not with a ticket back to here.

His time had come. The end of an era, the end of a bastard's reign who had done nothing good for anyone.

The three of us kept moving despite the screams and despite the gunshots. Our monstrous forms were barely containing themselves. We were hunting, and that made us want to become one.

My blood burned with rage as I ran faster, following her scent. Our men followed us, spreading out and fighting whoever Hercules had hired to work for him.

They didn't have loyalty to him. They didn't have respect. The moment they saw that we were going to win, they'd get the hell out of this place.

"She's close," Minos called.

I gave him a slight nod. She *was* close. I burst through a set of doors, ducking right as more bullets flew. I growled, letting out a monstrous roar.

"*Where is our wife?*"

Our mate. Our love. She was ours and they had stolen her from us. She was meant to be our wife, to be our future.

If she was hurt...

One of Hercules' men ran straight for me and I grabbed him with my claws, slamming him down to the ground. He gasped as his bones cracked, his face twisting with pain.

"Where is she?" I snarled. "Where is our fucking mate?"

"She's in his room," the man gasped, his voice shaking.

"*Where* is his room?"

"Down the hall to the right. Second door, can't miss it. Has his face carved into it."

Of course it did.

Minos and Damon both heard what the man said. I let him go of him, taking his gun. The three of us moved, a unit of creatures determined to find her.

The air shimmered around us with heat as we went down the hall, our blood becoming hotter and hotter. I could feel our bonds to each other, could feel how close we were to joining together to become one.

The hall fell silent. We slowed, Damon giving us both a nervous glance.

We came to the supposed door, one that indeed had Hercules' face carved into his. His ugly mug grinned back at us, taunting us.

Warning bells rang through my mind. Minos let out a low growl. Her scent clung to this space, but it was stale.

There was something wrong here, but we didn't have time to figure out what it was.

I took a deep breath, trying to center myself. My mind was so chaotic, filled with fear and anger.

"Go," I whispered, waiting for him to open the door. "I'll open it—"

Minos was already moving forward. He kicked it in, hitting the carving of Hercules with every ounce of force he had.

Boom!

The world around us immediately exploded. *Fuck.* My body was tossed back and I smashed into a pillar hard enough to crack it. I hit the floor with a grunt, pain radiating through me as the stone began to crumble.

"*Aaecus!*"

My head was spinning, my hearing muffled. I slowly got up, my world tilting.

Those fuckers.

They'd rigged the door with explosives.

Was Minos okay? Was Damon?

I blinked, my ears ringing.

"*Move, Aaecus!*" Damon's harsh command was heard, but I couldn't understand what he meant.

I heard the *cling* of metal, and felt the presence I had been seeking out. I stepped to the left at the same time a sword cut through the air, a snarl coming from none other than Hercules.

"Oh look," I taunted, spinning. "You've finally joined us."

Hercules gave me a cruel smile, swinging his sword again. I ducked, my balance still slightly off and hearing echoing with a continuous ring from the explosives.

His sword struck the bottom half of a fallen pillar, sticking for just a moment. I lunged, dragging my claws over his face.

Hercules howled, falling back as his golden blood poured from the new wounds.

Damon and Minos came to my side, both of them looking slightly beaten.

"Together," Damon huffed. "We have to become one."

It happened in a matter of seconds. Crunching bones and snapping muscles, the bonds that had bound us together for centuries drawing our three bodies into one. I felt our most primal instincts grow stronger as our monstrous Cerberus form came to life.

We towered over Hercules now, and he still wore that grin. Even with blood dripping down his face, his eyes glinted with the look of someone who believed they'd already won.

"*Where is our mate?*" we asked, our voice a deep baritone snarl.

"Trapped," he said. "I chained her to my bed and intend to keep her there once I get rid of the three of you. When she wakes up, she will find that her mates are dead and she belongs to someone new."

Fury took control. That he would even suggest taking our mate was too much.

We lunged and he swung his sword, missing us narrowly.

Our claws raked through the air as he swung again, his blade striking true this time. Pain burned from the touch of his steel, slicing across our shoulder.

Blood began to run down our body, red smearing over the white marble floors.

We swung out, smacking his body. It had been so long since we'd fought a demigod, we had forgotten how fucking hard their bodies were.

Hercules hit the ground, letting out a snarl. "Does it make you mad, Cerberus? The idea that I might take her from you."

Our roar echoed through the hall, the building rumbling around us. *"Where is she? Where is our mate?"*

"You'll never see her again."

We fought, side stepping his swinging blade and throwing out our claws. It was a violent dance, wounds opening from sword and from talons.

His sword swiped over our back, followed by his taunting laugh. More pain erupted, blood seeping onto the floor.

We had to get to her. We had to defeat him.

We tackled him to the ground, his sword sliding away. Our three jaws snapped at him, my jaws managing to sink into his shoulder.

The taste of demigod blood filled us with more anger and desperation.

Our mate had been stolen from us.

Taken.

He had wanted to hurt her.

To keep her.

Hercules brought his knee up, using all his strength to throw us backwards.

We smashed into one of the pillars, the stone snapping. Broken marble fell down, hitting our body.

More pain, our vision dotting. We slowly stood, and Hercules did the same, golden blood falling over his wounded face.

Rage soared through us, shattering whatever hesitance there might have been to kill. Fates and gods be damned, we would bring down Hercules.

Chapter 29

Ashley the Thief

Ashley

I slowly opened my eyes, my head throbbing with pain. I could feel blood crusted around my mouth, and could taste it on my tongue.

He hadn't pulled his punches.

I let out a soft groan, blinking until my mind cleared. I raised my head, realizing I was bound to a four-poster bed. I glared, studying the kind of chains around my wrists and ankles.

They jangled as I yanked on them, refusing to budge.

He was going to pay for everything. Clotho had told me I had to kill him, and she was right. He would never stop.

My head plopped back on the pillow. I had to get out of this.

Explosions and shouts echoed through the house. I drew in a deep breath, feeling that my mates were close—but that only worried me more.

"I need them to come after you, so that I can finally send them back to Hades. I'm going to slaughter your monster mates, and I hope you feel their pain."

Those had been Hercules' words before he'd knocked me out again.

I yanked against the chains, this time putting more force behind it. Even with giving it all I had, they refused to break.

"Damn it," I whispered.

I squeezed my eyes shut, cursing everything. Demigods, monsters, the gods themselves. How in the hell was someone like Hercules allowed to run around and be a tyrant?

I had to break these chains.

I twisted my neck looking up at them again. There was a golden lock on each one of them.

My gaze narrowed. Hadn't papa Hermes said the key would unlock anything? And that it would always be there for me?

I snapped my fingers, hoping to see it appear, but nothing happened.

"Abra cadabra," I whispered.

Nothing.

"Unlock me," I said.

Again, nothing.

"Bingo. Yahtzee. Chains undone. Key."

I gasped as the card appeared in my hand, slipped between two of my fingers.

"Unlock me, you son of a bitch," I whispered.

My heart beat faster as the lock clicked, the chains around my wrist sliding free. I gripped the card and swiped it over my other wrist, letting out a gleeful laugh as the chains slipped free.

The house rumbled again, a piece of the ceiling loosening above me.

"Godsdamnit," I said, leaning forward and undoing the chains around my ankles quickly.

My nerves were running high now. I rolled out of the bed and winced, feeling like I'd been run over by a train.

My vision wavered for a moment, voices rising up again. *The Thief, The Thief.*

The same voices I had heard before.

I shook my head and the voices faded. Hopefully that meant someone had my back.

I had to get to Damon, Minos, and Aaecus. Hercules had known they would come for me. If he hurt them, I would destroy him.

I ran to the door of the room, swiping my card and listening for the telling click of locks being undone.

If I ever saw Hermes again, I might even thank him.

I burst through the door, and cursed. Smoke filled the halls, shouts from men echoing. I looked to my right and watched as one of the many marble pillars in this ridiculous mansion tumbled.

A roar thundered around me and tears blurred my vision.

My mates. I could feel them. I could feel their desperation, their pain.

I took off running, letting every instinct take over. My heart drove me down the hall and I ran faster. I came to a massive foyer with a fountain and paused, seeing the only sharp object I'd spotted so far.

It was a statue of Zeus, and in his stone hand was a massive lightning bolt.

When in Rome...

I stepped into the fountain and scaled the statue, gripping the lightning bolt and yanking as hard as possible. There was a pop, followed by a crack, and I gasped as it broke free.

"Shoot the girl!"

Fuck. I could feel men surrounding me, closing in with their weapons.

I jumped out of the fountain, wincing as my pants were now wet, and took off running again—stone thunderbolt and plastic key card in hand.

Gunshots hit every spot behind me, narrowly missing me. *Lucky.* Adrenaline coursed through my veins, pushing me harder. Another roar rumbled through the mansion, followed by the echo of Hercules' laughter.

The bastard had lost his mind. He was no longer a hero, but a villain.

I rounded a corner and came to a halt, nearly stumbling over a body. I grimaced and stepped over it, my eyes drawn up.

Hercules was standing in front of a massive monster—*my* monster.

This was Cerberus. The creature of countless myths and legends, the beast that had been whispered about for ages. They were massive, with three hellhound heads attached to a large body that stood upright. Their eyes burned red, the room shimmering with waves of heat.

Fires raged around them, bodies of men strewn across the floor. Nausea hit me as I realized the ground was red from their blood, pooling at their feet. Cerberus was bleeding profusely.

"No," I whispered.

They'd been stabbed multiple times. Hercules held a gleaming sword, his muscles rippling as he let out a maniacal laugh. He lunged at them and I watched in frozen horror as he brought them to the ground, raising his weapon high again.

"Hercules!" I shouted.

My feet were already moving. I raised my stone bolt as I ran towards him.

He snarled, his distraction working to my advantage. Cerberus managed to knock him back, but he rolled to his feet.

"You escaped," he growled.

"I did, you son a bitch," I seethed.

He only smiled, his eyes flashing. I felt the power in the room shift, my mating bonds tugging so tightly in my chest that I lost my breath.

Run, Ashley.

Their voices echoed in my mind, but I shook my head. *No.*

"Fight me," I challenged. "I'm a demigod. Fight *me*, Hercules. Not them."

"Why?" Hercules snarled. "Because they'll lose? Sorry, but I like that much more."

He turned, lifting his sword again and driving it straight into their chests.

I screamed, panic and fear sending me over the edge as their pain became mine. I felt the sword go through, and something inside me broke.

I threw the bolt like a javelin, aiming straight for Hercules' heart.

It entered through his chest, burying itself and coming out of his back.

He gasped, stumbling back from them. I met him, slamming him down onto the floor. I scrambled to Cerberus, pulling the sword free.

We love you, little thief.

Damon's voice was a soft whisper in my mind, filled with so much longing.

My vision blurred and I turned. Their blood dripped off Hercules' blade and I walked to the demigod slowly.

Rage. Rage and pain. Everyone I'd ever loved had been taken from me.

Every. Single. Person.

Hercules doubled over, the stone bolt still lodged in his

body. He coughed, blood dripping from his mouth, the gold mixing into the red that covered the floor.

The house rumbled around us again, pieces of stone crashing to the floor.

This whole place could come down, I didn't care.

I kicked Hercules, sending him onto his back. He gasped, wheezing. His eyes widened as he looked up at me, and I finally saw it.

The fear.

I'd never considered myself a hero.

I'd never considered myself a villain.

I hadn't wanted to hurt someone. I'd never wanted to cause others pain or be the hand that dealt death, until now.

"You won't do it," Hercules rasped. "You can't. You're weak."

He was wrong.

I gave him a soft smile, my entire body burning with anger. With vengeance.

"You were a hero," I whispered. "But you've lived long enough that you've become the villain, Hercules. I hope you have fun in the Underworld."

He raised his hand, and I brought his own sword down. The blade drove into his neck, the sound making me feel sick as his head was severed from his body.

I stared into his eyes, watching as the life faded.

Demigod or not, he wasn't coming back from that.

Boom!

I winced as there was a blinding flash of light, every hair on my body standing on end. A lightning bolt struck the room and I looked away, wincing as light flooded over me.

I fell to my knees, tears filling my eyes. I looked up, seeing the figure of a man—but I knew he wasn't a mortal.

He stared at me, regarding me with an almost cruel curiosity.

"He's dead," I whispered.

"I know," the man said. "You're a demigod, but I do not know of you."

I swallowed hard, my words failing me. What did I say to a god?

"Are you Zeus?" I asked.

The man nodded. "I am. And you are?"

"Ashley," I said. "Ashley the Thief, as my mates call me."

He raised a brow, turning his head slowly to look at Damon, Aaecus, and Minos. I turned too, realizing they had changed back into their mortal forms.

I could see their chests rising and falling.

"Oh gods," I whispered desperately. "They're alive."

"They are, but my son is dead. Killed by another demigod that should not even *exist*." His words sent a chill down my spine.

"I didn't choose to exist," I said, my hands curling into fists. "In fact, I'd say that's really my dad's fault, considering he's an all-powerful *god*."

Zeus's gaze became a glower.

Well, this would be how I met my end. I sucked in a breath, but refused to look away from him.

"I will remember this, Ashley the Thief," he said, walking closer. He leaned down, picking up Hercules' head. Golden blood dripped from the severed neck, his expression still frozen.

A sick part of me felt a hint of satisfaction from that.

Fuck, I was going to vomit on him.

"Isn't this what demigods are supposed to do?" I asked. "Kill the bad guys? Or was that just the stories?"

"Well, first, they're supposed to kill *monsters*—not mate them."

"I guess I just like to do things my own way."

Zeus snorted and turned, walking away from me. "Look away, child, unless you want to be a blind thief."

I closed my eyes right as he burst into light, leaving me alone in a crumbling hall with my injured mates and countless bodies.

I slowly got to my feet, swallowing back my nausea again. I heard a cough and turned.

"Damon," I gasped.

I ran to the three of them, throwing myself at Damon right as he sat up. He groaned, his arms wrapping around me and he pulled me down with him.

"We're okay," he croaked. "Fuck. Where's that son of a bitch? I'm going to kill him."

"He's already dead," I said quickly.

"I feel like death," Minos groaned.

"Minos," I breathed, reaching over and planting a kiss on his mouth. He grunted, cupping my face for a moment, and then I felt Aaecus pull me towards him.

"My turn," he said, kissing me hard.

Tears started to fall and I drew in a shaky breath. I settled between Damon and Aaecus, staring up at the cracked ceiling.

Minos slowly sat up, looking around. "Ah shit, we need to get out of here."

"Can the three of you walk?" I asked.

"Yes," Aaecus grumbled. "We're healing quick, though."

Aaecus' arms wrapped around me and I squeaked as he lifted me. "You're injured," I hissed.

"I don't care. We're never letting you go again, baby girl."

Chapter 30

Three Fates Mafia

Damon

It had only been a few hours since everything had happened, but the Three Fates Mafia was ruthless. The moment that Hercules' death had become known, there'd been a meeting called for all of the monsters and demigods.

I wasn't happy about it, but I knew that it was unavoidable. The events that had occurred would change everything.

Ashley had killed Hercules.

The demigod that had been alive for centuries. We had fought him and had lost, but our mate had taken him down.

Killing him was a big deal and I knew it hadn't sank in yet.

Our car pulled into a parking lot on the outskirts of Moirai. There was a building with no signs and boarded up windows waiting, the presence of monsters and demigods emanating from it.

We had cleaned up after the fight and had changed into

fresh clothes before driving here. Ashey was wearing a dark red dress, her long blonde hair tumbling over her shoulders.

She didn't look like someone that had just beheaded an ancient demigod with his own sword.

"I'm nervous," she admitted.

I nodded, looking at her. Aaecus and Minos both gave me concerned glances as well.

We had never heard of another demigod and monster being mated. And perhaps it would not have been a big deal, except that she had inherited Hercules' mafia branch when she killed him.

Our little thief was now a mafia queen.

"If you don't want the mafia, you don't have to take it," Minos reminded her softly.

We all knew that wasn't how it worked.

"You can just announce that you don't want this," Aaecus said. "And the rest of us will vote on what to do."

Ashley drew in a short breath, her gaze hardening. "No," she said softly. "I want this. I can make a difference with this type of power. I'm claiming what belonged to him as my own. I'm tired of playing by others' rules."

Aaecus, Minos, and I all stared at her for a moment. There was resolution in her words. She reminded me of a goddess right now, her eyes burning with determination.

"I love you," she said. "All three of you. But I'm doing this for me."

Her words knocked the breath from me, and I let out a soft growl. "We love you too."

"We'll follow you wherever you go, baby girl," Aaecus said.

"From Elysium to Olympus," Minos murmured.

She nodded, swallowing hard. I watched as all the signs of nervousness evaporated. Her shoulders pulled back, her spine straightened, and she gave us a subtle nod. "They're waiting for us."

I opened the door and stepped out. Storm clouds were gathering above us. The hairs on the back of my neck stood up, telling me that we were being watched.

Aaecus and Minos got out of our car. Minos held out his hand for Ashley, helping her stand. Her crimson dress wavered in the wind as we walked towards the door.

I opened it for her, giving Aaecus and Minos one last nod.

The meeting home for the Three Fates Mafia was the exact opposite of safe. Four demigods that hated us waited inside, and all of the other monsters would be against Ashley.

Hell, I would have been too.

We went down a dark hall, the lights flickering above us. At the end, there was a steel door. Two men stood to either side, their expressions stoic.

One of them opened the door for us, and I went inside first, Ashley walked in behind me, followed by Aaecus and Minos.

We had rehearsed the story over and over again since the call for a meeting had been made. There were some things that would need to be omitted for the time being until we figured out what it meant, such as the fact that the Three Fates were pulling us all into their battle.

The silence in the room was oppressing. At the center, there was a massive table. On the left side, there were five seats. Four of them were filled, one empty. The demigods Orpheus, Theseus and Jason stared at us with a burning hatred. Perseus, the only demigod that I didn't absolutely despise, was the only one that wore a soft welcoming smile. She raised a brow as she watched us.

To the right sat the monsters. Creatures that I had known for so long, but suddenly I didn't trust any of them.

Argos, Bash, and Pierce were the leaders of the Hydra.

They sat the furthest away, all three wearing knowing smirks. Next to them was Medusa, or Madeline, as she was known in the mortal world.

Then there was Ian, the Colchian dragon. His iridescent eyes didn't even meet mine, instead going straight to my mate. Assessing her. Watching her.

To his right were the Chimera twins. Neither one of them looked pleased.

"Well," Minos said, breaking the silence. "We're here."

"Take your seats then," Orpheus said.

I had instructed Ashley that she would sit between Aaecus and I, but she moved past me—taking the chair that would have belonged to Hercules. This brought about a series of growls and snarls, and I fought to contain the wave of rage that crashed into me. That any of them would look at her with such malice.

Her poise never wavered, though.

I took the seat next to her, Aaecus and Minos joining us.

"You would sit where he sat?" Orpheus asked, his cold gaze turning on Ashley.

She raised a brow, regarding him. "Yes."

Medusa let out a dark, feminine chuckle. "This is the person that killed that piece of shit? Her?"

"Watch your tongue," Jason growled, shooting her a murderous look. "Hercules was a hero. The fact that he has fallen is the mark of terrible times."

"Perhaps for the demigods," Ian said. "Us monsters have no ill will towards someone that brought Hercules down. He has been a tyrant for years."

Orpheus and Jason both started to stand, but I slammed my hand down on the table. The movement made almost everyone in the room jump.

"We have come here to settle this," I growled, the air

around me prickling with heat. "Ashley has slain Hercules. She has inherited his branch in doing so."

"There haven't been new demigods in ages," Orpheus exclaimed. "And you're telling me that this woman is one? The Three Fates and Zeus himself decreed that none would be born or allowed."

"Yes, and the Three Fates have obviously changed their mind," I growled, trying to keep my temper at bay. "Very obviously, a new demigod is in our presence. She is the daughter of Hermes."

"She is also mated to Cerberus," Jason said.

There was a series of growls around the room again. A giggle slipped through, and even I turned my head.

Ashley held up a hand. "Sorry, I'm still not over all the growling."

Minos snorted next to me and I had to keep myself from smiling. "Anyways," I continued. "Yes, she is our mate."

"It's unacceptable," Orpheus scoffed. "She cannot have an entire mafia branch to herself as your mate."

"And where is that written, Orpheus?" Ashley asked.

Once again, I found myself fighting not to smile. She could hold her own in this room and that made me proud.

"It's not written anywhere," he sneered. "And don't speak to me as if we are equals."

"We *are* equals," Ashley said, leaning forward in her seat.

"Before we continue, I'd like to know what happened exactly," Argos, one of the Hydras, said. "In detail. That will help us all, I believe. From the very beginning, please, Ashley."

She nodded, drawing in a soft breath. I slipped my hand under the table, taking hers and giving it a soft squeeze.

Ashley explained her story, including how she came to work for Hercules and how we had discovered that she was our fated mate and a new demigod. She was thorough enough that they didn't question some of the gaps, although I could feel the occasional glance towards me to read my expression. When she mentioned that Hermes found her, and revealed he was her father, that brought a series of *hmms* and gasps.

"If anyone were to make children without Zeus knowing, it would be him," Ian, the Colchian dragon, said.

"Indeed. Continue, please," Argos said.

Ashley nodded, clearing her throat as she continued explaining all that had happened.

"You're omitting the part where Aaecus shot Hercules in the head," Jason said casually.

"And she's also omitting the part where Hercules was going to kill her," I growled, the tension in the room heightening.

Jason and I glared at each other, but Ashley continued.

"That eventually led to this morning. I was alone at their penthouse when Hercules broke in and kidnapped me."

Medusa glowered, her gaze sliding over to the other demigods. "Not surprised. He's always been the type."

Well, we could count on her aligning with Ashley, then.

Ashley concluded her story of how she slayed Hercules, ending with the reason she had killed him. "I thought that he had murdered Damon, Minos, and Aaecus. They're my mates. And so, I killed him."

Silence fell over the room, but it only lasted a few seconds before Jason stood abruptly, glaring at her. "You murdered him."

"It was self defense," she said. "He was going to kill me. Is that not against your rules, Jason?"

"You little—"

"Finish that sentence, and I will spill your blood," I snarled, cutting Jason off. "Do *not* speak to her that way again."

"He wasn't a hero to me," she bit out.

Jason sat back down in his chair, crossing his arms. "It's not right. None of this is right."

"We are unbalanced now," Orpheus said in agreement.

"Unbalanced?" Medusa hissed. "Why? She *is* a demigod." Her eyes slid over to me, her diamond pupils gleaming with a hint of malice. "She has blood from the gods. A daughter of Hermes. The agreement that was made upon the foundation of this mafia was that there would be five demigods, and five monsters."

"It has never been fair, as you outnumber us," Theseus chimed in, breaking his silence.

"That was the decision of the Three Fates, Theseus, not us," Ian growled. "None of us would have chosen to work with any of you. The gods have never been kind to us."

"She is mated to *them*," Orpheus snarled. "To Cerberus."

"I *am* mated to them," Ashley said. "That doesn't mean I'm not capable of running my own branch or making my own decisions. I'm sure they would testify to that."

That was more than true. I felt a streak of pride as she held her own.

His eyes were the color of sea glass, and sharper than knives. "I highly doubt you are capable."

I growled again, but Ashley squeezed my hand.

"Why? Because I'm not some crusty male demigod? Medusa and Perseus are the only other women that sit at this table. You can kiss my ass."

Fucking hell, this woman. I already knew that I was in love with her, but every moment that passed, I was falling all over again.

I snorted, feeling eyes shift to me. I cleared my throat, trying to give a menacing look. "You will *not* kiss her ass, only we are allowed to do that."

I said that as seriously as possible, and enjoyed the way everyone took it that way.

"Besides," Ashley said. "We are to be married soon as well."

What?

Aaecus, Minos, and I all swiveled in our seats—looking at her with wild gazes. My cock responded as well, my desire to call her my wife making me thankful that we were sitting at a table.

She winked at us, relaxing. "Was this meeting called so that you can be sure Hercules is gone... or?"

"Is he truly dead?" Ian asked.

He watched her with his iridescent gaze, his short silver hair glinting in the overhead light. He had never kept his mortal form quite as human looking, and there were parts of him that gave away that there was a dragon hiding beneath.

"He is," she said. "Zeus took him."

That brought about a series of grumbles, but Jason surprised us all by standing from his seat. "I've heard enough," he said. He looked at her, cocking his head ever so slightly. "Welcome to the table, Ashley. We all have businesses to run and messes to clean up. As you are taking on Hercules' mafia, you will need to make sure that your men are not misbehaving or crossing boundaries previously set. There are promises that Hercules made that he will not be able to keep now. All of us—myself, Orpheus, Perseus, and Theseus—will need to meet with you separately to potentially renegotiate. I'm sure they will want to have conversations with you as well. As for today, I am finished."

"I think it's safe to say this meeting is adjourned," Medusa said. She eyed me carefully, rising from her seat. "Yes, Damon?"

"Yes," I said. "If that is all, then we will handle everything else separately. I would also like for it to be known that my future wife will be in charge of her own mafia."

Jason all but rolled his eyes, shoving his chair forward and stalking out the door. The others followed him, and I watched them file out. I wondered what would be said about us after they left.

"Good luck, demi," Medusa said, giving Ashley a subtle nod.

Ashley nodded in return, her composure still perfect even as she squeezed my hand harder.

I let out a low hum as the door slammed shut behind us, Pierce the last one to leave. I didn't like the knowing smile that he wore.

All that remained was the four of us, Ian, and Perseus.

Perseus ran her fingers through her silver hair, letting out a tired groan "Everyone is so stuck up in this family."

"Hardly a family," Minos said.

Perseus shrugged. "I have never had as many issues as the others. You know this. I have a question for you, Ashley."

"Yes?"

"When you killed Hercules, what did my father say?"

"Zeus?" Ashley asked. "He wasn't happy about it."

Perseus frowned, raising a brow. "He's never happy about anything. Everything will get easier, I'm sure. You did kill our brother, and Jason was particularly close with Hercules."

"I don't trust him," she said simply. "And as I explained, the reason I killed Hercules was because at the time, I believed that he had killed Cerberus."

"The others don't believe you," Ian said.

"Colchian—"

"Please. Call me Ian," he said firmly. "I will be blunt. I am not happy to see a demigod and monster mated together. This has never happened before, and it makes me feel uneasy. The

Three Fates put us here for a chance to run our own world, and having this type of change leads me to believe they have other motives."

"They do," she said, sitting up in my seat. "None of you can sit here and tell me that they don't."

The silence that settled over us was uncomfortable.

Perseus let out a soft hum. "Well. If you need anything, let me know. And if you have questions about... well, being a demigod, we can always meet. We're not always enemies."

With that, she rose from her seat, leaving all of us.

Ian stood too, but he waited until the door shut again before he spoke. "Why didn't you call me, Damon?"

"Would you have helped a demigod, Ian?" I asked, narrowing my gaze. "Truly?"

He snorted, and a puff of smoke blew from his nostrils. "For you, perhaps."

"I'll remember that then," I said.

He stood from his seat, letting out a soft hum. "Our world will not be the same."

He left us with that. The four of us were silent as he exited through the door, leaving us alone.

"Fuck me," Minos mumbled, rising from his seat. He came to Ashley's chair, his hands sliding over her shoulders and rubbing. She instantly groaned. "That was not a fun meeting," he said.

"They hardly ever are," Aaecus muttered.

"I'm ready to go home," Ashley moaned as Minos kept rubbing her muscles. "Fuck today. I'm ready to sleep for a week."

"Let's go home," I said. "I'd like to find out what our future *wife* has in mind for us when we haven't properly proposed yet."

Chapter 31

Cerberus

Ashley

Damon, Aaecus, and Minos all knelt down in front of me on one knee. Despite the disasters today had brought, it had also given me a clear vision of what I wanted.

My monsters.

I wanted them. I wanted to build a life with them.

"Will you, Ashley the Thief, be our wife?" Damon asked.

He held a velvet box in his hand and opened the lid, revealing the most stunning ring I had ever seen. There were three gorgeous stones—one diamond and two crimson rubies.

"Oh gods," I whispered, tears springing to my eyes. "Yes. Yes, I will be."

I held out my hand, trembling as Damon removed the ring from its box and slid it onto my fourth finger. The jewels glistened, a symbol of a future we would make together.

I threw my arms around the three of them and was quickly picked up. I kissed each of them and then melted into their arms, my body finally feeling a wave of exhaustion from all that had happened.

"Our little thief turned mate turned mafia boss turned wife," Aaecus teased, kissing the top of my head.

I giggled, grinning. "It's not quite The Odyssey, but I'm fine with it."

They snorted.

Minos stole a kiss from me, letting out a satisfied hum. "I think it's time we all get some rest. What do you think?"

We all agreed and I was carried down the hall, the four of us piling into Damon's bed together.

When I woke up the next morning, I felt like a new woman.

I laid there, listening to the soft snores of my mates. I ran my hands over my body, feeling the black silk night dress that I had thrown on after our midnight shower.

I was a motherfucking mafia queen.

I smiled to myself, wondering what all of that would entail. I had so many questions, starting with what the hell was I supposed to do.

"Go back to sleep," Aaecus grumbled. "I can feel your thoughts racing."

I smirked, turning to look at him.

The four of us lay in bed, the three of them surrounding me with their warm and naked bodies. Aaecus opened up one eye, letting out a loud groan.

"She has that look," he mumbled.

I reached under the blankets, running my hand down his hard muscles until I came to his cock.

"Fuck."

He was already hard too.

Damon let out a low growl, turning over on his side and spooning me. He tugged me close and hiked up my dress, his cock pressing against me.

"Morning," I said, my voice husky.

I heard Minos chuckle and raised my head, seeing that he was waking up as well. He gave me a sleepy wink, spooning Damon too.

"I have a question," I announced. "What do I have to do to try out the Cerberus form?"

All three of them growled, Damon's cock now fully hard against me.

"Princess," Damon groaned.

"I just want to make sure I know what I'm getting into with my future husbands," I teased.

"Fucking hell," Minos groaned. "I want to breed her together."

Excitement ran through me. Yesterday had been fully terrifying, but the dreams I'd had last night had made me waking up wanting more.

I already loved being knotted, and now wondered...

Would I be able to take them in that form? They were huge when merged together...Beasts.

"Please, Daddy," I whispered, pressing my ass back against him. "Please breed me together."

Damon nipped my neck, letting out a low growl. "How can I say no to you, princess?"

My heart sped up and I could hardly hide my excitement, but I forced myself to try and contain it. Aaecus saw it though and smirked, leaning in and stealing a kiss.

I groaned against his mouth. I wanted them so bad right now that it was hard to think of anything else.

Damon's hand slid down between my legs, finding my clit as Aaecus kept kissing me. I moaned as he began to stroke me, playing with me lazily as we kept kissing.

Aaecus pulled back. "You think we'd even fit in this little pussy of yours, baby girl?"

"I want to try," I huffed, moaning as Damon kept playing with me.

They were so *big*. I wanted them to fill me with all of their cum, breed me as theirs.

"Gods," Minos groaned. "I can smell how turned on you are."

"Please," I whimpered.

I bit my lower lip, fighting off a groan. Damon kissed my neck, his chest rumbling with a growl.

I couldn't stop thinking about how their cocks would look. In everything that happened with Hercules, I'd never taken a moment to observe...how their *equipment* looked.

Was each cock stacked vertically or horizontally?

Either way, how the hell was I going to do that?

As my mind played through scenarios, Minos sat up on the other side of Damon.

"You know your safeword," Minos said, his voice soft.

"I do," I whispered, biting my lower lip as pleasure rushed through me.

Damon drew out a pant from me. I was so wet already, and all he had done was touch me.

He chuckled, giving me a gentle rub. "And you will use it if you need to. Correct?"

"Yes, Daddy", I said, swallowing hard.

"Get up, baby girl," Aaecus ordered, stealing one last kiss.

The sweet way he usually looked at me now hardened, a tinge of fire behind his eyes.

He wanted this too.

All three of them did.

I all but scrambled as they moved their bodies to allow me

room. My hands dug in the satin sheets, and I pulled myself across the bed until my feet touched the floor.

"Princess?"

I paused, turning to look at them. I was met with a very twisted, evil grin from Damon.

He arched a brow, a growl rumbling from his chest.

"Run, little thief."

His growl made my heart leap, and my feet moved on instinct. I was prey, but where would I even run? The penthouse was only so large—would they even be able to fit inside?

I made it to the door, and when my hand grabbed the cool metal of the doorknob, I could hear their bodies begin to change. My heart beat fast as the sound of bones cracking followed me, my three mates becoming one fierce monster.

The snapping of their teeth was the last sound I heard as I ran out into the hall. I went to the right, heading for the art room where I'd first met them.

I slammed the door shut, the excitement of being hunted turning me on even more. My eyes fell on the piece of art that had started it all.

Three werewolves ravaged a woman, and she was having the time of her life—because she was. The first time I'd seen it, I'd felt a bit jealous, and rightly so.

There was nothing like being taken by three monsters.

The door burst open and I squealed, turning to try and dodge them.

A loud snort was all I heard, a mocking laugh from Minos as I was knocked to the floor.

My face collided with the rug, and I hit the ground so hard that my breath left me.

I pulled myself up on my hands and knees, only for one of their huge paws to slap against my back.

"So wet for us," they growled. "Our little thief."

I should have screamed, but instead, I moaned.

The silk night dress split down my back, and a large paw splayed against my bare skin, warm and applying pressure in just the right way.

"She likes it," Aaecus' chuckled. "Don't you, baby girl?"

"Yes, gods, yes." I gasped as a hot breath gusted against my back, and teeth delicately yanked the rest of the fabric away.

Damon's voice made me shiver. "Ass up for us, princess."

The paw gave way, and I did as they commanded me. I pushed my ass up, my pussy dripping with need.

I felt the head of a cock press against me, teasing me.

And then I felt another.

And then a third.

"Fuck," I whimpered. "I want to see them."

"You will soon enough. Ass up, princess."

I knew that I had to, or he'd make me pay for it. Part of me wanted to refuse just to see what punishment I'd get, but I didn't.

A long inhale sounded through the room, and I felt another nose against my waiting cunt.

I wanted them to devour me.

"That's right, little thief," Minos groaned. "So perfect for us. I'm going to make you scream."

His long tongue ran over me, the friction of it against my clit making me cry out.

One broad lick became several as his tongue lapped and swirled against me.

"Oh gods," I groaned.

I was going to come like this. Bent over for my Cerberus mates, taking their tongues. I panted, their growls reminding me that they were desperate to have me.

To taste me.

"We have to make her come as much as possible before she

can take us," Aaecus said right as Minos drove his tongue inside me.

I cried out, pleasure curling through me. His tongue plunged in and out, every thought in my head turning to dust.

"Don't worry," Damon huffed. "She will take us."

Damon's voice made my head raise but only enough to feel a large paw push my head back to the floor, followed by a snarl.

"I'm so close," I gasped.

"Not yet," Damon hummed, his voice deep and sultry.

I closed my eyes, fighting the need to come right now.

"Please," I rasped.

"Not yet, princess."

Minos' tongue kept thrusting in and out of me, their claws digging into my back. The pain was refreshing, but it only drew me closer to the edge.

"Good girl," Damon said. "Come for us now."

I cried out as the wave of my first orgasm washed over me.

"That's it, baby girl, scream for us," Aaecus groaned.

My hips bucked as Minos milked another orgasm out of me tirelessly.

"Fuck!"

They drew back from me with a deep growl.

"Up," Damon said.

I could hardly move, much less think about it. Everything felt like trembling jello.

"Wha—" I stammered as I allowed my body to sink to the floor in a pile.

Minos chuckled. "Is that all you can handle, little thief? I thought you wanted to ride all of our cocks."

My pride had me rolling onto my back and I sat up in a euphoric daze.

I was faced with them in their full Cerberus form. Three

beautiful monsters bound together, their eyes burning red and fangs gleaming.

They were massive, towering over me. I saw their thick cocks still outfitted with their knots between their legs, though now each was as large as my calf. My gaze ran over them, falling on the crimson spiked tail they had that trailed on the floor.

They were magnificent.

I knew I could take them. I was a demigod, right?

No more fighting monsters, just fucking them.

I needed to fit them inside me.

"Come ride your mates, baby girl," Aaecus said.

The three of them sat on their haunches and then lay on their back, with their feet in the air. It was a strange sight until they settled in a lounging position.

Their three cocks were upright, leaking with glistening precum. My mouth instantly watered, wanting to taste them.

On my hands and knees, I crawled over toward them. I'd be able to control how hard I rode them. The thought alone excited me, my pussy pulsing with need.

I crawled between their legs, looking up at them. Each of them stared longingly up at me with a lustful haze in their eyes.

"Our gorgeous mafia queen," Minos said lovingly.

"Get on our cocks or they're going down your throat, princess," Damon said.

Aaecus moaned, his expression one of pure primal lust.

Straddling their stomach, my hands teased the sides of Minos' and Aaecus' cocks. The long slick feel of their precum leaking down their shafts made me groan.

"I can't wait to fit you inside me," I whispered, sliding my hands down both of their shafts.

My fingers hardly closed around them, but the way their eyes glazed over I knew they liked it.

I bent my head down to Damon's thick cock, licking the tip of him while my hands continued to stroke the other two. His eyes rolled in his head and he groaned.

"Fit it all in your dirty little mouth, princess. I want to see you take it."

Looking down at his swollen cock I took it into my mouth, the head of it barely fit without my cheeks aching. I swirled my tongue around it, loving the way Damon watched me like I was the center of his world.

I ran my tongue over his shaft, swirling over the head before taking it into my mouth. All three of them moaned while I stroked the other two, sucking the middle one.

This was heaven.

"You're so sexy," Damon groaned.

I sucked in a breath, reveling in being called sexy. I loved this more than I thought possible.

The more I sucked him, the more their cocks began to move together. It was as if they curved closer to Damon's until they were nearly a triangle.

My cheeks rubbed the sides of Minos and Aaecus' cocks and I closed my eyes. Their hips began to pump him further into my throat until my eyes watered. Tears slipped down my cheeks, but I didn't stop.

More. I needed more.

"I need you on my cock," Damon huffed.

My eyes fluttered open and I nodded my head around Damon's thick shaft. I let his free with a wet pop, their gazes scalding me with need.

I was so fucking wet.

"Are you sure?" I asked, fighting the urge to smirk.

I knew that he was sure. And I knew that I wanted it just as much as he did.

Aaecus growled. "Get on top, baby girl, before we flip you over and rut you."

"Yes, Sir," I said.

He moaned in response.

I looked down at their body for a minute, trying to figure out how the fuck I was going to do this.

"Stand on us while you lower yourself down on our cocks. When you're fully seated, you can ride us however you want," Minos grunted.

Being a thief for so long meant that I was fairly flexible, but this was to be a true test of that skill.

I sucked in a breath as I balanced on them, lowering my pussy until I felt the tip of Damon's cock slowly spread me.

I rubbed myself against Damon's cock, until it was wet with me and slowly pushed against it. Just the tip of him inside me made me groan.

He was massive.

"It won't fit," I groaned.

"It'll fit, princess."

I eased more of his cock inside of me, letting out a long moan. I was burning with need for them, my blood pumping with adrenaline.

His cock was large enough to split me in two, but it still felt perfect. I was so wet for them, more than I'd ever been before. A little cry escaped me, my body throbbing as I took inch after inch.

I used my hands to drag myself down further, and as I did I noticed the slight mischievous look in Minos' eyes. I could see him glance toward Damon and when he did, Damon's hips bucked upward.

Just that one movement forced him to enter me deeper. My hands gripped his shaft and my eyes rolled backward.

"You look like a goddess like this," Minos said. "Taking your monster's cocks."

I felt like one too. The way that they looked at me was like they worshiped me. I gasped as I took the last bit I possibly could, reveling in the control I had.

They didn't move, allowing me the chance to acclimate until I was certain my stomach showed the outline of Damon's cock.

I looked down at myself, amazed.

I could see the bulge of him, could feel the heat of his shaft pulsing inside me.

"You're doing so good," Aaecus grunted. "So fucking perfect."

I started to move my hips, a yelp leaving me. My hands fell to my sides, finding the other two cocks that were waiting to fill me. I started to rub them, finding a rhythm that allowed me to work all of us together.

I bent to the side taking Aaecus into my mouth while I continued to stroke Minos. I wanted them all inside me but I wasn't capable and that made me try harder.

Every hip thrust we made in tandem made me moan around Aaecus and drive him deeper inside me. My hand stayed around Minos, trying my best to continue to stroke him too.

"That's it, baby girl," Aaecus groaned.

"I'm going to fill your pussy," Damon grunted.

It wasn't enough. None of it felt like enough. I wanted *more.*

Aaecus' cock thrust up, hitting the back of my throat right as I felt Damon's knot against my pussy.

I groaned, wanting him to knot me. I needed to feel it inside me.

A tap on Aaecus shaft was my way of signaling I wanted a pause. I tapped three times and their hips stopped moving.

I sat up, drawing in deep breaths.

I needed more.

"Minos, I need you in my ass."

"Yes, ma'am," he chuckled.

They rolled us onto our sides, Damon's cock still buried inside of me.

Being immortal now had its perks.

With one of my hands I coated it in my juices and made sure I was slick for his cock. Then I guided him against my entrance.

It took all of two minutes before every hole was filled and I was positioned side-saddle. We moved together, our bodies finding a glorious rhythm. I felt my orgasm creeping up, my cries becoming louder and louder. I felt claws around me, digging into my skin as they pumped me.

Fuck, I was so close to coming.

With one more powerful thrust, I felt myself unravel. I tried to scream, choked by Aaecus as the first wave crashed over me and they continued to ruin me.

"We're going to breed you, little thief," Damon grunted. "Our mafia wife."

My eyes rolled at his words, pleasure pouring through me.

Minos was the first to fill me, the first knot hit me and then the others filled me even more. I couldn't move or breathe as his hot cum burst inside me.

Damon's hips bucked faster until I couldn't do anything but choke on Aaecus and then Minos' knots felt like barbs. I didn't care in the slightest until cum hit the back of my throat, Aaecus' roar music to my ears.

Damon still hadn't come yet, holding on until the end. His knot began to swell, his breaths turning to pants until finally—I felt his cum fill me and his growl tore around us.

"Good girl," Damon panted. "You did so well, princess."

Not even two weeks ago, I would have thought I'd lost my mind for feeling proud of myself for taking Cerberus' three cocks.

But here I was, basking in the sunshine of their love.

Seven days of sin had turned into forever, and I wasn't mad about it.

I loved them.

I smiled to myself. Being mated to mafia monsters wasn't so bad after all.

Three Months Later

Ashley

I walked down the beach of my island, the sun warming my skin. Sand shifted beneath my feet, waves lapping at the shore and revealing pink seashells scattered everywhere.

Our honeymoon had been wonderful. The four of us had managed to book a ticket out of Moirai for a week, and it had been glorious. This was our final day here, with the plane taking off in just a few hours.

Part of me didn't want to leave, but the other part of me was happy to get home and start working on my new empire.

It wasn't the monster-free beach I'd dreamed of before I met my mates. In fact, it was so much better.

The island we were on was one of several that Hercules had owned in Greece. Now they belonged to me and I fully intended on visiting them whenever possible.

I glanced up at the sky as the sun started to rise. I needed to make it back to my three husbands before they woke up and realized I was gone. I didn't need them to raze this place looking for me.

I sighed happily, closing my eyes for a moment before walking into the softer sands that led to a line of palm trees.

Thunk.

I paused and scowled, tapping my foot on the ground.

"What the fuck?" I mumbled.

The ground right here had a hollow sound to it. I crouched down, pushing the sand away until I saw what looked like rusted bronze. I stared for a moment, deciding if I actually wanted to keep going but hey... buried treasure was a thing, right?

My fingertips buzzed with excitement. This wasn't like stealing, but it still gave me a little thrill.

I worked pushing the sand back for a few minutes, digging out whatever the hell this was. What if Hercules had bombs under the island? Or maybe it was filled with expensive relics?

Fuck. I hoped it was the latter.

I shouldn't have been excited about beheading him and taking everything he owned, but it was hard to not be a little giddy.

Finally, I stood and planted my hands on my hips. My skirt waved in the wind, and I was sure I looked like a blonde surfer and not a mafia boss that was digging up a random beach door.

"Maybe it's rum," I giggled.

There was a latch at the top with a seal, and unsurprisingly, it was the Three Fates Mafia eye.

"Oh fuck no," I said, shaking my head.

Nope. No. I knew better, right? I knew better than to open this door.

I stared at it, squinting. The sound of the ocean calmed me and I breathed in the fresh sea air.

It was still a no.

There will be a door, and you will open it. I pressed my lips into a thin line, unamused by the Fates at the moment. Specifically Clotho. Had she known the door would be on my island?

Fucking hell. Of course she'd known.

I sighed and leaned down. *Fine, lady. You win.* I gripped the latch, tugging on it. It didn't move, instead staying firmly closed.

"Fine," I mumbled. "Be stubborn. *Key.*"

The key card Hermes had given me appeared in my hand and I swiped it over the latch. There was a heavy *click,* followed by a metallic groan that echoed around me.

Ah shit, that wasn't good.

I could feel my mating bonds start to tighten, which was a sign that my hubbies had woken up. I heard a growl from far away and looked up, not surprised to see Damon hauling ass down the beach toward me like a track star.

"Run, Damon, run," I whispered, waving at him.

I leaned down and worked my fingers under the latch, pulling with all of my strength.

"Ashley! Don't you fucking dare open that—"

The door fought me for a moment, and then gave way. I gasped as it flew open, a puff of smoke blowing straight into my face.

Damon tackled me into the sand right as two red eyes blinked at me in the darkness of whatever that was. I grunted as the two of us rolled, and he pinned me beneath him.

"What the fuck did I tell you about wandering around?" he hissed.

"Well, I didn't expect to find a door!" I blurted.

He cupped my face and planted a quick kiss before letting out a frustrated breath, looking back over his shoulder. He moved off me, the two of us sitting up. We both stiffened as a low growl echoed from the hole in the ground, followed by more smoke billowing out.

"What the hell?" I whispered.

"Damon! Ashley!"

We both looked up, seeing Minos and Aaecus barreling through palm trees and high grass. Damon wrapped his arms around me and pulled me tight as another growl came from the hole.

"Look at what's in it," Damon barked at Minos and Aaecus.

They both made a face as they came closer.

"I'm not looking in the hole," Aaecus said, crossing his arms. "And you, wifey. You didn't even leave us a note."

"Sorry," I said sheepishly. "I just wanted a little walk on the beach."

"Yes, and now we have a mysterious hole in the ground," Minos chuckled.

We all looked at him expectantly and he groaned, running his hands through his long hair. "Why me?" he mumbled, but he was already shifting into his monster form.

I watched appreciatively as one-third of my Cerberus husband crept toward the steaming hole. He cocked his head to the side, then let out a curse.

"What the fuck are you doing in a hole on a tropical island, Ryan?"

Two golden horns emerged, followed by the head of a bull, followed by the sculpted chest of a bullish man.

Holy fuck, he was a *minotaur*.

Damon clamped his hand over my eyes right before Minos pulled him all the way out—in all of his naked minotaur glory.

"Let me see!" I mumbled, tugging at his hand.

"No! You're my wife, you are not seeing that thing."

"Oh my gods," I giggled.

"Hercules fucking threw me down there a couple years ago," a low timbre voice snarled. "And no one came to try and find me."

"Right..." Minos drifted off. "Well, we rescued you now, bud. We're flying back to Moirai in a few hours."

"I'll join you."

I giggled again as Damon let out a low hiss. "Aaecus, give him your shirt."

"For fuck's sake," Aaecus sighed.

"I want to see," I hissed.

Damon leaned in, his breath tickling my ear. "I will bend you over and spank you here and now, princess."

"I'd like that."

Damon snorted. "Ryan, this is our wife, Ashley. She has replaced Hercules. The fucker is dead and this is her island now."

Damon pulled his hand away, finally allowing me to see. Aaecus had sacrificed his cherry red Hawaiian shirt, and it was now wrapped tightly around Ryan the minotaur's hips, although it didn't disguise much.

"Well, then, the world is truly ending," Ryan said bitterly.

His eyes burned like molten gold and he studied me for a few moments, before turning. "I'm leaving now," he said. "Thanks for finding me. I have people to kill."

"Have fun," Minos muttered.

We all watched as he walked away, disappearing down the beach.

"Who the fuck was that?" I asked.

"The Minoan bull," Damon said. "He goes by Ryan in the city of Moirai. He disappeared a couple years ago and, to be honest, we all assumed he'd just gone on vacation. It's not uncommon for that to happen."

"Is he not a mafia boss?" I asked.

"No," Damon said. "He works for the Chimera twins."

"Oh," I whispered. "Are his horns really made of gold?"

"Yes," Aaecus said, plopping down in the sand next to the two of us. "He also has some mechanical parts to him. He is a monster, but he was not made like us. And you, baby girl..." Aaecus gripped my chin, turning my head towards him. "You got our blood pumping this morning."

"That she did," Minos said, standing over us.

"Did I?" I asked, raising a brow. "Maybe you should show your *wife* what that means."

"Maybe I should," he growled, smirking. "Maybe we should do a little beach chase. It's only fair we get to hunt you after running all this way."

"I like that," Damon growled. He gave me a hungry look. "Get running, princess."

"If you can even catch me," I teased.

The three of them were already shifting now, and I cursed, rolling to my feet right as their massive Cerberus form appeared.

I grinned and took off down the beach into the sunrise, just a thief-turned-mafia-boss running from her monstrous mates.

THREE FATES MAFIA

CERBERUS

CLIO'S CREATURES

Hello Creatures!

My name is Clio Evans and I am so excited to introduce myself to you! I'm a lover of all things that go bump in the night, fancy peens, coffee, and chocolate.

IF you had the chance to be matched with a monster- what kind would you choose?!

Let me know by joining me on FB and Instagram. I'm a sucker for werewolves (and plague doctors ;)) to this day.

ALSO BY CLIO EVANS

CREATURE CAFE SERIES
Little Slice of Hell

Little Sip of Sin

Little Lick of Lust

Little Shock of Hate

Little Piece of Sass

Little Song of Pain

Little Taste of Need

Little Risk of Fall

Little Wings of Fate

Little Souls of Fire

Little Kiss of Snow: A Creature Cafe Christmas Anthology

WARTS & CLAWS INC. SERIES
Not So Kind Regards

Not So Best Wishes

Not So Thanks in Advance

Not So Yours Truly

Not So Much Appreciated

FREAKS OF NATURE DUET
Doves & Demons

Demons & Doves

Thank you

There are so many people that I would like to thank! WENDY- thank you for jumping in on this book and even pulling an allnighter. You're the GOAT. April, Ashley, Mimi, Beatrix, Lo, Vera— thank you so much for all of your support on this book.

Ingram Content Group UK Ltd.
Milton Keynes UK
UKHW021307150623
423501UK00020B/510